RESOLUTION
The Perfect Crime?

A Novel

James Hebert

RESOLUTION
The Perfect Crime?

Dedication

Fourteen mountains worldwide are 8000 meters or higher.

Writing one's first book is like taking on the challenge of climbing one of these mountains. One of the most challenging aspects is converting the story into a book format that is accessible to a broad audience. Without Mat's comments after reading the rough draft, Stavroula's editing expertise, and Gene, my artist friend who crossed over into graphic design, I would never have reached the summit. Thank You!!!

DEAR READER,

It's a lifelong dream to put pen to paper and create one's first crime drama for everyone to enjoy. Also, being a "Classic Rock" fan, I like to quote from a great song, "Turn the Page."

Enjoy!

James Hebert

Prologue:

What is the perfect crime?

Definition: 1) A crime never solved by the authorities. 2) An illegal act committed to obtain a substantial financial reward. 3) The criminal act must have no motive or ties to the party committing the crime other than monetary gain. 4) Anyone with the proper planning can commit the crime. 5) Execution of the crime must be done to leave no trace behind. 6) The monetary gain must be secured to leave no trail back to the person(s) committing the crime.

Are you capable of planning and committing the perfect crime?

Chapter 1

eam One is checking in with base and is on station for the pick-up of target one. We will confirm when we get visual on target one and then transmit a text confirmation of the pick-up.

A white cargo van with no markings and very tinted windows was parked in the adjacent space next to Target's vehicle in a public parking garage in Bethesda, MD.

Peggy Turner volunteers ½ day every Tuesday morning at the offices of a non-profit that helps homeless veterans. With a CPA degree, Peggy does pro bono work managing the donations and grants provided to the non-profit. Her husband, Alan Turner, founded AX Tech Corp approximately 15 years ago, and it has since become a highly successful defense contracting company, generating over $300 million in annual revenue. This allows Peggy to use her time and skills to help half a dozen charitable organizations, which she finds very rewarding.

Peggy approached her car. The vehicle sensed her key fob in her purse, and the driver's door clicked open. Before she could reach the door handle, the side door of the white cargo van parked next to her car flew open with one masked man lifting her off the ground with one arm and using his other arm to put his hand to cover her mouth and stifle any screams or pleas for help. A second masked man immediately pulled a hood over her head and then dragged her inside the van; they immediately zip-tied her hands and feet. The van driver backed out and sent a text message to their base advising them that target one was secured. The van exited the garage and proceeded to a safe house in rural Virginia with their hostage. Terrified, Peggy asked, "Why did you take me?" None of the three men in the van spoke to her; she only felt a mighty hand placed over her mouth, indicating she was not to talk again.

Team Two is checking in with base, reporting on station, and waiting for visuals on target two.

Another unmarked white cargo van was parked near one of the main cross streets at George Washington (GW) University in Washington, DC.

Carly Turner, the 29-year-old daughter of Peggy and Alan Turner, was completing her Tuesday morning classes to expand her knowledge of environmental disciplines, including global warming and the sustainability impact of products used by most consumers daily. While waiting for the crosslight to turn in favor of pedestrians, Carly contemplated the harm plastic products did to our oceans, having just attended the lecture. She was saddened to know that the vast majority of plastic in the oceans today was not discarded plastic water bottles, but tons of plastic netting that had served its purpose and then was randomly discarded by fishing fleets at the bottom of the ocean. Over time, these nets broke into smaller plastic pieces, polluting every ocean worldwide.

The traffic light turned in her favor, and as she stepped off the curb, the white van raced upon her. Thinking the vehicle was running the red light, she froze and stepped backward to avoid being hit. The van braked hard, and the side door flew open. Two sets of arms, from men wearing masks, grabbed Carly and pulled her into the van. Her call for help was muted by the door slamming shut and the vehicle racing off. The stunned pedestrians could do nothing to help Carly but tried to take a photo of the van's license plate as it sped away. A black hood was placed over her head, zip ties were placed on her feet, and her hands were secured. The driver immediately texted his message to their base of operations, stating that target two was secured and in transit to the safe house.

Team Three is checking in and waiting for Target Three to exit the Pentagon's secured parking facility. Per the surveillance data provided, we will follow him to his lunch location before approaching and securing the target.

Zach Turner, the 35-year-old son of Peggy and Alan Turner, was sitting through Tuesday morning briefing sessions at the Pentagon. After serving ten years in the U.S. Army, his father convinced Zach to leave the military and enter the family business. AX Tech Corp grew from being a management and distribution advisor for government warehouses to the principal company handling the procurement and distribution of small arms and weapons to all U.S. military bases. The Tuesday morning sessions were mostly redundant, and Zach was looking forward to his standing lunch date with his best friend and Army buddy, Cody Wall. Tuesday lunch between Zach and Cody was a great time to swap stories of recent events and keep the strong bond they formed in their army days together.

Cody had also left the Army around the same time as Zach, and with his background in Army intelligence, saw the need for private companies not to get "hacked," potentially causing them to suffer substantial financial losses. For this reason, Cody started a cybersecurity firm for private corporations and added a personnel protection division for anyone of high-profile importance visiting Washington, DC. Over the past several years, his company, Fail-Safe, has achieved great success in both areas of endeavor, mainly due to his strategic hiring of dedicated staff with exceptional expertise.

Zach climbed into his nondescript company car, a Chevy Malibu; his dad required U.S.-made vehicles to support his corporate image with all his government contracts. Upon leaving the Pentagon parking lot, Zach called Cody to advise him of his arrival time for their lunch date. Traffic, as always, was a challenge in the DC metro area.

After traveling several miles from the Pentagon and making multiple turns to find the least congested route, Zach's Army training kicked in, and he observed a white van several blocks behind, mimicking every turn he had made.

Chapter 2

Zach and Cody met after spending several years in the Army. Both were assigned to the United States Army Intelligence and Security Command, a/k/a INSCOM, whose headquarters were located at Fort Belvoir Army base south of Alexandria, VA.

The skills they acquired through Army intelligence training were always to observe their surroundings and assess every situation in terms of the degree of risk or threat. Then, all the data will be analyzed, and a course of action will be chosen to get the most favorable and safe results. Army intelligence's primary function is to gather information using any resources available. Officers trained in Army intelligence were taught fieldwork skills but instructed to avoid confrontations that could cause loss of life whenever possible. It was better to outthink the enemy than put your life at risk.

Zach and Cody bonded into two brothers, although Cody was several inches taller at 6 2", very handsome, and had developed an interest in yoga after leaving the military to stay fit with his gym workouts. The other quality that Zach envied in Cody was his "zen" like attitude learned in yoga that women seem to melt over. Zach knew Cody well enough that he could not make any long-term commitments in a relationship. Even though Cody dated some gorgeous women, he always seemed to move on before the relationship entered the danger zone. Zach always ribbed Cody; he would be glad to be the safety net when Cody dropped out of any relationship.

Zach immediately redialed Cody's cell phone, informing him of the white van's movements, which may or may not pose a threat or a problem. The decision was made by the two of them to err on the side of caution and have Zach drive directly to Cody's office building in Old Town Alexandria and enter the secure, below-ground parking garage using the provided gate code. Then, they could assess or approach the van if it stopped near his office building. After arriving, Zach parked in the garage, where Cody met him and said Let's take a quick walk around the block. Not taking Zach's instincts lightly, Cody had grabbed a 9mm pistol from his desk and told Zach he was packing in case of trouble. Their 10-minute walk around the block saw no white van in sight anywhere. Cody offered to drive to lunch a few miles away at their favorite Mexican restaurant in the Del Ray community. During the short drive, the white van did not make another appearance.

Cody asked Zach if he was allowed to carry a concealed firearm while working for his father. Zach indicated he did not have a concealed carry weapons permit and saw little need for one. Through his company, Fail-Safe, Cody provided personnel protection for high-profile visitors to the DC area and held licenses for certain employees, including himself, to be armed with a handgun.. Zach felt like he could take care of most situations, but indicated he owned several loaded handguns, kept them at his condo, and regularly went to the local gun range to keep his shooting skills up to par. Given the unresolved white van incident, Cody offered his 9mm Beretta to Zach and indicated that he could return it at their next lunch appointment. Zach declined the offer because the white van was not present after their walk and did not reappear on the way to lunch.

Chapter 3

After lunch, Zach headed back to AX Tech's corporate offices, located in Arlington, VA, which his dad had chosen due to their reasonable proximity to the Pentagon. On the George Washington Parkway, heading north, just after passing near Ronald Reagan National Airport, Zach observed the white van again, several hundred yards back in traffic. To confirm this wasn't his imagination, he immediately pulled into Gravelly Point Park, the next exit off the GW Parkway north of Reagan Airport. This park is a local favorite and is usually busy because it sits directly at the end of the principal runway for Reagan National Airport. The park commands a great view of planes taking off and landing. Zach looped onto the bypass road to reach the public boat launching ramp rather than entering the parking lot. He felt that if the van were tailing him, confirmation would come if the vehicle approached the boat launch area rather than the general parking lot. The one white van turned into the park but stopped near the entranceway.

After about 10 minutes, Zach sat in his car and dialed Cody on his cell phone. Zach explained to Cody about the appearance of the white van and how it followed him into Gravelly Park, but quickly added that a second white van had just appeared. Still on his cell phone, Cody advises Zach to sit tight; he could get there in 10 minutes or less for backup if the situation worsens. Zach told Cody the two vans were moving slowly in separate directions, covering the roads to seal off any exits back onto the GW parkway. Zach, unaware of the threat or intention behind the vans' pursuit, warned Cody that he had only a couple of minutes before a confrontation. He also indicated he wished he had accepted Cody's handgun offer at lunch. Zach did not like the odds of dealing with two vans, each likely containing multiple people.

Zach quickly decided to take action: he started his car, rolled down all four windows, popped his trunk open, jumped out, and grabbed his driver's out of his golf bag. Slamming the trunk shut, he opened the rear door and climbed into the car's back seat. He made two requests of Cody before hanging up the phone: first, call Alan, his dad, and advise him that the company car was going into the Potomac River near the boat ramp at Gravelly Point Park. It would need to be towed out of the water, and second, he asked him to drive immediately to Reagan Airport, where he planned to swim after exiting the sinking car. Bring some dry clothes and somehow think of a way to release him from the Airport's Security custody.

Zach knew that when his vehicle hit the water, the front airbag would deploy, pinning him in the front seat of a sinking car, with no idea of the water's depth. Located in the car's back seat, he reached over the driver's front seat and put the Malibu into drive; with one hand on the steering wheel, he pushed the grip of his golf driver on the accelerator pedal to the floorboard from the back seat. Knowing if the front airbag deployed, he wouldn't be trapped in the car. He needed to launch the car off the embankment into the tributary separating the Park from the Airport grounds. Knowing that going straight down the boat ramp, the impact with the water would instantly stop the vehicle. Zach steered the car toward the highest side of the embankment, and the Chevy Malibu reached enough speed to go airborne and land squarely out into the water. Zach had ducked behind the front seat, felt the car impact the water, and immediately scrambled out through the car's open rear window before the water started to flow into the sinking vehicle. The tributary for the boat launching is only a couple of football fields wide, with the Reagan National Airport runway positioned on the opposite bank. Zach's plan worked great until he realized that swimming fully dressed with shoes on was extremely difficult. The several-hundred-yard swim was like taking on the English Channel. He was exhausted when he climbed out of the water onto the property of Reagan National Airport. Once on the Airport property, an 8-foot high-security fence with twisted barbed wire on top stopped him from entering the Airport property. He sat down, dripping wet, waiting for security to arrive.

Zach's logic was that whoever was in the white vans couldn't pursue him; bystanders at the park would dial 911 instantly, and the U.S. Park Police would respond accordingly. Reagan National Airport security had Zach in custody less than a minute after exiting the water. Zach welcomed the company, hoping Cody could find a way to get him released. The two vans were no longer in sight when he looked across the inlet before entering the airport security patrol car with his hands handcuffed.

Chapter 4

Cody, scrambling to get to National Airport, dialed Alan Turner, Zach's father, to advise him of the bizarre circumstances leading to Zach ditching the company car into a tributary of the Potomac River. Alan indicated that he had left several messages on Zach's phone in the last 20 minutes, but there was no return call.

What happened next caused Cody to pull off the road and try to understand what Alan was telling him. Witnesses had been able to provide DC police with Carly Turner's name as the person who was abducted while crossing an intersection at GW University. Alan had put the police on hold and tried to contact his wife, Peggy, with the horrible news. When she didn't answer and it was well past the time she usually came back home on Tuesday from her volunteer work, he provided the police with a description of her car, including the license tag number, as well as the address of the non-profit organization and information on where she usually parked. Police indicated they would contact the precinct in the jurisdiction where the parking garage was located. Alan then spent the next 30 minutes using his Department of Defense contacts to find someone influential in dealing with the top people at the FBI. Alan was provided a number, and a call was made to the FBI deputy director's phone advising him of the details supplied by the DC police about his daughter's abduction right off a public street in DC.

During his urgent request for the FBI to get involved in the abduction of Carly, his phone beeped with an incoming call from the Montgomery County, Maryland, police department. Placing the FBI on hold, he was informed that Peggy's car was found, unlocked, in the public parking garage with her key fob lying on the floor just beneath the driver's door. No signs of a struggle were evident, and police tried to see if any cameras were in the garage or vicinity to provide video footage of the incident.

Alan then conveyed the news to the FBI deputy director, who committed to dispatching a team to his house in Great Falls, VA, to investigate and gather all data available from local authorities about Peggy or Carly's disappearance.

Cody was visibly shaken when he updated Alan on Zach's being pursued by a white van and ultimately cornered in the Gravelly Point parking lot. Cody told Alan details about Zach's evasive action in ditching his company car into the water near the boat launching ramp and then swimming across the creek onto Reagan National Airport property. He also indicated that he was 10 minutes from the airport and expected to find Zach in airport security custody.

Upon Cody's arrival at the airport security office, they confirmed that Zach Turner was in custody and that their office had just been contacted by the FBI several minutes earlier. The Bureau explained Zach's actions to airport security and cleared the way for his immediate release. Cody was relieved that Alan had wasted no time using his influence with the FBI to resolve this.

When Zach was brought out, still dripping wet, Cody asked security for a private room to talk to Zach about his sister and mother and get him changed into some dry clothes he had brought. Zach was in total disbelief at the possibility of his sister and mom being abducted earlier in the day. It hit Cody and Zach simultaneously that they both clearly understood the white vans in question intended to kidnap the entire Turner family, including Zach, on the same day. The next decision was for them to immediately head to Turner's home in Great Falls and get updated on all the information the authorities had gathered about Peggy and Carly.

Chapter 5

Cody pushed his turbocharged Mustang to the limit, sensing the urgency of the situation, but DC traffic was miserable. It made a 20-minute commute into almost an hour. As they pulled into the Turners' estate in Great Falls, the car pulling in the driveway behind them looked like a government-issued vehicle, and they presumed it was probably the FBI team assigned to the case.

Cody and Zach approached the car and introduced themselves to the FBI. The senior agent introduced himself. Shaun O'Hara looked like a no-nonsense type with a lot of experience. His partner, agent Kimberly Ross, was even gorgeous in slacks and a sports coat. Agent O'Hara indicated the Bureau was giving this situation a very high priority, given Alan's business contacts. The four walked into the house together, hoping to find Alan and gain insight into what had happened that day.

Alan, expecting everyone, had cleared the conference table in his office that would easily accommodate the five of them. Shaun took the lead; he had received reports from the local police on Peggy's incident. The parking garage had cameras that filmed all vehicles entering and exiting the facility. The camera's primary purpose was to capture license plate numbers if any vehicle exited without paying the parking fee. The footage had been reviewed, and a white van entered the garage about 30 minutes before Peggy exited her volunteer job. The van paid a one-hour parking fee with a stolen credit card that had not yet been canceled. The camera at the entrance caught a portion of the lower front windshield, but it was tinted dark enough to prevent identification of the driver. The license plate was a commercial VA Tag ZZP-169. They confirmed that the keys on the garage floor operated Peggy's vehicle. No purse or other personal possessions were found. No one has stepped forward as a witness to the incident to make a police statement or report a person screaming or in distress.

Carly's abduction had numerous witnesses; they all indicated the two men seizing her wore hooded-type masks, gloves, and all-black, nondescript-type clothing and were very efficient in their manner and actions. They also stated that the white van had severely tinted windows, making it impossible to see inside, including the driver or the number of people inside the vehicle. Several witnesses confirmed the license plate number was a commercial VA Tag ZZP-169. Shaun indicated that, based on the time and locations of the two abductions, there were two vans used with the same license plate. The VA license plate number was traced to a commercial painting company in Richmond, VA. Authorities in Richmond confirmed they belong to a white commercial van owned by a painting contractor. The vehicle with the actual plates had been parked at a job site in Richmond the entire day. They checked the VA DMV reorder to see if any information on the specific plate number had been hacked from the DMV system. He also mentioned that finding a white commercial van and jotting down the plate number was extremely easy, without needing to hack into a computer database. Making duplicate plates would not raise a red flag during most traffic stops, even without the registration to back up the plates. Duplicate plates were becoming more common than stolen ones and were usually reported to the police fairly quickly. Easy access to good-grade 3D printers made it easy for criminals to be in the license plate business.

Zach indicated he never got close enough to get a plate number. He recounted his story of being followed twice, before and after lunch, and stated the approximate time of each incident. Shaun stated clearly that three vans were involved. One had to believe they all had the same VA plate number. After hearing Zach's details, Shaun said the sequence, timing, and execution of the three abductions showed a very high level of organizational planning. Three vehicles, assuming two persons to carry out the kidnapping and one driver, reflect a lot of resources in play. He advised that the best situation would be a ransom demand, because the alternative motive for this type of crime is often vengeance against the family.

Taking in all the facts and information exchanged, Alan asked for a specific course of action to get his wife and daughter back safely. As the no-nonsense CEO of a large company, he wanted details and resources to be used to get his family back. Agent Ross responded to Alan, indicating that an FBI van would arrive momentarily and unload numerous electronic equipment to monitor all communication devices, including phones, computers, and tablets. The FBI would keep a Tech person on site as long as needed to trace any communications from the persons responsible. The tech person would also scan everyone, including Peggy's & Carly's computers, tablets, secondary phones, etc., looking for any hacks or viruses that may have been planted with cookies to obtain information on their habits and routines. Backtracking or identifying prior hacks may provide a channel to determine the parties involved. She asked Alan and Zach to provide any persons, either through business dealings or personal relationships, who would have reasons to try to kidnap three members of the Turner family. Alan and Zach looked blankly at each other, indicating they knew no one with the motivation or ability to commit this crime.

Alan made two statements directed at the FBI: he, with help from his administrative assistant, Beverly Hardesty, would run his company from his home study till this situation was resolved. He wanted updates from the Bureau on any information that was uncovered or available. I want to be in the loop on every development of this case. Shaun O'Hara replied, We certainly can keep the lines of communication open with any new data or developments.

Cody knew, with so little to go on, that it was evident to all parties that they were in a waiting game to hear from the kidnappers as to the motive for the crime. The only goal was to get Peggy and Carly back safe and sound. Shaun did offer Alan and Zach that the FBI could assign an agent to each of them at any time they left the premises. He said at this point, we don't know if you're still targets. Alan and Zach indicated the persons responsible would be foolish to expose themselves again after failing to abduct Zach after two attempts. Zach didn't mention it, but he knew he would be carrying a firearm everywhere for the next week or so.

The FBI Tech Van had arrived and worked with Alan to set up all the monitoring equipment. Cody pulled Zach aside and asked if he could stop by his office the next morning around 9 a.m. Cody indicated that he would commit all his corporate resources to help in any way possible to get his mother and sister back safely and sound. Zach expected nothing less from his Army buddy and indicated he would be there at nine sharp if nothing developed overnight.

Zach saw Agent Ross approaching and asked if she could step outside with Cody and him for a brief conversation. The three walked out the front door toward a beautifully manicured garden on the side yard of the driveway. Zach provided Agent Ross with details about his Army relationship and subsequent long-standing friendship with Cody. He also mentioned that Cody has served with Army Intelligence and worked on numerous cases involving terrorist or criminal elements. Zach intended to keep Cody in the loop on all developments and always valued his opinion and insight. He wanted to ensure that the assigned agents understood this.

Zach told Agent Ross he wanted to share some background on his dad, Alan. She immediately said that both of them call her Kim and that she looked forward to any insight they had that may help the Bureau. Zach indicated that Alan started his company about 15 years ago, and, like any new business entering the defense government contractor arena, one faces a highly competitive marketplace. He shared Alan's full name with Kim – Alan Xavier Turner – pointing out that AX Tech Corp was founded using his father's first two initials. Zach mentioned that in those early years, many competitors' toes were stepped on, and Alan became known for his business tactics as "The AX Man".

The point Zach said he wanted to make was that if this event had happened ten years ago, there would be a list of prospects that may, indeed, want to harm his family. Cody also mentioned that after leaving the Army, Zach has worked at AX Tech Corp and would have a good feel for the day-to-day operations. Zach said that AX Tech Corp has blossomed over the past 5-7 years into a well-run and respected business within the government contracting sector. Therefore, it's not possible to ID anyone today who would want to harm their family. Kim thanked Zach for his candid comments and insight on the past and said she would share his views with Agent O'Hara. She also indicated that, given their background, Cody's involvement was okay as long as it did not hinder their investigation. Cody's only thought was that Kim was too beautiful to ever step on her toes.

Chapter 6

Zach promptly entered Cody's conference room at 9 a.m. the following day. Sitting around the table were four key employees who worked for Cody. Before formal introductions were made, Cody asked Zach for any updates or developments on the abductions of his mom and sister. Zach advised them that there was no communication from the party responsible overnight. He indicated that local authorities had pulled his car from the river inlet. A transponder was located, attached under the car's rear bumper. It appears that the device's make was common, had a range of a couple of miles, and would be hard to trace. His mom's car was towed from the parking garage, thoroughly searched, and no new information was provided for authorities to use. The FBI believes her car probably also had a transponder attached, but it was removed once she was secured in the white van. Everything was still pointing to a well-planned, executed, and funded kidnapping.

Cody kicked off the meeting by again committing to Zach that all resources he and his company could provide would be available until his mom and sister were back home and safe. Sitting in the conference room were four key persons directly responsible for Cody's company's success and growth over the past four years. Zach knew them all by sight when he stopped in to see Cody at the office, but was unaware of their roles or skills. Fail-Safe was principally a cybersecurity consultant, but also provided personal security to VIPs visiting Washington, DC for business purposes.

Cody started with Karen Clarke, sitting next to Zach. He stated that Karen could research any topic and provide a "business plan" to execute to reach any end goal. Her organizational ability was off the charts when given a complicated task.

Next to her was Carter Wagner, whom they affectionately nicknamed "Q" from the James Bond movies. Carter had his workshop in the Fail-Safe basement. The storage area was well-equipped with equipment that Carter could design, manufacture, and modify as needed for the company, including, but not limited to, frequency monitors, cameras, jamming signals, secure communications devices, and drones for capturing wireless communications, such as Wi-Fi transmission from modems. Aerial video surveillance by drones is used when VIPs are transported from place to place. Cody had access to high-end tech equipment, specifically designed for government use, through his contacts in Army Intelligence. This equipment was built to a far better quality and is far superior to anything sold over the counter. The drones they had acquired were military grade and very sophisticated, even before Carter made any modifications.

Next was Jack, a person Zach knew by reputation, who never used a last name because he was retired from a special forces unit that was not on the books of any military branch of the service. Cody told Zach that Jack's handle or name he went by was "Stoney," and he ran 100% of all Fail-Safe personal security details. Stoney had 3-4 former retired team members available as needed for any personal security-type job.

The last person on staff was a charming employee Zach would love to get to know better under different circumstances; her name was Susie Mathews. Cody indicated Susie had a computer between her ears, multiple degrees in computer science from Stanford University, and an I.Q. to match. She was the company's principal I.T. specialist and could forensically analyze customer systems for firewall gaps or any malware embedded in their drives. Cody bragged that Susie could hack into almost any system without a trace. What amazed Zach was that Susie, besides having brains and beauty, had probably not celebrated her 30th birthday yet.

Zach activated an old phone this morning, as the river had claimed his phone the day before while he was swimming onto the airport grounds. It pinged, indicating a text message had just been received. Typical of Alan, a short message and to the point: ***RETURN HOME ASAP - WE HAVE BEEN CONTACTED***

Zach asked Cody if he wanted to go with him to meet with Alan. Cody declined, saying he did not want to be in the way, and asked Zach to provide an update on what was communicated.

Cody then handed Zach a small tote bag, advising him that he had added Zach to the payroll of the Fail-Safe security team, headed up by "Stoney." Inside the bag were his concealed carry permit and a 9mm Beretta handgun with spare clips. As soon as Zach left, Cody briefed everyone on yesterday's events and what little they or the authorities knew. Karen, Susie, Carter, and Stoney were committed to helping Cody in any way they could.

Cody asked Carter, also known as Q, to prepare several drones with the best video surveillance capabilities and the quietest, stealthiest operation. He indicated that the FBI seemed to have the equipment to monitor communications, so their frequency-monitoring drones would not be needed unless things changed. Cody thought out loud about possibly installing aerial surveillance over Turner's property to see if any white vans or other vehicles were loitering around and to gather intel on who was coming and going. Susie was asked to research all roads leading in and out of the Turner property to see how feasible it was to cover the area effectively from the air. The meeting ended with Cody telling everyone to check their email for updates. He would loop them in on the details as soon as he heard anything from Zach.

Zach made record time in his BMW from Cody's offices in Old Towne Alexandria to his parents' house in Great Falls. Gathered again in his father's office were Agent's O'Hara and Ross, his dad, and Beverly Hardesty, who was Alan's assistant at AX Tech Corp. Since Alan needed to run the company from his home during this crisis, Bev was summoned to handle most of the day-to-day administration matters for AX Tech Corp. Alan had extensively searched several years ago for the right person to be his administrative assistant. Bev's resume, according to Alan, had been impressive, and he made her an offer she couldn't turn down. Bev had embraced the growing responsibilities delegated by Alan and became an integral part of the company, instantly handling matters that freed Alan to continue growing his business.

Alan had read the email a dozen times and passed out copies he had made to Agents O'Hara & Ross, Zach, and Beverly. Alan received the email through his corporate address. It read:

Subject Line: FAMILY

There will be NO Negotiations!! Your wife and daughter will be returned at a time and place we determined based on the following payment being made:

1.0 million dollars for each person – Uncut diamonds ranging in size from 4 to 6 carats with a current market value of 2 million - You have four days to acquire the stones – On the fifth day an email will provide a general location in Washington DC, your delivery person will have 45 minutes to get into the vicinity identified–Then another email will be generated with specific delivery instructions that must be followed within 15 minutes

If you do not comply with our demands, one person will be eliminated on day five. We will then state our demands one final time for the remaining family member.

Chapter 7

Alan took the lead, stating he had the financial means to get this done, but he had no idea where to acquire uncut diamonds. Shaun O'Hara said that his IT people ran traces to identify where the email originated. They determined that the email was coded so that a reply could not be returned to the sender. The "NO Negotiations" comment was indeed a one-way street. Agent Ross said she would use FBI contacts in New York City's diamond district to identify what broker or brokers could assemble the number of uncut diamonds needed to meet the kidnapper's demands.

As the lead FBI agent, Shaun saw an opportunity to formulate a plan and muster all the needed resources to be in the general area of DC on the fifth day. Then, those resources could be deployed within the 30-minute window to the actual payment location. He believed they would need to be prepared to track the diamonds, rather than apprehending anyone, and possibly lose the ability to see where Peggy and Carly were being held. Shaun added that in a hostage situation, until you can determine their exact location and safety, any action taken must be passive and not threatening. He didn't need to say what everyone was thinking - hostages are killed and disposed of if authorities get too close for comfort.

Shaun indicated to everyone that the only positive aspect of this note was that the motive was financial gain from the abduction, not vindictiveness. He also added that the death threat has to be taken very seriously when dealing with the timeline stated. Until we can establish communication with the persons responsible, there is no leeway to meet the stated requirements.

Kim said she had not encountered a previous case in her training about exchanging uncut diamonds for a ransom payment. She said she had no expertise in buying or selling diamonds, but it seemed that when uncut diamonds are cut and polished, they should become untraceable when put on the market.

Agents O'Hara and Ross both voiced their opinions. They believed this was a very sophisticated organization behind the kidnapping, the resources and manpower to commit the crime, the planning and execution, and now the one-way communication stream. Kim Ross said she expected to have details from NY by early afternoon and hoped they could operate within the four-day window to acquire the necessary quantity of uncut diamonds.

Alan asked Bev to contact their corporate insurance broker. He recalled from a previous review meeting on insurance coverages that the company had purchased Kidnap and Ransom (K&R) coverage for the firm's key executives. If the broker confirms that we have coverage in place, instruct the broker to notify the insurance underwriter of the kidnapping by filing a claim. Alan instructed Bev to serve as the primary contact with the insurance company's claim department for all documentation and information exchanges.

The meeting broke up. Everyone knew the next 4-5 days would be challenging, and they would all be anxiously awaiting the following email.

Zach excused himself as the meeting turned into a general discussion about the ransom note. Since no other tangible evidence had surfaced, he didn't feel the need to sit and listen to the chit-chat. Zach jumped into his car and drove to a local coffee cafe in Great Falls. Since the FBI has sophisticated monitoring equipment at the family's house, placing a call to Cody with an update didn't need to be recorded or analyzed.

Cody immediately saw the incoming call and asked Zach about any new developments. Zach spent the next 15 minutes advising Cody of the ransom note directed to Alan via email, the basic demand for ransom, and the non-negotiation situation with the persons responsible. He then conveyed in a wavering and distressed voice to Cody the death threat made toward one of the captives for non-compliance within the timeline allotted. Zach then advised Cody of Kim Ross' inquiry to New York City to establish contact with a diamond broker or brokers that could provide the uncut stones needed to meet the demand made by the kidnappers. Lastly, he shared the details of Washington, DC, with Cody, along with two forthcoming emails outlining where the ransom would be paid and how the exchange would occur. Zach added that the FBI review of garage cameras, license plates, eyewitnesses where Carly was taken, and tracking the IP address of the email sender have all turned up negative. He said the FBI has abundant resources at its disposal; nothing tangible is surfacing that would help solve this nightmare. Cody asked Zach to sit back and objectively look back at the abductions. Cody and Zach, having worked together in Army intelligence for some years, collaborated on many situations that were unclear about who, what, and where was involved. They had to collectively find a course of action or solution for the most favorable path. Cody brought up that the abductions were intended to be of all three family members. Was this done to increase the ransom by another 1.0 million? Did this pressure Alan to meet the ransom terms without outside intervention? Despite the non-negotiable situation, the payment was made, but it did not guarantee the release of Peggy and Carly. Cody was thinking out loud again: untraceable stones worth several million, two witnesses in captivity that could become a problem, and a ransom payment that leaves no trail.

Cody's focus was on the next contact with the criminals. Where in DC would the place be chosen? Formulating and executing any type of plan requires a minimal timeline of 15 minutes. He knew the FBI would have extensive resources on the ground. Cody shared his thoughts with Zach on using Fail-Safe drones to provide video surveillance over the Turner home in Great Falls. Unfortunately, Karen, on his staff, researched the road system near the house and found too many ways into and out. They could not effectively monitor for any type of loitering traffic that may present an opportunity to capture valid license plates to trace, mainly since fake plates were used in the abductions. It would be a long shot for a real plate to present itself. Cody told Zach that he would talk to Q (Carter) to see if using drones to cover DC was feasible, now that they knew where the ransom would be paid. Based on everything discussed, Cody told Zach he would get everyone together and share any information. He added four more minds looking for a solution; couldn't hurt. Cody told him to stay in touch, day or night, with any new developments.

Chapter 8

The persons who committed the crime selected a location approximately 110 miles west of Washington, DC. Their destination was just outside the small town of Clary, VA, which is located at the northern end of the Shenandoah Valley. This place was selected because it's a straight drive on Interstate 66 directly west of Washington, DC. Outside the township, a remote cabin in the woods had been rented for six months, paid for in full in cash. Two of the rooms had also been renovated with secure doors and windows. Carly and Peggy Turner were being held hostage at this remote cabin. The rooms were equipped with a small couch, a bed, and a bathroom. Their captors never spoke to either hostage; when meals were brought to them, the captors still wore full ski masks, black clothing head to toe, and black latex gloves. This apparel made it extremely difficult to identify any one of them. Carly and Peggy's means of communication was a white dry-erase board with a felt-tip pen. The bedrooms had a CCTV camera mounted in a corner of the ceiling to keep them both under surveillance.

One of the first encounters each person had was when their captors entered their room and had them hold up a sign and take their picture. Shortly afterward, Peggy was shown Carly's picture, and Carly was shown Peggy's picture. Because each was holding the same sign, they read the board that confirmed to them:

You are both being held hostage at this location. If you try to do anything to escape or cause us difficulty, the other hostage will be severely punished. You both are being held for ransom. Alan has been made aware of our terms and will facilitate both your releases if he complies. Expect to be here for 1-2 weeks, solely dependent on receipt of the ransom payment.

Carly screamed out loud, which resulted in her being bound and a bag again being placed over her head. She knew her outburst had led to this punishment, so she decided to act more subdued going forward.

In viewing Carly's picture and reading the note, Peggy was more composed now that she understood their abduction was all about money. Given the circumstances, they both had to comply and wait, however long it took for the ordeal to end. Given the nature of her abduction, she had the feeling these people were professional, and the chance of rescue by police authorities was minimal or non-existent. She wrote a request on her whiteboard, asking her captors if she could correspond with or see Carly, but the immediate written reply was 'no'.

Chapter 9

Zach reached out to Cody and told him the FBI would do a briefing early in the afternoon, and he would like him to attend. Cody jumped at the chance to leave the office and participate in the meeting. He arrived on time at the Turners, where Zach met him at the front door, and then they proceeded to the conference area. Alan and Agent Ross were the only others attending – Kim Ross called the meeting to discuss the information they had developed on the ransom payment made in uncut diamonds. The New York City Diamond District could indeed handle securing the quantity and size of stones needed for the ransom. It would most likely involve two diamond brokers to obtain the amount required. She explained they would be dealing with approximately 1000 uncut stones. Kim indicated her contacts told her each stone would yield ½ the weight of a polished and finished diamond. She stated that a 4-carat uncut stone would produce a 2-carat diamond that would be untraceable. If and when the diamonds were cut and polished, their value would be more than double that of the uncut stones, or simply put, a two-million-dollar ransom becomes a four-million-dollar payday. Lastly, she indicated that with the 4-day window referenced in the ransom email, decisions would need to be made promptly to complete the wire transfer of funds required to meet the deadline.

Alan advised Kim to get Bev, his assistant, who had set her office up in the study down the hallway, to coordinate the wire transfer for payment to the diamond brokers. Bev also confirmed to the group that AX Tech's corporate insurance policies did cover the family of corporate executives for the peril of kidnapping. Alan asked Bev to ensure the insurance company was aware of the exact cost of acquiring the uncut stones. Bev indicated that the insurance carrier wanted a contact at the FBI so they could monitor if the criminals were ever apprehended; they would have certain legal rights to any recovery after the claim was paid to AX Tech Corp. Kim said to provide her name and contact information as she handed Bev her business card. Alan then requested that Kim deliver the stones to the FBI for safekeeping until the actual ransom payment was made. She indicated arrangements would be made for the safekeeping of the stones.

Cody made an offer to Alan and the FBI to have Jack, also known as Stoney, be the person to deliver the stones wherever the instructions were received. He briefly mentioned Stoney's special forces credentials and a person who could handle any situation that may crop up at the exchange point. Alan embraced the idea of having someone other than an FBI agent involved in delivery, primarily because if the criminals identified this person as an FBI agent, it could lead to backlash when making the ransom payment.

Kim closed the meeting by stating that the Bureau was formulating a plan to have substantial resources in the general vicinity of DC, which had yet to be determined. The key was deploying their resources to the exact location within the 15-minute window for delivering the ransom payment. She said any plan the FBI formulated would be presented for discussion, focusing on the minimal risk of endangering Carly and Peggy. She addressed Alan, indicating that the use of Cody's employee, Stoney, would be discussed with her team, but based on his abilities, she thought it would not be a problem to use him to deliver the ransom.

Cody, Kim, and Zach all walked out to their cars together. Cody wanted Kim to know that Zach and he had made a great team in Army Intelligence, and that his sole purpose was to assist, not interfere, with the Bureau's handling of the kidnapping investigation. Kim, very professionally, said she appreciated any input or insight that Zach or Cody could provide, then handed each of them a business card with her contact information. As Kim walked toward her car, she turned her head and flashed Cody a million-dollar smile and a wink of the eye. Cody flipped over the business card she had handed him and saw the handwritten notation, "Call me," with her cell phone number. Cody shouted back, "Will do." Zach looked confused at Cody's out-of-the-blue comment.

Chapter 10

Twenty-four hours later, the FBI called for another meeting and an update at Turner's home. Still within the four-day window, no new messages or communications had come from the kidnappers. Senior Agent Shaun O'Hara led a meeting with Agents Ross, Alan, Zach, and Cody, who were in attendance. O'Hara indicated the only good news was that the diamonds would be in FBI hands in DC tomorrow. The negotiations, acquisition, and transit of the stones had gone exceptionally well. He told Alan that Beverly, his assistant, had efficiently handled the wire transfer of funds to pay the diamond brokers in New York. Kim added that on the negative side, the Bureau has uncovered no new tangible leads to identify who committed the crime. Our focus is on finding someone responsible for the crime that could lead us to where Peggy and Carly are being held captive. Our informant network associated with criminal types had not yet yielded anything valuable for us to pursue.

Shaun wanted to outline a plan that the FBI has formulated to track the uncut diamonds, possibly. He believed the stones would lead them to discover who was responsible and potentially end up at the exact location of the captives. If the area were not positively identified as holding Peggy and Carly, they would want to execute the ransom payment as advised.

He indicated that any type of electronic tracking device embedded with the stones that sent a frequency could be detected, hence putting the hostages at risk. The FBI has the technology to put a clear coating on all the stones that emit a low level of radiation. The radiation was at a dose that would not cause anyone harm. Still, with sophisticated equipment, our detectors could pick up elevated radiation levels at a range of 100 feet or more. We would plan to have upwards of 10 vehicles available with radiation monitors in the general vicinity of Washington, DC, as denoted in the kidnapper's following email message. Once the exact location of the drop was identified, the FBI would deploy these vehicles in 5-7 minutes to set up a solid perimeter on every street or alley. We estimate that we will be able to cover a 1000-1500 foot perimeter or where the payment will be made. When the diamonds are moved, they would cross our perimeter and provide us with an ID of a person or vehicle possessing the stones. We have the manpower to establish covert tracking operations without being detected. O'Hara said our Bureau has mastered the ability to track a car or person. Once the hostages are released, we'll use the information we obtain to track the stones and go after the criminals involved. He felt this posed little risk to the hostages since the payment would be made using the quantity and quality of stones requested.

Kim said that as a backup to the radiation detection, they felt that Washington, DC, provided numerous residential and commercial buildings where they could enter and set up a visible perimeter around the drop-off area. Communications between all field agents, detection vehicles, and trackers were secured. She indicated the Bureau would be committing its best field agents to this operation, giving them an excellent chance to track or identify the persons involved.

Since the FBI intended not to take any overt action against the criminals before Carly and Peggy's release, Alan and Zach provided no pushback against the FBI's plan. Once the hostages were safe, they wanted the criminals apprehended and brought to justice as swiftly as possible. Zach said the main reason he felt every means should be used to ID the criminals was that, without an arrest, this is highly likely to be done to another family.

Alan asked Beverly to stay behind to discuss some company business. He mentioned this kidnapping must not jeopardize AX Tech Corp. opportunity to secure a massive contract to supply small arms to the Hungarian military. As a NATO member, it was quite possible AX could land numerous other contacts in Europe if Hungary signed a deal. Beverly assured Alan over the past several years that there were no problems that couldn't be resolved when working together.

Chapter 11

Cody asked Zach if he could meet at his office this afternoon around 3 p.m., when he planned to get the team together for a briefing. After the FBI update, Zach said there was no reason for him to hang out at the family home, knowing the following message was still days away.

The team assembled at three o'clock in Cody's conference room - Susie, Karen, Carter(Q), and Jack AKA Stoney - as Zach arrived and took a seat. Cody provided the rundown from the morning meeting with the FBI. He advised Stoney that he offered his services as the delivery person for the diamonds. Cody expected the FBI to have him mic up with voice communication on a secure channel. Stoney, who was trained for action, indicated that the role of the delivery person should not be a problem, and he was ready to assist in any way.

Cody floated the idea of getting two of their stealth drones up on the day of the payment drop. Air space over DC was heavily controlled, with the White House and the Capitol at risk for air-type attacks. Cody asked Carter, AKA "Q," if their best cameras could film surveillance, especially when the final drop area was identified. Q indicated the stealth drones changed colors like a chameleon; looking at them upward, they mirrored the sky; if you were looking down on them, they mirrored the ground below. The height was the tricky part, as it needed to be low enough not to be detected by government monitoring. As for sound, their electric motors are almost noiseless from ground level. Since the FBI had not mentioned drone usage, they felt no need to ask for permission or inform them of their intentions. Q indicated with two drones programmed for a race track, figure 8 pattern, one drone covering north & south, and the other east & west. This provides them with excellent ground coverage surveillance of any area.

It was agreed that Zach would be the conduit, stationed at the family home and providing real-time information from any messages received from the kidnappers. Stoney asked if any of his retired comrades who worked with him on security details should be ready. Cody stated that the FBI tried at all costs to avoid confrontation until Carly and Peggy were safely released.

For this reason, he felt additional manpower was not needed, but it would be prudent to ask them to be ready to respond if circumstances change. Cody added to Stoney that we have no idea how the exchange will be done. Just because you're playing the role of UPS man, there may be an element of danger we don't know about. Stoney said with a straight face that any hiccups along the way would be dealt with expeditiously. With so little information from the authorities, they were resigned to sit tight and wait for any new developments to emerge.

Cody, after heading back to his office from the briefing with his team, placed a call to Kim's cell phone. When she picked up by saying, "Hello Cody," he knew she had obtained his cell number and programmed it into her phone. When dealing with an FBI agent, one has to expect that they have unlimited resources available for getting information. Cody asked Kim if he could treat her to a picnic lunch the next day, guaranteeing it would only take 45 minutes out of her busy schedule. He offered to pick up bagel sandwiches from the best deli in Old Towne Alexandria. She agreed to meet him, indicating that her time would be very tight, and then requested hummus on an everything bagel with lettuce and tomato. Cody advised her to drive into Old Towne from DC around 1 p.m., make a left turn on Princess Street, and follow it to the park on the Potomac River. He would have a blanket ready for their lunch, and mentioned the weather looked delightful. Since Cody was not in a relationship, he was excited to get to know Kim better and hoped the feeling was mutual.

Kim arrived a few minutes early, wearing her standard FBI blouse and slacks. Her attire did not detract from her stunning features, and Cody did notice for the first time that she had let her dark brown, shoulder-length hair down from the tight bun she always wore. Cody greeted her unexpectedly with a big hug and told her that a hug gets the touchy-feely part of their relationship out of the way. She responded with a kiss on his cheek, indicating she needed that hug, as the investigation was not producing any tangible results.

They agreed not to discuss work and kept the conversation light. Cody ran over the menu, which consisted of bagel sandwiches, celery and carrot sticks, natural fruit juice, and a large bag of kettle-cooked potato chips, as his philosophy is that healthy food always needs a crunch factor. For dessert, he advised Kim that they would be splitting a dark chocolate bar with 90% Cacao bitter chocolate. He knew that type of chocolate was very healthy for you, but had no idea what the benefits were. She wasted no time with her tight schedule, enjoying the food and the beautiful view of the river. During lunch, Kim asked Cody if he was in any relationship, which he thought was a pretty direct question. Cody honestly replied that he was not, but that he could see one in his immediate future. He gave her his best smile and a wink of the eye. The gesture was not lost on Kim, and she said that she was expecting to get a goodbye hug when lunch was over in a few minutes.

Before leaving, Kim told Cody she had not dated anyone for quite some time and was maybe a little rusty. Her world was consumed by studying to become an FBI agent, training at the Quantico Marine Base, and working out at the gym during her free time. Her only other activity was sleeping 6 to 7 hours a night. Cody said he hoped he could change her routine in a very positive way – he then said their next date would be on the 27-foot sailboat he kept at the Washington Sailing Marina. He indicated that being out on the water with the wind powering the sails was the most peaceful time anyone could spend. Cody did mention to Kim that boating attire did not include business suits and white high-neck blouses. Kim replied that she would look forward to their next get-together and that her attire would suit the occasion. The goodbye hug was mutual and tender, and then Kim hurried off to DC feeling fabulous.

Chapter 12

Upon returning to the Turner estate, Zach was advised by Alan that an unexpected message from the kidnappers had been received. They proceeded to Alan's home office, and he called up the email, which Zach read:

No negotiations: Your delivery person must wear construction site clothing, including a green vest with the words' DC Public Works' stenciled on the back and a hard hat. They should be using a canvas-type toolbox to transport the stones. If you do not comply, our prior email cited the consequences you face.

After Zach read the message, he immediately called Cody and provided the updated information. Cody told Zach that a construction site, given the number of workers employed by numerous contracting companies, would create a great environment to make an exchange. Stoney-wearing DC Public Works garb would become invisible on any job site.

Cody's cell phone rang with a request from the FBI to schedule a meeting at Cody's office with Stoney to review the timetable for the delivery of the diamonds. They asked if Cody was up to date on the latest email, and he indicated that he had been advised of the message's content. The FBI stated that if Stoney could provide his clothing, shoe, and hat sizes, they would secure the construction clothes and vest required in the email. A meeting was then scheduled in two hours with the Bureau. Cody found Stoney and linked him into the call to provide the necessary sizing information and confirm his availability for the meeting.

Two hours later, two FBI agents arrived at Cody's office and produced their credentials. They said their job involved communications and logistics, including securing construction clothing. The four met in Cody's conference room. The senior agent took the lead and explained to Stoney that they would like a live camera and sound built into the clothing. He explained that the audio and video devices would be concealed and invisible to anyone. The audio would be transmitted on a secure frequency that could not be intercepted. He added that this would provide them with detailed footage of the drop and a means for Stoney to request help.

The agents believed either the stones would be left in a particular place and retrieved later, or Stoney would meet a person face-to-face in making the transfer. One agent indicated a drop-off was less likely unless secured in a locked compartment. If a person showed up, they expected the individual to be hired "blindly," with no knowledge of what they were getting and probably no relationship with the organization responsible. If Stoney were requested to remove his clothing before the exchange, all cameras and microphones would be sewn into the clothes' pockets and not be visible. They asked if Stoney felt a full-body search was a risk to him; they would not embed the equipment into the clothing but would rely strictly on a very tiny earpiece/mic to communicate. Stoney replied to the agents that he had no problem with the camera and mic, asking only if a weapon could be provided for him to use. After some thought, the senior agent indicated that placing an LCP (a light, compact pistol) made by Ruger on top of the hard hat webbing should be possible. The gun would be a .380 caliber, which held one in the chamber and six bullets in the magazine. The agent indicated this was not a powerful weapon, but with hollow-point bullets, it would be very effective at close range. The gun should not be easily visible if he had to remove the hard hat. Stoney liked the idea of having access to any type of gun if the situation warranted.

Stoney was then asked to spend the night at the FBI headquarters in DC before making the payment. The primary reason was his deployment to the general vicinity of DC and subsequent movement to the specific area within the 15-minute window. His only questions to the agents were how good the food was and if he could get his steak rare.

Cody's only request to the agents attending was that Stoney be provided with some type of lightweight body armor if the situation turns into gunplay for any reason. They acknowledged that it was already accounted for and that it would be provided underneath the construction clothes.

After the agents left, Cody asked Stoney if he had to change his pay grade to construction work wages. He laughed at the comment and said

to Cody, "*Most people don't shoot the messenger.*" Stoney then stated that this job assignment was his contribution to Zach and his family and that he was excited to get it done. Cody's only thought was, "*Once a warrior, always a warrior.*"

Chapter 13

At FBI Headquarters, Shaun O'Hara and Kim Ross were heading up the last major meeting with close to 40 agents assigned to attend the briefing. The first order of business was a review of the email received that morning. Given the requirement for contractors' clothing and the need to post DC Public Works on the day-glow type vest, the conversation centered on what indication this provides regarding the drop or exchange location. Consensus after a lengthy discussion pointed to an active construction site, midday, with numerous workers, to avoid distractions and cause difficulty in monitoring the diamonds. No general contractor would question someone walking on a construction site representing DC Public Works. Knowing the criminal's kidnapping plan had been executed nearly perfectly, without leaving a trace, they must expect diligent planning from them on how they would get paid.

Shaun O'Hara voiced his opinion on the way he would execute the delivery. He spoke of the old shell game, where a ball is placed under a cup and then switched with two other cups. Shaun believed the diamonds would be deposited in a standard container that could be locked and secured. Then, at quitting time, the stones put in something as simple as a water cooler and walked off the site with the dozen other workers. This placed the sole burden on their radiation detectors to track the stones and determine when they crossed the perimeter set up and left the job site. The person exiting would have to be trusted with $ 2 million, so they needed to identify the individual. Other theories were floated, but no one could say for sure what would take place.

The task force, comprising over 40 agents, was divided into four principal subgroups during the briefing. Approximately 15-20 vehicles, including cars, vans, motorcycles, and electric bicycles of all types and years, would be available. Rapid deployment was the key once the final location was identified and the transfer process was determined.

Jack, AKA Stoney, had a limited resume in special forces, which was shared with all the agents as the individual selected to deliver the uncut stones. Everyone was advised that Stoney could provide video and audio feed, provided his clothing wasn't removed. Kim closed the meeting, stating they were dealing with a sophisticated and cunning organization. The focus was to gather information covertly that could be used to identify the organization, following the release of the two hostages. Her final comment to everyone is that they must remain flexible in their approach and communicate exceptionally well to succeed.

The morning of the fifth day, when the ransom of uncut diamonds would be paid to the kidnappers, brought extremely high tension and apprehension in Turner's home, FBI headquarters, and Cody's firm, Fail-Safe. Cody had Carter (Q) and two of his best IT technicians spend the night in a centrally located hotel in Washington, DC. They could not risk getting instructions early in the morning and had to deal with rush hour commuter traffic to get in position. Q was instructed to drive immediately to the general area of DC, as indicated in the 1st email message, and then deploy both drones over a several-mile area. This should provide around 40 minutes of general surveillance until the second message from the kidnappers indicates the exact payment location. At that point, Cody would contact Q to reprogram the drones to create figure 8 circles exactly over the specific payment area. Stoney would make the payment within the next 15-minute window, as per the requirements stated in the email. The drones had approximately 2-2½ hours of battery power before coming down and getting a new set of batteries. Like any aircraft, the drone's power usage depended heavily on airspeed and wind velocity. Video links from the drones were sent back in real-time to Cody's computers at Fail-Safe for permanent download and review.

The FBI had formulated several principal plans of action and numerous contingency plans to react to the upcoming information from the kidnappers. Given the limited timeline, the task force's size would require perfect coordination to get all its assets in place. Shaun O'Hara and Kim Ross would be in the central FBI field command post, monitoring all developments and communications.

At the Turner house, Zach thought his dad was showing signs of stress, wanting to get this behind them. Once Alan made a business decision at AX Tech, Zach knew his dad always wanted to focus on the next issue at hand; it was just his nature. Alan told Zach that he believed Stoney was the right person to trust in executing the payment drop. Alan said he couldn't wait for the message that indicated both family members were released.

Zach knew it was crucial to update Cody quickly on any information received, enabling him to advise Q on the data needed to position the drones.

Chapter 14

The message arrived in the early afternoon at 1:30 p.m. at Alan's Office email address; only four words were typed in the email:

COLUMBIA HEIGHTS, Washington, DC

FBI agents at the house immediately informed the task force of the general area in DC. Zach's text message to Cody provided the same information. Based on the mapping information, the FBI decided that the Powell Recreation Center was the most centrally located place in Columbia Heights. The FBI would then deploy their four divisions from the Rec center, using a simple compass to head North, South, East, and West. This approach ensured that one unit would be very close to the final ransom area, allowing for quick deployment of the other three units. Stoney was in the mobile command center on the way to the Rec center. He was well-outfitted with well-worn construction clothes, boots, a stenciled vest, and a hard hat that did indeed hold a small semi-automatic pistol. The body camera and mic were almost invisible, and he had solid voice and video communication with the command unit. His only question to Shaun and Kim is, Where did the FBI get used clothes that fit perfectly and allow room for the body armor underneath? The last item provided to Stoney was a two-ply thick set of latex gloves. They indicated to Stoney that the diamonds were sealed in a plastic bag, and a knife was provided to slit the seal, allowing for radiation coating to be exposed. The levels were shallow, but as a precaution, he should wear gloves if required to handle the stones, as they may cause minor skin irritation.

Q responded, drove to Columbia Rd NW and 14th St NW, and found a vacant alley where he promptly programmed and launched the two drones. His watch showed 1:41 p.m., indicating he had 34 minutes until the next message with the updated final ransom location would be released. At Cody's office, several people were tasked with watching the live feed of the surveillance video and making time notations if anything appeared odd, out of place, or suspicious.

The second and last message was longer and more detailed, as expected: It arrived in Alan's email 45 minutes later at 2:15 p.m. – the message read:

Payment will be delivered at Meridian Hills Park. To access it, use the entrance located mid-park on 15th St NW and Chapin St NW. Then, proceed on the paved path crossing the park toward the west side. Your person will approach a water fountain just off the park path, encircled with yellow tape indicating it's out of order. If our instructions were followed, he would act as a DC construction employee and appear to be fixing or tinkering with the water fountain. He will remove the strainer screen over the drain and deposit the uncut diamonds down the drain pipe. He will replace the drain screen and ensure all the yellow tape remains in place. Then, he will immediately exit the park. A contractor unrelated to our organization will remove the water fountain

before the park closes. Do not impede or interfere in any way with its removal. When we secure the payment and assess its value, a final message will be sent regarding the release of the captives.

Given its length, Zach could screenshot the entire message and send it to Cody. Q immediately took Cody's call and obtained the longitude and latitude coordinates for the center of Meridian Park. Q did not need to land the drones; he reprogrammed them directly from his laptop. Q advised Cody he was about a half mile away and would stay in the vacant alley until it was time to leave. Q closed the call, advising Cody that it's been good; the drones were doing their job.

Shaun and Kim knew, as with everyone on the task receiving the message, that this was a dead drop ransom payment and not a meeting with another person to make a face-to-face exchange – the 15-minute meter was ticking, and a car with Stoney on board was sent to the park entrance. Stoney was briefed on the message and asked if his acting skills as a repair person were in order; Stoney indicated he could pull this off without any problem. Secretly, he wished there might be something more complex and challenging than stuffing a lot of uncut diamonds down a drain pipe. He suspected the bad guys might have eyes in the park, so he had to play his part in making this happen. His last thought was that a UPS deliveryman might look OK on his next resume. Kim spoke to Stoney through his earpiece, emphasizing that the last thing to avoid at all costs was for a homeless person in the park to witness $2 million worth of uncut diamonds being dumped down a water fountain drain pipe.

FBI tech personnel briefed everyone on the logistics of the park:

Meridian Hill Park had ten entrances, with five on the west side off 16th St NW and five on the east side off 15th St NW. The park spanned approximately 4-5 city blocks, starting with Euclid St NW on the north side and ending at W St NW on the south. Two reasonably high apartment buildings outside the park were *Enoy* on the west and *Adams Garden* on the east. These buildings' rooftops should be considered for an observation post, but mature trees may block any line of sight.

Shaun and Kim deployed the various vehicles with the radiation detection equipment - each should be near each of the 10 entrances/exits. Any agent dressed appropriately and with field skills should enter at different access points and spread out throughout the park. All persons exiting the park should be photographed with date and time stamps. They were down to their last few minutes of the timeline and had to advise Stoney to make his entrance and perform the drop.

Flashing their credentials, the FBI got apartment maintenance to allow them rooftop access. Agents on both buildings reported limited visual sight lines due to tree cover, but would remain in place if needed.

Chapter 15

Stoney lumbered in, shuffling his feet like a person paid by the hour, not by the job, and entered the park at 2:27 p.m. This stayed within the kidnappers' 15-minute time window, allowing the FBI maximum time to set up and cover the drop location. He knew there was a good chance the bad guys had one spotter in the park and that they could probably communicate with their bosses. Finding the water fountain was easy; he started unwinding the yellow caution tape and appeared to be trying to figure out the water fountain's problems. Stoney casually said into his mic that he did not see anyone near the fountain.

After removing the drain screen, he placed the tool bag containing the stones on top of the fountain, slit the bag open, and slowly scooped handfuls of uncut diamonds and dropped them into the drain pipe. No one in the immediate vicinity seemed to be paying him any attention. Being a pleasant middle-of-the-week spring day, the park had mild activity but was not busy or crowded.

After opening the plastic bag, Stoney told the FBI he was questioning whether the drain could hold all the diamonds. He indicated he would fill it without exposing any stones in the catch basin. Taking his time to drop nearly a thousand stones, he announced the job was done, and the drain screen was reattached. His last comment to the FBI command post was that he expected this fountain had been altered somehow to hold the entire quantity of uncut stones. Taking time to reattach the yellow tape around the fountain, he finished his part in paying the ransom.

He tried to move his body in different directions while slowly walking back to the park exit. This allowed his body camera to record what he was observing. Nothing seems out of the ordinary, but the video film may show some clues or leads the FBI could follow. His total time in the park was about 12-13 minutes from start to finish.

When Stoney returned to his vehicle, he knew there'd be an extensive debriefing session at FBI headquarters. His only thought now was whether he got to keep the construction outfit, including the hard hat with that nice little compact pistol stored in the hat's webbing, as a memento.

A few minutes after 3 p.m., the FBI identified a pickup truck hauling a small garden trailer parked on 15th NW near the Chapin St entrance. Agents on the rooftop reported the license plate number. They indicated one black male, approximately early sixties, unloading a hand truck and a tarp, and appeared headed for the park entrance. Before Romeo Gardner set his tool bag down next to the water fountain, the FBI knew his name, age, and that he advertised himself as a local handyman. A criminal record check was run through their database and showed no arrest or prior record for Romeo Gardner. Shaun O'Hara informed his field force that Romeo Gardner appeared to have been hired to deliver the fountain, likely for cash, and would then take the fountain to the location of the actual exchange.

Romeo thought *this was my lucky day, as he planned to buy several lottery tickets later with the $500 cash he received for removing the water fountain.*

He received a phone call offering to move a broken water fountain for $500 in cash. He accepted the offer and was instructed where to go: to unbolt the fountain, roll it into a large tarp, and deliver it to 2000 14th NW. This location was less than a half mile from the park and would use minimal gas. Feeling the bolts sticking up posed a tripping risk to people using the park, so he wrapped some yellow tape around the four now exposed bolts. After duct-taping the tarp tightly closed, he loaded it onto his hand truck and rolled it back to his trailer. Every movement was witnessed by an FBI agent in the park and communicated back to the command center.

As Romeo exited the park, an old van denoting AAA Painting Company was parked about 100 feet from Romeo's vehicle. This van was one of the 10 vehicles covering the park exits carrying the radiation detection equipment. They reported not getting a "hit" but indicated Romeo turned away from where they were parked, increasing the distance between them. Shaun and Kim immediately contacted the FBI's technical experts. They inquired whether the solid 4-sided metal housing of the fountain base and the wrapping in the tarp might have affected the radiation emission level that could be detected. The FBI tech agent's reply to Shaun indicated that the effectiveness of reducing radiation emissions from the fountain depended on the thickness and type of metal housing, but it was possible.

Romeo's vehicle and trailer reached 2000 14th St NW in 5-6 minutes. The FBI had no problem tracking it for the ½ mile distance; it was astonishing when Romeo pulled into the DC Public Works facility. After conversing with the gate guard, Romeo was shown the way to their maintenance area. Romeo did need to ask another worker for the city where they wanted the water fountain dropped off. It took him several minutes to unstrap the fountain, roll it off his trailer, and head home.

Chapter 16

The facility was identified on the FBI computer, which indicated that it closed at 4 p.m. daily in 20 minutes.

Shaun O'Hara openly asked for input and opinions on how the DC Public Works location would be used to transfer the stones without detection. There was a significant consensus that DC Public Works needed an insider. One thing was sure: they needed a camera on the fountain to see who approached it since the facility was closing. Shaun said it may be risky, but we can't be sure that our radiation detectors will detect the stone's movements. All the detection vehicles were moved from the park, and a tight perimeter around the DC facility was formed.

Cody's tech team, monitoring the live feed from the two drones, immediately alerted him in his office, advising that they had observed the removal of the water fountain from the park. Cody believed the FBI was responsible for conducting surveillance on the transportation of the fountain to another location. He contacted Q and advised him to retrieve the drones ASAP and return to the office. He felt fortunate that they had managed to capture just under 2 hours of video covering the ransom area without his drones being detected in the sky. If they could spot just one vehicle of interest and get a license plate number, the FBI might have the lead they need to ID the organization responsible—a long shot at best, but worth the risk. Cody instructed the two employees monitoring the video stream feed to rewind the video and play it in slow motion, as the drones were approaching. This tedious task was necessary to look for any clues that might help.

The FBI felt it was worth the risk to approach Romeo as soon as he left the immediate area of the DC Public Works facility. They had to know how he was hired and what instructions he had been given. When two FBI agents approached him, Romeo had not finished parking his vehicle and trailer in the alley behind his house. His reaction was that this would not be his "lucky day" after all. They asked if they could talk privately, and Romeo invited them into his house. He told the agents he lived alone because his wife died of breast cancer several years back.

The agents asked Romeo, who had hired him, to remove the water fountain in Meridian Hill Park a short while ago. He replied that he took a phone call two days ago, and the person indicated they represented a minority contractor hired by DC Public Works to do odd jobs in maintaining city property. The person calling indicated his minority-status company had no employees, the contracts they were awarded with the city were lucrative enough, and he would subcontract with people like Romeo to get the work done, pay them well, and still make a nice paycheck for his company. He remembers the fella saying, "It's all our tax dollars at work - the city spends without many questions." The man said he was behind in repairing a water fountain in one of the public parks, hence this job offer.

The FBI asked him if he had ever mentioned the name of his company; Romeo indicated he hadn't and had never thought to ask. The fellow on the phone said a non-operational water fountain needed to be removed and dropped off at the Public Works facility. Said he would pay me $500 in cash if I could do the job. He needed it done today at 3 p.m. because the DC Public Works facility where it would be dropped off closes at 4 p.m. If I were OK with that, he would send a bike messenger to my place with the payment for doing the job. This friendly fella indicated that if I got the job done as instructed, he could probably throw me a new job every week. It was easy money; someone was going to make it. I told him I was very reliable and good at my word. He went over the details on the park entrance and the location of the fountain, how to unbolt it and wrap it up tight, and the address of the Public Works facility - I knew where it was located, not too many blocks from Meridian Hill Park.

Yesterday, a kid on a bike rang my doorbell and handed me an envelope with my name printed on it. Inside were five $100 bills, along with a note stating that the Fountain in Meridian Hill Park would be removed at 3 p.m. on the date of the note.

The FBI lead agent asked if he still had the envelope, note, and money. Romeo said the note and envelope were in the recycle bin, and the $500 was in my wallet. The agent pulled out a plastic bag and wooden tweezers and then placed the note and envelope in an evidence bag. He indicated they would provide him with a receipt because the money also needed to be fingerprinted and loaded into a separate bag. They asked Romeo for a set of his prints, which they knew were on the note, envelope, and money. Romeo watched enough TV - one never said NO to the FBI.

The last question concerned the bike messenger. Did he know him? Could he recognize him? Did the kid say anything about who hired him to deliver the envelope? Romeo stated he had no idea who the kid was and didn't make any small talk with him. He may be able to recognize him, though he added that all young teenagers tend to look and dress alike these days.

They left their cards and advised him that a severe crime was ongoing and that if he thought of anything that he had not mentioned, to contact them day or night. Romeo's last thought was that his lottery money just disappeared.

Shaun O'Hara felt the DC Facility was picked because someone believed they had a foolproof plan to get to the stones without leaving a trace. He ordered two of his agents, who were in very casual clothes, to go into the DC Public Works facility and seek out the director. They should take one of their smallest high-resolution cameras with them. In a private room, convey to the director the urgency of locating a camera on the blue wrap tarp holding the water fountain, indicating that it must be inconspicuous. This way, they could monitor the live feed if anyone approached the tarp fountain all night. Shaun said it would be risky if the Director started discussing our surveillance with anyone who worked at the facility.

The two agents selected approached the facility's director. They stressed the importance of keeping this strictly confidential due to an ongoing investigation and locating the camera so that it would not be seen. The agent's feedback to Shaun was that the director seemed concerned and, being a responsible person, said he would find the wrapped fountain and locate the camera personally. He only asked to be notified when there was no longer a reason to keep the camera on his premises so that it could be removed and returned. Shaun told Kim he felt they closed the back door to get the camera placed. Someone with access must enter this facility to remove the stones and take them off these premises, and we should be aware of this.

Chapter 17

Kim then left the mobile command unit and was at the FBI headquarters to debrief Stoney on his 10-15 minutes in the park. Kim met Stoney in a secure room at the Bureau and advised him that she would like to tape the conversation and be able to replay it to other agents if needed. Stoney was okay with the taping; his attitude was to do what it took to get the family members back. Kim sat back and told Stoney she had no specific questions but wanted him to provide his thoughts and impressions from when he entered the park until he exited.

Stoney said he took a slow walk into the park to see if anyone made eye contact or showed interest in him. Before he entered, it made sense that the bad guys might have a spotter in place, given the amount of ransom being paid. He indicated that his combat training gave him a better understanding of danger than the average person. He said he did not feel watched at any time, entering or exiting the park. If he was, they were very good at surveillance.

Stoney said he didn't lift the canvas tool bag with the stones until he got the OK to enter the park. He said the weight was pretty substantial, and when I cut open the bag, the quantity was larger than I expected. I thought an ordinary drinking fountain drain would never accommodate this load. While tinkering with the fountain to resemble a repairman, I removed the drain screen. I observed that the drain pipe was approximately 1½ inches in diameter, exceeding the standard size for water fountain drains. The pipe was also made of PVC plastic, which is relatively common, just oversized in diameter. After slitting open the sack, I decided it was best to hand-scoop the stones into the drain rather than pouring them, as the latter might draw more attention. I thought the drain would never hold the quantity of stones in the bag. When the first several handfuls were dropped in, I heard a metallic sound, as if the stones were hitting the metal floor panel or being collected in a bucket at the fountain's base. The drain did not clog or refuse to accept new stones until all were deposited. Stoney continued to say that after the first 4-5 handfuls were dropped, the metallic noise disappeared, and I heard stones landing on other stones.

I believe this fountain was customer-built and never intended to be a water fountain. Not sure how you find the person who built it, but if you did, it would point you in the right direction. I replaced the drain screen and rewrapped the yellow caution tape as best I could to indicate that the fountain was still not operational. Then, knowing time was on my side, I took a very slow, casual walk out of the park to allow your video to survey the area. That about sums it up!

Kim felt she owed Stoney a brief update on the removal of the fountain, including where it was taken and stored. She told Stoney they could monitor anyone approaching the fountain while the facility was closed tonight. The handyman hired to remove the fountain has been cleared of any connection to the crime. He was employed by phone and paid in cash by a messenger.

Kim thanked him on behalf of the entire Bureau, accepting the job of going into an unknown situation with a fortune in diamonds in an old tool bag. She told Stoney she heard he was attracted to his construction hard hat, pulled it out of a cardboard box, grabbed a Sharpie pen, and wrote on the inside of the visor KR-TY. She told him that it meant Kim Ross/Thank You. He felt it was a nice gesture on her part and would show it off to the team back at Fail-Safe. Stoney, always observant by training, noticed that no one had removed the Ruger LCP pistol from the webbing of the hard hat. After a well-done job, Kim arranged for a car to get Stoney back to Old Towne Alexandria.

She then typed up Stoney's comments and observations and circulated them amongst the task force. Kim had advised Shaun that she would contact Alan and Zach and update them on the ransom payment. She wasn't looking forward to the call because of the events at the park, and the removal of the fountain didn't provide a clean exchange of the uncut stones to trigger the hostages' release.

Alan picked up on the first ring and told Kim he would put her on speaker and wait a minute while he found Zach so he could listen in on the call. While both were listening to the call, Kim started with a brief recap of Stoney playing the city worker and depositing the stones in the fountain's drain. She didn't feel the need to convey Stoney's comments during the debriefing season at FBI headquarters. Kim explained that approximately 20 minutes after Stoney exited the park, a local DC handyman arrived, unbolted the water fountain, wrapped it in a tarp, and hauled it off ½ mile to the DC Public Works facility. They identified the handyman from his license plates, ran him through criminal records, and he came back clean, showing no criminal record. They tailed him home and felt it was safe to approach him to find out who hired him. She reviewed what Romeo said about the phone call and the money delivered by a bike messenger for payment. The FBI has the payment envelope and is running it for fingerprints. The delivery messenger seems like a dead end - a young kid riding his bike was hired to drop off the payment to the handyman. They were not optimistic that this would result in identifying who hired and sent the messenger.

Kim added that the criminals had not tripped up in their planning and that hiring and paying the handyman would probably lead to another dead end. We believe the handyman has no connection to the crime but was only doing his job to transport the water fountain. We have the fountain under passive surveillance, without going into any detail, assuring them that if the diamonds were to be moved, they would be aware of it. Knowing the organization that structured this crime, we believe they must have a foolproof way to retrieve the diamonds from the Public Works facility. Until the criminals have the stones in hand, validate that they are real, and the quantity justifies the value they requested, we probably will not see any movement on the release of your family.

The Bureau will continue to monitor all your communication devices. If you notice any activity or contact outside of your usual devices, please notify us so we can analyze and respond accordingly. The Bureau plans to remain defensive or passive until your family is released. Kim did not want to suggest that they had little to no leads and were doing everything possible to gather tangible evidence that could break this case open.

Chapter 18

Zach told Alan he was headed to Alexandria to have dinner with Cody. He needed to break the tension of waiting for the following email to pop up, knowing it may contain instructions on when and where Carly and Peggy would be released.

Zach drove straight to Cody's office and found the team, Susie, Carter, Karen, and Stoney, all present in the conference room. Everyone shouted a welcome to Zach as he grabbed a beer from the small office refrigerator and pulled up a chair. Stoney needed Zach to hear a recap of his time in the park dropping off the stones. He commented that he did not feel anyone was observing or watching his moments in the park. The one point he made dealt with the water fountain's construction, which looked relatively new and not in a style or shape he had ever seen in a basic water fountain.

Stoney added that any casual person seeing the yellow tape would know it was not operating and would think it was an actual water fountain. He said that to hold the 1000+ or so uncut diamond stones, the fountain could not have an ordinary drain. The base of the fountain, being sealed on all four sides, would have the capacity to hold the number of stones dispersed.

Cody took over recapping the drone timetable and how many videos had been recorded. After watching live and playing back in slow motion, there was no specific situation on film that did not appear to be relatively routine. They will commit tomorrow to another viewing with the team in the conference room. If Zach wanted to sit in, the meeting was calendared for a 10 a.m. start time.

Cody advised Zach that he had to make two quick business calls and would be back in 10-15 minutes to leave for dinner. Zach told his buddy not to rush; he found something to do to kill the time. Cody was back fairly quickly and asked Zach if he had any food preferences for dinner. With everything going on, Zach said they'd better stay local in case another email came through to Alan's work email address. Cody grabbed his phone, found the contact list, and dialed the restaurant he had in mind, which was centrally located in Old Towne Alexandria. Reservations for 2 for dinner sitting outside were booked. They hopped in Cody's Mustang for the 5-minute drive. Cody announced they were eating French food and backing it up with a good red Bordeaux bottle of wine. Zach indicated he was all in on the dinner recommendation.

Cody asked for a more secluded table so they could brainstorm, similar to how they did in the Army when a significant issue arose and was thrust upon them. The maitre d' was accommodating and sat them off in a corner of the outside patio, giving them some distance and a little privacy from the other diners. The restaurant was bustling in the middle of the week due to a ½ price offer on their wine list today.

Cody knew Zach and openly asked how he and Alan were holding up. Zach replied that over the last 2-4 days, Alan, with help from Beverly, has immersed himself back into the daily routine of running AX Tech. This was his way of coping with the crime, feeling the diamonds would get his wife and daughter back from the kidnappers. Bev had moved into the family s guest house to eliminate a long commute. Both of them have been putting in some long days to keep the company running smoothly.

Zach expressed his current feeling of helplessness to Cody and said that he would have liked to be taken that day and be on the inside rather than on the outside, waiting for something to happen. Cody told his friend that being locked up and under armed guard would present a daunting task to do anything when two other lives were at risk. He believed the FBI had resources they did not openly discuss, and maybe they had data that had not yet been shared with his family. Zach told Cody that unless some development happens before 10 a.m. tomorrow, he'd like to sit in on the meeting with the team. Zach said he felt an energy in the room during the past meetings with the sole focus on helping in any way possible.

Cody shifted gears to lighten the conversation and told Zach about Kim's business card request to call and the subsequent quick picnic lunch. Zach expected nothing less, knowing Cody always connected with beautiful women with his easygoing personality and handsome looks. Zach asked if the 2nd, 3rd, and 4th dates had been arranged. Cody admitted that he planned to take her sailing at the next get-together, but he did not expect it to happen soon, given that this case was still ongoing. Zach told Cody he was glad to hear of the new relationship and to keep him apprised of any details she may share with him that might end this ordeal.

Zach then advised Cody that while returning some business calls before they left for dinner, he walked down to Susie Mathews's office and chatted with her. Zach admitted to Cody that he found Susie attractive and a little intimidating because of her IQ when dealing with computers. After 10 minutes of chit-chat, Zach asks Susie if she would like to get together when this situation ends. Cody then told Zach that he might need to clear any get-together with Susie's boss, who may or may not be on board with this relationship. Zach said she had already given him the green light, stating she would love to, without mentioning asking for the boss's blessing. Both had a good laugh over the exchange, and as on cue, the waiter showed up with two wine glasses and a Chateau bottled 2010 Bordeaux. Dinner ended with Zach driving back to stay in his old bedroom at the Turner family home. Everyone was hoping for a positive message to be received from the kidnappers.

The following morning at 8 a.m., this message appeared in Alan Turner's work email:

The diamonds are being analyzed, and a random sample is being taken to determine the quality level of the uncut diamonds. If we decide it is sufficient and meets the required dollar value, one hostage will be released. Our experts detected a coating that was placed on the stones. This has been removed, but you were warned not to impede the ransom payment in any way. One hostage will remain in our custody until we determine their fate!

Shaun O'Hara and Kim Ross had been at FBI headquarters since 7 a.m., going over reports and updates from their fieldwork. There was not much substance to go on, which had not changed since the investigation's outset. The message was instantly relayed to them. Both scanned it, and Shaun let go of every foul expletive he knew. He immediately recognized that the radiation coating they used had been somehow discovered, and the life of one of the two hostages was now in grave peril.

Once composed, Shaun started barking orders. First, get some agents immediately to the DC Public Works facility and confiscate the water fountain. Do not unwrap or touch the unit without gloves on. He requested the wrapped fountain be sent to the FBI forensic unit ASAP for fingerprinting and analysis of the metal and the age of the parts used in its construction. The most important question is, who built it? Was it custom-made, as Stoney inferred in his debriefing? Custom-made or commercially bought, who had it built or acquired it? He had to assume the diamonds had been removed per the message received. How and when were the central questions? He sought confirmation that the camera feed had not been interrupted since its installation for monitoring the fountain at the Public Works facility. Then, get the radiation units stationed around the perimeter to check that no spike had occurred overnight. Lastly, he asked Kim to get a car and driver to pick them up in front of the Bureau headquarters in 2 minutes and have the vehicle's GPS programmed for Meridian Hill Park.

The FBI black Suburban had lights and sirens going in, trying to navigate Washington, DC's morning rush hour traffic. The anxiety level seemed like the drive took an hour, but they pulled up to the park's entrance in about 12 minutes. Shaun and Kim entered the park using the same means, by Chapin Street that Stoney had taken to pay the ransom. The westerly walk to the yellow tape that Romeo, the handyman, had left to make the bolts stick out was still in place. With gloved hands,

Shaun removed the tape as Kim made a film recording. The bolts appeared firmly held to a metal plate under the grass. As Shaun gently worked his hands between the metal plate and the grass, he cleared enough grass away and let a similar curse rant to the one he said after reading the message from the criminals that morning. Kim's only thought was that this was one Irishman you didn't want to piss off twice in the same day. Shaun and Kim were looking at a round manhole cover, not a metal plate, with a 3-inch access circle in the middle that had been removed. It was shockingly evident that the water fountain drain ran directly through the manhole cover into the sewer or tunnel system underneath the ground. The fountain itself had been installed and bolted to the manhole cover with a firm layer of grass sod covering everything.

Shaun instructed Kim to contact the DC government and arrange for their top city engineer, familiar with the sewer and tunnel systems, to be sent to FBI headquarters promptly. Ensure the person sent can provide computer access to view the sewer/tunnel system records, showing the line's route and purpose or usage. He then wanted an agent posted by the manhole until they got some answers, expecting they would need to send a team into the system to determine if this was how the diamonds were retrieved.

Shaun's last comment to Kim stated he believed the water fountain removal was done to keep law enforcement occupied until the diamonds were securely in the criminals' hands. He expected that the stones would never have been stored in the fountain's base when the fountain was analyzed. His opinion on the ransom payment was that the FBI was set up like a dog chasing its tail and going around in circles. He would find out who was behind this crime and punish them personally. Kim's only thoughts were with Alan and Zach Turner on reading the message and knowing one of their family members was in grave danger.

Chapter 19

During their drive back to FBI headquarters, they were informed that a 25-year career DC city engineer named Hank Evans was being picked up and should arrive in 15 minutes at Bureau headquarters. He would be escorted into conference room 4 on the first level. Shaun & Kim arrived back at FBI headquarters and were informed that Mr. Evans was seated in conference room 4 with an agent awaiting their arrival. Shaun expressed his gratitude to Mr. Evans for promptly responding to their request. He introduced Kim Ross to the city's engineer. He indicated that, unfortunately, they would not be at liberty to discuss the ongoing case they were involved in, but surely needed his expertise. Hank Evans was a bit confused, but he assured them he was there to help and answer any questions they had.

Shaun asked if he could log into the city records and pull up data on the tunnel-type conduit that ran under Meridian Park in Columbia Heights. Hank logged in to the records and asked what they wanted to know. Kim indicated that a paved walking path runs east to west just off the Chapin St entrance to the park. Just off the route was a manhole cover. What size is the conduit or tunnel beneath this manhole cover? What is the purpose of this tunnel? Where does the tunnel start and stop?

Hank Evans took a few minutes to research the records and read the data that should provide the FBI with the answers. He explained that the tunnel in question is designated for communications lines, primarily phone & TV, but has been upgraded to handle fiber optic for Wi-Fi and cable TV. The tunnel also has gas lines and, in some sections, underground electrical lines to service residential units. As to the size of the tunnel, it appears to be approximately 5 feet in diameter. These types of tunnels were built in the 1920s or 1930s, during the development and construction of the DC road system for automobiles. As to where it starts and stops, there is no correct answer. Hank explained that the tunnels principally follow the major streets or avenues, then branch off to secondary streets to provide adequate services to both residential and commercial structures. The tunnel in question, running under Meridian Hill Park, is a branch tunnel that was a junction off the main tunnel running up 14th St NW on the park's east side and connecting to another main tunnel running under Kalorama Rd NW on the west side.

This format continues where the branch tunnels' T" in the main tunnel, so the system does not have an exact starting and stopping point.

Shaun wanted to confirm that the tunnels had room and clearance for service technicians to walk and do repair-type work. He also asked what the average number of manhole covers was that gave people access to the tunnel maze.

Hank indicated that the city had a maintenance staff working 24/7 in tunnels throughout the city. Manholes were designed and placed approximately every 1000 feet or so, using three football fields as a visual reference to Shaun and Kim.

He added that, besides our city workers entering the system, other contractors, especially the major cable providers, have daily access to the tunnel system.

Kim then asked the most pertinent question, "Who has access to the tunnel plans, directions, size, etc.?" Hank gave them the reply they did not want to hear. He noted that most information is now public record and accessible, except for details about the White House or U.S. Capitol grounds. At one time, when everything was on paper blueprint documents, there was limited accessibility to the blueprints of the underground tunnel system. However, when the paper blueprints were digitized and uploaded to a database, it became apparent that too many contractors needed access, and the decision was made to make them public records.

Shaun then requested that he wanted to put an FBI team of 4 people in the tunnel, using the manhole in Meridian Hill Park as the entranceway. Could Hank restrict access this afternoon to prevent his team from dealing with any interference? He explained that two agents would go east toward the 14th St NW main tunnel, then one agent would continue north, and the other would go south. Two agents would be tasked with heading west to the main tunnel under Kalorama Rd and splitting at the "T" intersection in each direction. He could only guess the time they needed, but indicated approximately 2-3 hours should be adequate to provide them with any data or information relating to their case.

Hank stated that with his seniority in the city's engineering department, he would be able to block access to that section of the tunnel system, but needed to get back to his office to get this done. Shaun and Kim again thanked Mr. Evans for his time, information, and cooperation. They were provided with Hank's contact numbers and email if they had any follow-up inquiries. They closed the meeting with the city engineer, indicating that all discussed items must be kept private for now, as failure to do so could seriously impact their investigation. Hank understood the message from the agents and said everything would be kept strictly confidential.

After Mr. Evans left, Shaun & Kim both knew the uncut diamonds left Meridian Park via the service tunnel, probably within minutes from when Stoney dropped the diamonds into the fountain's drainpipe; the timeframe for leaving DC was solely dependent on where in the city they had entered and exited the tunnel system. They had to expect the entry and exit to be a fair distance away to evade any detection by authorities. Once Meridian Park was disclosed as the drop location in their email message, someone was probably already in the tunnel waiting for the stones. They both knew that if the water fountain could not be traced to the person who bought it or had it built, it would provide the criminals with close to 16 hours to cover their tracks by having it removed by the handyman.

Shaun directed Kim to get four forensic specialists at the bureau ready to go into the tunnel system that afternoon. Provide them with basic information on the crime without any names being referenced. Going forward, they were going to compartmentalize details on this case. They would be the only ones to get data from all sources or teams in the field. Kim knew this was very irregular and asked Shaun if he believed there was a leak from within the bureau to the criminal organization. Shaun hesitated before saying that money can corrupt many good people.

Shaun told Kim that the coating they applied to the uncut diamonds was close to invisible. Still, somehow, it was detected, as referenced in the email received that morning. No matter how sophisticated this criminal organization was, the odds of them having and using a Geiger counter that could detect radiation were slim to none.

If his reasoning was correct, he added that someone inside the investigation provided the criminals with that information. With the FBI task force of nearly forty agents, counting their administrative staff backing up the field agents, this would come close to 100 persons at the Bureau who had access to and knowledge of that information.

Shaun told Kim that if she stayed with the Bureau long enough, a mole or insider would surface sooner or later in one of her cases. The way to ferret the person out was to compartmentalize requests and not let anyone know or see the big picture. Once this is in place, some disinformation can be filtered to specific teams, and if that data surfaces, the problem can be narrowed down very quickly. Shaun stated they did not have the time to start and monitor a disinformation campaign, given the stakes are too high and may involve the life of either Carly or Peggy Turner.

Shaun's last thought with Kim was that every day that passed, they didn't hear from the kidnappers, which could be a positive sign. Kim was unsure where his train of thought was going until he indicated that if the organization had a foolproof backup plan, it would respond very quickly with their plan "B". If there was a delay or lag in receiving the following message, the criminals had to formulate a new, foolproof strategy and leave no trace back to them. Shaun added: Did they treat the kidnapping as a business venture and see an opportunity to profit again by using the coating substance as their leverage? The worst situation would be for the kidnappers to take the ransom paid, polish the stones, which would then make them untraceable, release one hostage, and kill the 2nd person, closing out their involvement. Kim shuddered as a chill went through her body, knowing Shaun's logic for either scenario seemed very likely.

Shaun then asked Kim to make a tough call to the Turners and give them the basic outline of how they believed the kidnappers secured the ransom payment.

After consulting with Hank Evans, the city engineer, Kim received confirmation that no interference should occur when placing the FBI teams in the tunnel system. Kim again thanked Evans for his information and help in working with the Bureau. She could only hope their team could secure some evidence left in one of the tunnels that may provide a solid direction for identifying the kidnappers.

Her next call, per Shaun's request, was to the Turner home in Great Falls, asking for Alan or Zach to provide them with an update. Kim believed the housekeeper picked up the call and indicated that Mr. Turner was on an overseas business call and that she would like to speak with Beverly, Mr. Turner's administrative assistant. Kim asked if Zach was available, feeling it better to provide a family member with an immediate update that could be shared with Alan.

After receiving the message this morning, Zach immediately picked up the call and asked what had transpired over the past several hours. Based on the message, it was inferred that the criminals had the ransom in hand, prompting them to immediately send a team to the DC Public Works facility to secure and inspect the water fountain. Meridian Hill Park had been under continuous surveillance by the Bureau since Stoney had entered the park with the ransom payment. She indicated Agent O'Hara and her drove to the park to walk where the fountain had been. Kim then had to explain to Zach that the grass covering the metal plate used to hold the fountain in place was removed; it revealed the manhole cover and detailed the tunnel system running underneath the park. Inspection of the underground tunnel will commence shortly by the FBI. She said that they believed this was the most likely way to obtain the uncut stones, without detection. Kim asked Zach, once he shared the updated news with Alan, if Mr. Turner had any questions or wished to discuss, to just have him call her cell number, and she would pick up day or night. She could not share Shaun O'Hara's opinions with Zach on his second ransom theory versus killing the 2nd hostage to close out the crime. Zach walked in on Alan's business call and scribbled a note, indicating he had just spoken with the FBI and needed to share some information with him as soon as he got off his call.

Alan, after hearing the news, told Zach that the FBI has to be held accountable for their plan to coat the stones. One of our family members is still going to be a hostage and may never be returned. We have no idea who we are dealing with or how ruthless these people are. Alan then called O'Hara and shared his thoughts, and wanted some positive direction on this case.

After speaking with his father, Zach texted Cody to ask if he could come by when he got the "team" together. Cody immediately responded to Zach, saying he could just provide his timeline. Zach indicated that 30 minutes should work fine and got a thumbs-up emoji picture back from Cody.

Chapter 20

Everyone was present in the conference room at Fail-Safe – Susie, Carter, Karen, Stoney, and Cody, making small talk until Zach entered the room. Zach started off thanking everyone again for their time and concern. He asked Cody to turn on the flat-screen TV in the conference room and then proceeded to screenshot from his phone the message received at 8 am that morning:

The diamonds are being analyzed, and a random sample is being taken to determine the quality level of the uncut diamonds. If we decide it is sufficient and meets the required dollar value, one hostage will be released. Our experts detected a coating that was placed on the stones. This has been removed, but you were warned not to impede the ransom payment in any way. One hostage will remain in our custody until we determine their fate!

Cody asked Zach if any other new developments had occurred since receiving this message. Zach advised the team of FBI agent Kim Ross' call to the Turners' home a little over half an hour ago, updating them on finding the manhole in the park where the water fountain was attached. Based on the message's reference to having possession of the uncut diamonds, the FBI went to the DC Public Works facility to secure and transport the fountain for inspection and analysis. Zach went on to recap how the park had been under surveillance since the fountain's removal, but based on the note, Agent O'Hara and Ross went to the park for a physical inspection of the area. The last item Zach referenced was the grass sod covering placed over the manhole cover used to anchor the fountain in place. He then indicated this was a utility-type tunnel that ran underneath the park, but the FBI did not indicate where it connected. Zach shared Kim Ross's opinion that the tunnel was the most likely means by which the uncut stones were removed from the park. There was dead silence in the conference room as everyone was processing the information just provided.

Stoney was the first to speak, indicating he felt the water fountain was fabricated and used solely for this purpose. He expressed this opinion in his debriefing session at the Bureau headquarters afterward. He went on to say that the fountain's location in the park was very odd—not near or next to a public restroom facility, but out in the open next to a walking path.

Stoney went on to say the organization planning this kidnapping had to be given very high grades for two reasons: 1) using uncut diamonds that, when processed, would be virtually untraceable and double in value from the original ransom price and 2) setting a ransom payment/delivery system is usually the flaw when a kidnapping occurs, but this plan had a high level of sophistication, noting to get it done with close to a thousand stones, given the weight and volume would be extremely difficult. However, they found a way to use the tunnel to get paid and buy themselves time to cover their tracks with the fake fountain being removed—his last comment to the team about executing this plan borders on pure genius. No one in this room should take this organization lightly; they are pros and probably very dangerous.

Cody then asked his IT expert, Susie Mathews, to access her computer and determine the tunnel's location under Meridian Hill Park and its exact purpose. If the records were not public, hack into the DC government's system and extract the information through the back door without leaving a trace. Her reply was a piece of cake, and she broke off from the meeting to get Cody's answers. Cody then asked Zach for his input on the message statements; Zach believed the uncertainty of the second hostage not being released was very unsettling. He went on to state to the team several scenarios: 1) the stones were paid and met the demands made, and both captives got released, or 2) the criminals would use the coating of the stones to make a second demand for additional monies on the second hostage. Zach then choked, trying to address scenario 3, which Cody understood and said the 3rd option is never to release the 2nd hostage, closing off any further contact with the family or authorities. Cody then went on to say to the team, 'We will do anything humanly possible to ensure that does not happen.' Zach, showing great emotion, had to wipe away the tears running down his face.

Cody asked for everyone's take on the criminals being able to detect the coating placed on the stones that emitted a low level of radiation. Cody stated that he and Zach attended an FBI-run meeting at the Turners' house when the coating was proposed as a passive way to track the uncut stones. The FBI believed it represented a low exposure risk factor due to being a clear or nearly invisible type of coating and not emitting a frequency like a standard electronic tracking device. Yet the criminals detected the substance and have indicated that some kind of consequences will be decided on involving the hostage, who will not be released.

Stoney jumped in again, echoing what everyone in the room was thinking: there must be an insider leak that's notifying the criminals about the coating substance. This information has complicated Carly and Peggy's safe recovery process. He said anything said in this conference room never leaves the premises. Turning to Zach, Stoney said that it may be difficult for you to be on both ends, but the recovery and safety of your family have to be the only priority. We can know and control what we think or find out, but if the FBI leaks to its organization, it will make matters much more difficult.

Cody knew Stoney's training involved life-and-death situations, clandestine operations, and secretive missions. Cody said to Zach directly that he had to think the FBI also thought or suspected they may have been compromised by an insider leaking information to the kidnappers. After reading the message, Cody wondered if he could persuade Kim Ross to share her thoughts on whether they believed a mole was in place within the Bureau, without risking her career or their potential future relationship. It's not something he wanted to put on the table for open discussion, but he would have to think about broaching this subject with Ms. Ross.

As the meeting broke up, he asked everyone to be available tomorrow at midday. While Cody was chatting with Zach, he leaned over and specifically asked Q (Carter) to stay for a few minutes, indicating he needed help. During the meeting, Cody showed Zach a timeline he had scribbled on a legal pad. He then reviewed these notes with Q:

A message from kidnappers about the Ransom Area in DC was received at 1:30 pm

Q deployed the two drones approximately 10-12 minutes later, over the Columbia Heights area of Washington, D.C.

At 2:15 pm, they were advised of the Meridian Hill Park location for the drop and reprogrammed drones into a north-south / east-west surveillance pattern.

Stoney delivered the ransom just before the deadline of 2:30 pm

The contractor arrived at the park just after 3 pm, and removing the fountain took 15-20 minutes.

He added that we shut the drones down at approximately 3:20 p.m., which was very close to their maximum battery range.

Chapter 21

Cody's mind flips gears to consider the tunnels; he advises Q to get with Susie Mathews when she has specific information on the tunnel sizes and directions, and have her map them with a bold tracer line over a city street map of Washington, DC. Then Q was to provide Susie with two overlays from the drone courses as to the paths they flew onto Susie's tunnel map – One course when the drones were flying a general surveillance route during the first 35 minutes in the air – then a second overlay onto the map when the drones flew the two figure 8 patterns over the park location where the ransom was dropped. The film on these courses was approximately 1 hour and 10 minutes.

When we review the film again, we should be able to pause it each time the drone flies over the tunnel line connecting Meridian Park. This should give us a focused approach, possibly frame by frame, to look for anything tied to this crime. Q understood his task and said he and Susie should finish it early tomorrow. Zach clearly understood Cody's thinking and indicated he wanted in on the film review sessions if no other developments surfaced in the next 24 hours. Everything in the kidnapping case took a dramatic turn at 9:30 a.m.. Alan Turner's work email pinged with the arrival of the following message:

ONE HOSTAGE HAS BEEN released; they were dropped off at Alexandria House Park in Old Towne Alexandria. The person was instructed not to move or make contact with anyone until you send someone to pick them up.

Zach immediately advised his father, Alan, that Cody represented the closest person to the drop point, considering he worked and lived in Old Towne Alexandria and would only take a few minutes to be at the park. He said that Peggy and Carly knew Cody and should be thankful to see a friendly face. Cody could also quickly transport them to Alexandria Hospital if they had been injured or needed to be examined after their ordeal. Alan took a moment of pride that, after reading the message together, Zach came up with the best solution possible and suggested that Cody bring them home if he believed they were okay, as it would be the best thing for them after being held captive. Alan's last comment, let's hope this is not a hoax to give us false hope, then come back with some outrageous demands to get them both back.

With Cody's Caller ID noting Zach was calling, he picked up Zach's call on the first ring. He asked Zach if he was coming by today for their film session review. Zach cut in and asked Cody if he knew where Alexandra House Park was in Old Towne; Cody replied that his 3-mile jog took him past the park every other day. Zach recited the kidnappers' message and instructed Cody to head to the park immediately, stating that either Peggy or Carly should be waiting on a park bench. Cody ran to his car with his cell phone on speaker, advising Zach he should be there in 2-3 minutes. Before he closed the call, he told Zach he would update him on who was there and what mental and physical condition they appeared to be in.....

Alan dialed Kim Ross's cell number, and she answered, asking if he had received another message. Alan read Kim's email, which he had just received, and told her of Zach's plan to have Cody get to the park and verify if their family had been released and if they appeared unharmed to bring them home. Kim indicated they needed to interview while the details and circumstances remained fresh. She showed compassion to Alan, not knowing who had been released, and said she would respect his decision on how soon they could come out for their interview and debriefing.

Kim immediately contacted Shaun O'Hara and updated him on the message that one family member had been released. She advised Shaun that the family would contact her to verify who was released and whether they needed medical attention or were to be taken home to Turner's house in Great Falls.

Cody arrived at the park within several minutes of Zach's call. While parking his car, he saw a female sitting on a park bench, and his heart started racing, knowing this may be Peggy or Carly Turner. As he ran toward the person, they heard him approaching, and Carly Turner saw Cody. She jumped off the bench and hugged him so tight he could barely breathe. Cody whispered it was all right and said he planned to take her home if she felt okay and didn't need medical attention. With tears running down her face, Carly told Cody she wanted to go home and asked him if he knew if her mom was also released. All Cody could say to address Carly's question was that he didn't know if her mom was still being held captive; they had only just received the one message about her release.

Cody walked Carly to his car and quickly texted Zach, advising that Carly was with him; she appeared fine and wished to go home. He indicated that Carly was very emotional but otherwise seemed okay. As he closed Carly's door, Cody sent another quick text to Zach, stating, *"She knows Peggy was also taken. I'm not sure how she knows. Let her explain to you when we arrive."*

Cody reached over, held Carly's hand, and told her he knew she had many questions, but felt it better to have her dad and brother answer what had transpired over the past week. Since meeting Cody after he and Zach left the Army, Carly had always had a crush on him, but knew she would always be Zach's little sister to Cody. She expressed her gratitude to him for finding her in the park and taking her home.

Cody knew Carly would be interviewed shortly by the FBI for any information that could help ID the criminals, and that session would be very emotionally trying. To make some light conversation during the 30-minute drive, Cody asked Carly if she knew the recent history of Alexandria House Park, where she was dropped off, and she replied that she did not. Cody told her he jogged past the park every other day. On one of his runs, people who lived in the Alexandria House high-rise came onto their balconies at precisely 7 p.m. during the COVID-19 crisis to pay tribute to the medical community on the front lines of dealing with COVID. He told Carly that, besides banging pots and pans, some people started playing their musical instruments and waving American flags to acknowledge the first responders.

The story touched Carly and somehow gave her comfort, knowing that the park where she had been released was a place where good people celebrated every evening.

Cody did not openly express his thoughts to Carly, but expected the criminals to have chosen the park because Old Towne Alexandria has few CCTV cameras, and the drop-off at the park was most likely not on any film that the authorities could review.

Chapter 22

Alan and Zach waited on the front porch of the family's stately home as Cody drove into the circular driveway. Cody had not put his Mustang into park before Carly threw open the passenger door and ran into the arms of her dad and brother. From Cody's viewpoint, it was the most joyous reunion he had ever witnessed. As the hugs were given and tears were shed, Cody called Kim Ross's cell phone. She picked up and told Cody that Zach had reached out after receiving Cody's text message from the park. Cody told Kim they had just arrived at the Turners' home and added that Carly appeared in good physical condition but, as always, did not know the possible emotional impact of the kidnapping. Kim was waiting to hear from Alan and Zach about an appropriate time to come out and meet with Carly to get her statement on what happened over the past week. She indicated they would like to do it as soon as possible and asked Cody to convey that to Alan and Zach. Cody replied that he would pass on her message and probably would stay around for a while to provide any moral support.

Carly, Alan, Zach, and Cody went into the study, where the housekeeper had set up a variety of beverages and light snacks. Once Carly provided assurances to the three of them that she did not need any medical attention, but wanted to know if her mom had also been abducted and if she would also be released. Alan told Carly that Peggy was taken at approximately the same time from the parking garage at the non-profit where she volunteered her time. Zach then added that he believed an attempt was made to abduct him, but he was able to take evasive action and avoid being kidnapped. Alan then asked Carly if she and Peggy had been held together in the same room during the ordeal. She advised her dad that the kidnappers had indicated to her by showing a picture that Peggy was also being held captive, and if she did not follow their instructions, some harm would come to her mother.

Cody asked Carly if she was up to a 1-2 hour debriefing by the FBI to recount events during her captivity. She said that if there was any information that could help her mother's situation, she had only asked if the FBI could come to the house to interview her about what she had been through. Understanding this, Cody excused himself and said he would contact Kim Ross and schedule a meeting ASAP.

Cody returned to the study and advised Carly, Alan, and Zach that Shaun O'Hara and Kim Ross would arrive in about an hour to meet with Carly. Kim had advised Cody to inform the family that they were invited to sit in on the interview, provided they refrained from interrupting the questioning and replies. The session with Carly would be recorded, so they could listen to the tape if they needed to go back to clarify anything. After telling Alan and Zach they were welcome to sit in on Carly's interview, Cody did not press Carly for any details of what happened. They should just sit in on the FBI debriefing, allowing Carly an hour to rest or decompress from being a hostage to being home. They all agreed to reconvene in the study when the FBI arrived.

Cody asked Zach to take a short walk with him outside, and he had a couple of items to discuss. Zach took Cody to a beautiful garden with a small gazebo and several benches. Cody told Zach that the meeting in his office would be held later that day and that he would still like him to attend if Zach could get away for an hour or two. Despite the time spent together in Army intelligence, they remained a great team in finding solutions to problems.

Cody was looking forward to the map overlay of the DC tunnel system superimposed on top of the drone's video feed; Zach said he would look forward to the meeting as long as Carly was not so emotional that she needed his support at home. Cody then reminded Zach that they should not mention anything about the surveillance video taken by the drones to the FBI until they knew there was no leaking of information from the Bureau to the kidnappers.

One hour later, Shaun and Kim arrived at Turner's home and were shown to Alan's study. After setting up the recording equipment, they asked if Carly was available and ready to conduct their interview.

Everyone was present; Alan, Zach, and Cody sat off to the side to listen to Carly recount her story of being abducted and held captive.

Kim introduced Shaun and herself as the lead team from the FBI investigating the abductions. She told Carly they would like her to tell her story about all the events she could remember daily, ending up with her release that morning. She said they would like not to interrupt her unless they thought some clarification was needed in the recount of her time in captivity.

Carly composed herself and started talking into the microphone with the details of her abduction:

She talked about the two men who grabbed her off the street, pulled the hood over her head, bound her wrists and feet with zip ties, and placed her on a cot in the back of the van. She said her phone, watch, and purse were taken before putting her on the cot. Before the hood went over her head, Carly's best recollection was seeing three men, including the driver, all dressed in black clothing, each wearing a ski mask over their faces. Two men jumped out and grabbed her, leaving the driver. At no time, while she was in the van or held captive, did anyone speak to her. When she was secured in the van, one person pressed his hand over her mouth, indicating she was not to cry out or make a sound. She received the message, remained quiet in the vehicle, and admitted at the time to being terrified, not knowing what was happening...

Carly said it would only be a guess; the van traveled through DC traffic, stopping and going for 15-20 minutes. Then, the vehicle increased speed, likely entering a highway, as it didn't slow down for approximately the next hour until it exited. We slowed down with occasional stops, probably at traffic lights, but not very many. It wasn't long until we hit a bumpy stretch like a rural road needing paving or possibly a dirt road, then came to a complete stop...

Carly said she was taken off the cot with the ties binding her feet cut off so she could now walk. Two men holding each of her arms brought her inside a building that had five or six steps and escorted her to a room where the hood and wrist ties were removed. The room had a bed, a couch, and a small, separate bathroom. She indicated her captors used a dry-erase whiteboard to write down messages to her. One whiteboard was left in the room for her to write on if she had any issues or questions. She noted a camera mounted near the ceiling in the room's far corner to monitor her activity.

Kim asked Carly if she had heard any discussion or conversation outside her locked door or any noise outside the building. Carly replied that no one spoke to her directly, and it seemed that no one ever spoke inside the building where she could hear them. As to any noise outside, she only remembers birds chirping early in the morning. Sometimes she indicated tires were crunching on the road or driveway as they arrived or left. She thought they must have been somewhere very remote.

Carly stated that the first encounter that afternoon was with two men who came in and showed her the message board, which said, "Hold this sign up, and we will take your picture." They left, and another person came in with a tray of food. This consisted of a ham, lettuce, tomato sandwich, carrot sticks, a bag of chips, and a water bottle. She grabbed her whiteboard and wrote, I am a vegan and do not eat meat. No reply was made, but her meals from that point contained no meat products.

The subsequent encounter was shortly afterward; two men entered her room and handed her a picture of her mother holding the same sign she had held an hour earlier. On a separate whiteboard was a message to her stating:

Your mother is also being held captive by us. A ransom demand will be made, and it may take 1 week before you can be returned. Do not cause us any problems, or your mother will be punished.

She screamed at the men, demanding to see and be with her mother. One man took the board and wrote NO!!! She immediately knew any thought of trying to escape or get hold of a cell phone would only jeopardize her mother's safety.

Meals were brought twice a day, mid-morning and early evening. She was never allowed outside, so she had to develop an exercise routine in her room to occupy her time. Boredom was the most mentally challenging aspect of being held hostage. Over several days, a dozen or so paperback books with their covers ripped off and showing no library markings were brought in.

Carly said she had no idea if her mother was being held in the same building or someplace else. She believed Peggy was at the exact location, so why would the kidnappers use two buildings and have to use more manpower at multiple locations? She thought the books she provided were probably also given to Peggy. She considered writing a note in the margin of a book to her mother to find out if she was OK and in the same place. She also reasoned that if her note were found, it could harm her or her mom, and decided not to try this means of communicating.

Shaun asked Carly if the food had any packaging indicating where it was made or processed. Carly stated the food was basic, felt prepared on the premises, and was never presented in any type of container or wrapper. Plastic knives and forks, disposable paper plates, and napkins were served with every meal.

She ventured a guess that four men were on duty at any one time, and they changed shifts every 8 hours or so. They always wore black clothing, including shoes and socks, a black ski mask, and black latex-type rubber gloves.

Kim asked Carly if she could see around the eye openings of the ski mask—could she tell if the men's skin color was black, white, or brown? Carly felt all the people she encountered had male features with darker skin complexions, but not African American.

She was provided with fundamental clothing, a sweatshirt, sweatpants, slippers, and pajamas. Nothing fit her well, but she was allowed fresh clothes every two days. No labels or tags were on the clothes to identify where they came from. Carly then referred to the clothing she was provided as dollar store specials. Her original clothes were returned to her when she was released, but not her phone, purse, or watch.

The cameras in the room's upper corners showed a red light, which meant she was being monitored 24/ 7. She believed she had no privacy except when she was in the bathroom. She knew the cameras were real because she wrote a message, such as "I need something to drink," held it up to the camera, and within 5 minutes, a drink was delivered to her.

Carly recounted that one window in her room was sealed shut with a black film blocking the daylight. Late one night, she used her fingernail to scratch at the corner of the black film material covering the window and was able to lift a tiny corner. The only thing she saw was a heavily wooded area outside. She said that with the cameras in place, she did not try to remove any more film from the window for fear of being caught. Escaping by breaking the window was not an option, knowing her mother could be punished if she were to escape. Her other thought was, how would she navigate the woods to find someone to help them if she risked escaping?

Carly said her routine was the same over the next week: never being allowed outside, only reading books, having two meals a day, and not allowing any information on her mother. No further reference was made to whether the ransom was paid. Doing her exercises to combat boredom. She asked the FBI agents if they had ever seen the movie *Groundhog Day,* where the same thing repeats daily. That was her life until this morning, when she was instructed to dress and provide her original clothes.

In an hour or so, they returned with another message board: You are being released; do not cause us any issues, or your mother will pay the price. When you are dropped off, walk to the park bench, sit, and wait for someone to come and get you.

Carly indicated a hood was placed over my head, my wrist was zip-tied, and they took me down the 5 or 6 steps to the van and cot. The trip back was somewhat similar in terms of stop-and-go and highway time. When we arrived at the park where I met Cody, one man cut my ties, and the other man pulled the hood off my head and pointed toward a bench in the park's center. I strolled to the bench, sat down, and did not move as instructed. About 5 minutes later, Cody showed up, and I knew my ordeal was over.

Shaun then asked if it appeared to be the same white van that had abducted you and if you had noted the license plate number on the van that dropped you off. Carly responded, When my feet hit the ground, and the hood came off, I was directed to the park bench. I was like a zombie, and I walked straight there without ever turning around. The van left so quickly that I am not sure if I saw a license plate, and if I did, I couldn't remember the number. Kim broke in, saying it was okay to Carly, the criminals had used fake plates when you were abducted, and she saw no reason they would not use similar plates to drop you off.

Shaun asked Carly if anything she saw or happened during her captivity may have given her any idea where she was being held. Or any mannerism of the men holding her that could help to identify the kidnappers? He suggested several aspects of the room, including the decor, shag carpet, vinyl floors, pictures on the wall, the inside lid of the toilet tank's date stamp, and lighting fixtures. Mannerisms like soldiers versus civilians, height/weight, frame size of the men, hair color or eyebrows, jewelry, rings, watches, and any tattoos visible?

Carly sheepishly told Shaun that Zach was the family member most like Sherlock Holmes. Zach acknowledged the compliment and asked his sister to focus on anything that may help lead them to catch these criminals. Carly said she believed the men stationed to guard her were the same teams based on their height and size. She could not remember items like jewelry or distinguishing marks on any guards. The room was so basic, with no pictures, a wooden floor, a couple of lamps, a bed, and a couch. The men seemed fit, not overweight, but average in size. She added that she never looked in the toilet tank when using the bathroom.

Chapter 23

Kim was aware of Carly's concern for her mother's well-being, so she needed to inform Carly of the uncertainty surrounding her mother's situation. Kim spoke directly to Carly, telling her Peggy was abducted on the same day she was, and the photo of her mother was real. They were scrutinizing the ransom payment made to the kidnappers, and the criminals were not willing to release both hostages. Your family and the FBI have no means of negotiating with the criminals. Your dad's work email gets instructions from them that we must follow explicitly. We have tried with all our IT personnel to trace the IP addresses to find out where the emails are coming from, but have had no success. The message received this morning stated that one hostage was being released. Until Cody saw you in the park, we did not know if it was you or your mom who would be sitting on that park bench.

Kim went on to tell Carly she had no children, but could only believe any parent would never want to be on the park bench if their child was still being held hostage. The Bureau will exhaust every resource to bring Peggy home safely.

Sensing Carly's emotional state after Kim's update, Shaun thanked Carly for allowing them to interview her and said that if they had any follow-up questions, they would reach out through her father or brother. He then asked Zach and Cody if they could stay for a few more minutes to review some things with Kim and him. Alan walked out with Carly and put his arm around her, sensing her fragile state.

With the four people in the room, Shaun, the seasoned veteran investigator, knew they had so little to work on handling this case, and wanted all the input and opinions he could get. He started with a compliment, indicating that Zach and Cody, having served in Army Intelligence, must have had many sessions trying to draw a picture out of random facts. Kim and I would like to hear your take on Carly's recount of her captivity.

Zach jumped in first and said he wanted to address the distance and direction range possible for the area where Carly was held hostage. Based on her estimates, focusing on the highway travel timeline of about an hour, you have Interstate 95 South, which keeps you in Virginia, and Interstate 66 West, which would take you to the Shenandoah Valley or slightly further into West Virginia. Zach added I-95 north through Maryland to Delaware and Interstate 270/70 NW to Western Maryland. Given the wooded, remote, and rural criteria, I'd recommend taking I-66 West toward the Shenandoah / West Virginia, or heading on 270/70 NW to the Western section of Maryland. Zach finished by saying, "I-95 South, you'll hit Fredericksburg within 40-45 miles, and I-95 North will put you in Baltimore." However, neither option makes sense in comparison to what my sister described in terms of population density.

Zach said that if you buy into his two directions, it might take a lot of legwork. Still, looking for a white van using the 1-2 hour window from when Carly was kidnapped, with the fake license plate numbers known, I would try accessing express lane cameras first, then normal traffic lane cameras second, in those two directions, driving away from DC. If we could establish the road the van was on, it would surely provide a more limited area for study. If the van used the express lane with a transponder, it had to be owned or stolen, which may open another avenue for exploration. My best estimate for this remote place is 60-75 miles from Washington, DC. Unfortunately, that is still a lot of territory to explore.

Shaun and Kim noted Zach's comments and felt they would commit resources to pursue tracking the van to see if a location could be narrowed down or identified.

Cody expressed concern about Carly's lack of speech, as the only reason not to speak to her or in front of her was that their dialect would reveal their country of origin. The comment about a darker complexion was well worth considering. Thinking out loud, Cody said that a foreign organization has the resources, bankroll, manpower, and training to pull off this type of crime. His reply to his question was about any of the prominent Mexican or South American drug cartels. If you have resources or informants in these organizations, they may be worth checking out.

Cody also expanded on Zach's thoughts about where Peggy was being held. He asked if the place in the woods would be owned or rented. Since the kidnapping was a money-driven crime, the house, cabin, or building usage would only be for a couple of months. Several weeks were required to set up secure rooms, install the cameras, and prepare the space. Looking for remote rentals in the woods for 2-3 months would narrow their search if they could determine the direction of travel from DC. Cody also added that he would expect the rental to be paid for upfront with cash, which is not that commonplace today.

Shaun updated everyone on the water fountain they secured from the Public Works facility and told their technicians to review every part. He said the fountain was custom-made without marking or indicating where it may have been built. He did say its sole purpose was to resemble a water fountain, but its function was to serve as a funnel for the diamonds to pass through into some type of catch bucket located in the tunnel below the park.

Kim said they were still awaiting the forensic results of their tunnel examination under Meridian Hill Park. She indicated that the few items retrieved from the tunnels were most likely trash left there by other repair people. She was not optimistic about finding any concrete leads because the criminals knew the tunnel usage would be examined when the authorities saw it. Meticulous planning does not include leaving one's business card behind to help us out.

As the meeting broke up, Zach told Cody, after hearing Carly's comments, that his sole focus was on releasing his mother. He advised Cody to give him an hour or so, and he would head down to Alexandria for their film review with the team.

When Cody returned to his office, Susie Mathews told him she had worked up a mapping program for the Washington, DC streets surrounding Meridian Park. She was relieved that she hadn't hacked into the DC government database, as the tunnel system information for utilities and sewers was already publicly available. Susie easily took a DC road map with a color overlay of the utility tunnels. Carter, AKA Q, had then provided her with the telemetry of the two drones' flight patterns before and after they knew about the ransom drop point in Meridian Hill Park. The drone video footage was being merged over the top of Susie's map/tunnel program as requested. Susie told Cody that the final product would resemble real-time footage taken by the drones, showing traffic, people, and landscapes, but superimposed over her lightly shaded street map and tunnel program. Cody knew Susie was the best and would consistently deliver when challenged with a complex project. Cody then messaged everyone on the team to be available in the conference room in approximately an hour.

The team, Susie, Karen, Stoney, and Q, arrived in the conference room with coffee and assorted beverages, as well as pens and notepads. Zach was expected momentarily, so Cody took the opportunity to brief them on Carly's release that morning and provided them with a shorter version of her captivity during the past week. The only question was whether any new messages or demands specifically involved Peggy. Cody said Zach would be arriving any minute, but he had not received any other news since the release message that arrived this morning. The email followed the standard messaging means used by the criminals, sending it to Alan Turner's work email address.

Right on time, Zach walked in and, as always, thanked everyone for their concern and for being available to try and help out. Cody advised Zach that he had just updated everyone on Carly's release and statement.

Cody started the meeting by restating that the organization responsible has covered their tracks exceptionally well. He then referred to the first message received after the ransom was paid. Explain how the FBI coated the uncut stones with a clear radioactive substance that may give the Bureau a passive tracking way to follow the diamonds when they are moved. Everyone believed the stones were in its base when the water fountain was removed.

Stoney chipped in, saying he heard the first 4 or 5 handfuls of stones he dropped down the drain, making a metallic sound as they hit solid metal, which he believed was the hollow base of the fountain. He went on to say the reality was that a metal bucket was catching the stones as they fell into the fake drainpipe. Given the load of stones in his tool bag, he told the FBI afterward that no standard water fountain drain pipe could account for that quantity.

The primary point Cody wanted to make to the group was to deal with the message received that the coating used on the stones would result in some type of consequence for one of the hostages. He added that the only positive factor was the commitment to release one hostage, which the criminals were good to their word, resulting in Carly being home and safe.

Zach and I have kicked this coating thing around, and both feel there had to be a leak of information to the kidnappers. The odds of criminals having and using a Geiger counter seem very remote in our minds. I have no idea if our drone video will be helpful, but any theories or ideas from this team must remain within these walls. It's not that we don't want to help the FBI, but we must safeguard against another possible leak that could jeopardize Peggy's chances of being returned. After hearing Carly's commentary, Zach indicated in their debrief meeting that Cody and I made several common-sense recommendations to the FBI agents about the possible direction and location of where his family was held.

Zach jumped in, explaining that the ransom payment, facilitated by a manhole and utility tunnel, enabled the exchange without the authorities' immediate detection. It also had to occur within a reasonably quick time frame after Stoney dropped them in the drain pipe. The fountain removal provided them a cushion to be long gone before the tunnel's usage was uncovered.

Chapter 24

Cody advised the group on Susie's role in acquiring the tunnel plans and formulating a map overlay that can be overlaid with the drone video.

Cody asked Q to explain how the drones were deployed once in a general pattern over Columbia Heights and then again in a more specific figure 8 over Meridian Hill Park.

Q explained that he wanted the video surveillance of approximately a ½ mile radius of the area. The rationale is that any criminal in the vicinity as an observer would likely pose as a pedestrian walking rather than sitting in a parked car. The ½ mile distance takes an average person approximately 10 minutes to cover at a regular walking pace. There is no way to blanket a ½ mile circle, so the decision was made to fly one drone in a north-south pattern and the other east-west. After being stationed in DC the night before, Cody informed me that Columbia Heights was the general area for the drop, so I deployed the drones over that area at 1:40 p.m. Upon receiving a follow-up call from Cody that Meridian Hill Park was to be the exact drop location for the ransom, I reprogrammed the drones into two figure 8 patterns, N-S and E-W, using the park as the center of the figure 8 – Q went on to say he estimated an air speed of 5 m.p.h which would have each drone complete one loop of the ½ mile figure 8 in about six minutes. Their speed was set to capture good-quality video and keep the drones from being observed from the ground. If you notice anything in the video, you should get an opportunity to review the same area again approximately 6 minutes later. Q said to be mindful of the 2:28 p.m. exact time Stoney made the drop, and approximately 3:10–3:15 p.m. when the fountain was removed. Shortly after that, I pulled both the drones down.

Cody said, "With six sets of eyes, if you see anything that may be relevant, just shout out to Susie or Q to stop the video, mark the exact time and location, and note any comments made by the team."

When they started the video, everyone watching the entire video feed had to concentrate on all the activities they were viewing. The real-time traffic, parked cars, buildings, pedestrians, and the city streets and tunnels, all shaded by Susie's overlay program, complicated identifying anything out of the ordinary.

Cody asked everyone to take a break for 10-15 minutes. He then requested that Susie and Q slow the video feed down to half the speed and only show 20 minutes before the drop and 20 minutes after the drop. He speculated the person collecting the stones would enter the tunnel system somewhere and exit within that time. Cody felt they had a better chance of picking anything out in slow-motion mode.

The east-west drone was about to complete a loop when Zach shouted to stop the tape. Susie jokingly reminded Zach that VHS tapes had been obsolete for over 30 years, and he was watching a video stored on her hard drive. Cody, to lighten the mood, asked Zach how many VHS porno tapes he had kept from his childhood. Once the laughter settled down, Zach got out of his chair, walked to the flat-screen TV, and pointed to a white van parked atop the tunnel line. He read off the map program they were looking at, Kalorama Road, about a half block south of the 17th St intersection. The Meridian Park tunnel intersects right there with the main tunnel running under Kalorama Road.

Cody asked Q if he could zoom or enhance the vehicle in this frame. As Q made the necessary corrections, the video, frame by frame, clearly showed a white van with Verizon Fios labels on the side of the vehicle. Cody knew from a woman he dated who lived in DC that Xfinity was the primary TV/internet provider. Still, many people were switching to Verizon Fios for their lower monthly rates.

One frame showed a Verizon worker wearing a hard hat and bright green vest at the van's rear, with cones and yellow tape marking the work area. In a very excited voice, Cody shouted to everyone, "What is wrong with that picture?" The other five agreed that if they expanded the search area, they could probably locate another 5 or 6 Verizon service trucks. No one could reply to Cody's question or see anything out of order. Cody let everyone stare at the freeze frame for another minute before answering his question: "When was the last time you saw a cable company service truck not having a roof rack and multi-ladders attached? Not all service or repairs are done underground; without a ladder, you're not going up a pole to run a wire or make a repair." The five team members all had to agree with Cody, and the excitement level in the room went sky-high.

Cody grabbed his pad of paper and noted 2:21 p.m. on the video. He then told Susie and Q to run it to this spot at 2:27

p.m., 2:33 p.m., 2:39 p.m., 2:45 p.m., 2:51 p.m., and 2:57 p.m. He was zoning in on the six-minute loops made by the east-west drone. The first four loops of the video saw no movement of the worker behind the truck. Stoney commented: That person is either serving as a lookout or has to be the laziest worker employed by Verizon.

The 2:46 p.m. drone pass revealed a second worker entering the work area, which was marked off behind the van. He also had a Verizon hard hat, but did not wear a construction-style green vest. The 2:52 p.m., six-minute video showed the two workers had been busy little bees, cleaning up all the cones, tape, and tools, and loading them into the van's back doors. The man with the vest climbed into the driver's side of the van while the 2nd worker opened the passenger door, threw his hard hat in the back, then brushed out his hair.

Cody opened the floor for comments or opinions, and the team exploded. Q said we needed to review the video to see if we caught them when they set up. Zach said to have someone run down to DC and confirm there is a manhole cover at that exact location. We already know the tunnel exists at that location on our overlay map. Stoney said it is SOP (standard operating procedure) to get a decal wrap made to turn any personal vehicle into a commercial vehicle. He added that dozens of companies can produce decal-type products, and obtaining a Verizon logo would be very easy. Karen said the license plates are probably phony, like before, but worth trying to see if the drone has a better angle to capture them. Susie did some quick math and said even someone tall walking slightly bent over in a 5-foot-high tunnel should be able to get from where the truck was located to the park manhole in about 10 minutes max.

Cody's last request was for Susie to run the video one frame at a time and select the frame with the absolute best headshot picture of either man. Stoney said to focus on the guy who removed his hard hat and pitched it into the truck. Zach understood Cody's request for the headshot pictures. He looked over at Cody and said to him, Ruth Culverson? This name seemed meaningless to anyone else in the room, but somehow, it seemed essential to Cody and Zach.

Cody told everyone that we are barely on first base; let's all do our jobs, pool the intel, and then we can make solid decisions on how to proceed. The vibe in the room was electric, and Zach received many congratulations from the team on spotting the white van!

Cody tasked Susie and Q with finding every video piece from the Kalorama Rd location, then copying and splicing them into one sequence for viewing. He asked Stoney to make some calls locally to car wrap businesses, but added he did not have high expectations that they would get a lead. Karen was to send an intern to DC and verify if there was a manhole cover on Kalorama where the white van was parked. Then he asked everyone to regroup 1st thing tomorrow morning in the conference room. As Zach was leaving, Cody told him that if Alan and Carly needed him tomorrow, he could skip coming down in the morning, and he would find a secure way to keep Zach updated.

At 9 a.m., the conference room at Fail-Safe was buzzing with chatter, the energy level carried over from yesterday afternoon's meeting. Zach didn't make it down, wanting to spend quality time with Carly. He texted Cody, indicating he was very anxious about any additional feedback from the drone video.

Susie and Q had looped the video to show every time Kalorama Rd, just south of the 17th St location, was captured by their drone. Q indicated that when the drones were in their general pattern over Columbia Heights, they didn't pick up any footage of the location they had ID'd. Q added that when the drones were reprogrammed at 2:15 p.m., they did show the white van already in place with the cones and construction tape out marking the work area. Karen jumped in and reported their intern, confirming there was a manhole cover at that exact location, took a picture, and then walked north on Kalorama Rd, crossing the 17th St intersection, and found the next manhole, where we believe the tunnel forms a T-intersection with the park's tunnel.

Stoney reported that the half dozen major car wrap shops in the DC metro area had not recently done any Verizon Fios decals. The shops indicated that they could efficiently run off decals if needed, based on the graphics and dimensions provided. He expressed that expanding our search for who ordered the decals to other major cities was probably a waste of resources.

Susie said she spent a fair amount of time with her Photoshop program getting Cody his "headshot" of one of the workers. After viewing the film, she indicated that the 2nd worker, without the vest, when he removed his hard hat and brushed his hair with his hand, was the best picture they had of a relatively decent facial shot. Stoney chipped in, saying that when he played the construction worker in making the ransom drop, wearing a hard hat was heavy and took some getting used to. He added that having a small pistol in top of the helmet didn't help matters. He went on to say that the second worker was not used to wearing a hard hat all day; he would take it off at the first opportunity, which he did when entering the van. Susie told Cody to check his email; a PDF photo, which she was reasonably pleased with, was in his inbox.

Cody thanked everyone on the team for their time and input. He advised them that one more thing had to be done, and if this one piece of the puzzle fit, they would immediately regroup. He wanted Zach to be present, if at all possible. His reason is that we, as a team, may have to make some critical decisions going forward.

Cody reminded his staff that Fail-Safe was not a non-profit venture, and they still needed to complete their daily work to pay the bills, which elicited a few chuckles and a response indicating that the message had been received.

Chapter 25

Back at his office, he sent a text message to Ruth Culverson. She was Colonel Ruth Culverson of the U.S. Army. Zach and Cody were both under her command at Army Intelligence at Fort Belvoir. She had tagged them as the dynamic duo after Batman and Robin. To avoid ruffling either of them, she never labeled who Batman and Robin were, instead letting them sort it out between themselves. Cody's text message to her phone read, *"Call me back soonest without any ears on the line– CW."* A minute later, a text message came back from Ruth, reading, "Give me 30 minutes to reach out."

Very much Army protocol, precisely 30 minutes later, Cody's cell phone rang, and the opening comment from Ruth to Cody was – "How's the dynamic duo? You and Zach want to re-enlist in the Army and come work for me again?" Cody told her the Army could not afford Zach and the salary that his dad was paying him. He said that Zach and he had adjusted well to civilian life.

Cody countered her offer by saying that a job awaited her at his company if she ever wanted to retire from the military. Cody did inquire to Colonel Culverson when the one-star Brigadier General promotion was happening, saying she had been a

Colonel way too long. Ruth's reply and attitude were always to do your job correctly; everything else falls in line.

In a somber tone, Cody then asked Ruth if the line they were on could be taped, and she assured him it was private and secure. Cody said up front that if she heard anything from him that conflicted with her military position, she could walk away without any hard feelings.

Cody provided Ruth with a short synopsis of Zach's two family members' kidnappings. He alluded to feeling the FBI had leaked information that could jeopardize the release of Zach's mother. He then said he had a facial photo of a man he believed may be very involved in this crime. Knowing Army intelligence has access to the best facial recognition software, could she run the photo through the system and only let him know the results? All traces of the inquiry had to be wiped out because, at this time, he would not share any details with the FBI.

Ruth was devastated by knowing what Zach must be going through. She quickly committed to Cody, and one inquiry was a tiny favor to ask. She told him how to get the photo to her securely. She indicated that any reply generated from her would also be secure. Cody said the dynamic duo was very grateful and stressed the importance of a quick reply. She understood Cody's comment, knew what was at stake, and promised it would be a top priority. Cody hung up, knowing her answer to his inquiry may provide the key to getting Peggy back. Cody's final text to Zach was a somewhat cryptic message: it read –

"Ruth is on board doing research, may have a reply tomorrow." **Can you be available?**

CODY HEADED HOME TO his condo in Old Towne. He has lost track of the days since Peggy and Carly were taken; a quick look at the calendar told him they were on day nine. It also made him aware that tomorrow was Saturday, and everyone on the team was committed to coming and helping in any way they could. He knew Ruth would use her resources that day to cover her trail, so no one else knew about his inquiry. Cody hoped the person in the photo would be in the database, providing them with a name and pointing them in the right direction. The facial recognition database used by the military went deeper than just criminal records; it was a watch list of thousands of individuals who could pose a threat to the United States.

Cody had no energy for his 3-mile run or workout at the local gym. He uncorked a red pinot from the Willamette Valley in Oregon and decided to give Kim a call. She picked up and told Cody she was delighted he called; she recounted that her day had been stressful and probably wouldn't end for another couple of hours. She went on to say that she was all his for the next 10 minutes. Cody said he was calling to get his rain check for a sailing date with her set up. He mentioned the weather on Sunday was near perfect, with the temperature hitting about 75-80 degrees with a westerly breeze of 7-10 miles an hour. She sheepishly said she had never been on a sailboat and didn't know how much wind it took to make one move. He jokingly told her hurricane-force winds would not be a pleasant day on the water. He left it open, telling Kim he would like to make a day of sailing with lunch on board, or if her schedule was too tight, they could only go out for a couple of hours.

Kim admitted the investigation was stalled but provided no details. She said Sunday would be great if they could meet at

1 p.m. She would clear her calendar and love to spend the rest of the day with him. Cody then stated Zach was trying to get Susie Mathews, an IT person at his company, out on a date, and the boat could easily accommodate four. Kim didn't hesitate and advised Cody that with his sailing ability, they probably didn't need any extra crew. Cody got the message and was thrilled by her reply. They briefly discussed the lunch menu and the boat's docking location at the Washington Sailing Marina, just south of Reagan National Airport. She indicated she had to run but said to Cody that she would find an outfit suitable for sailing attire.

Cody settled in his favorite chair, poured another glass of wine, and thought to himself, "How can anyone not enjoy a great pinot?" With his love for great red wines, Cody had toured the Russian River Valley in California, tasting superb pinots, but felt the Willamette Valley in Oregon was still the gold standard for the world's best pinots. He then focused on Sunday's sailing date, which was only 48 hours away.

Zach had spent the day mostly with Carly, feeling she needed the bonding and comfort. He poked his head into the study, where Alan and his administrative assistant, Beverly, were busy either taking a call or sending emails to keep AX Tech running smoothly. He offered to pitch in several times, but Alan indicated things were under control and asked Zach if he could monitor Carly and see if she seemed OK emotionally. Zach, to appease his father, said he would, without mentioning he had already spent the morning with her and knew her only issue was dealing with the guilt of being released, and Peggy still being held captive. Zach and Carly had lunch together, and he asked if some physical activity like hiking, appealed to her. She accepted his offer and said they would need to stay in touch if anything happened. Zach checked his phone battery, which showed 85%, and suggested they could stop by the phone store to get her a replacement phone before their hike.

Zach, like Cody, was very focused and wanted to be more helpful in getting his mother back. He had read Cody's text and knew he would go down tomorrow morning to sit in on the next team meeting. Hopefully, their ex-commander in the Army would have some success identifying the person of interest from the video. Zach kept expecting some update from Kim or Shaun as the hours passed, but received nothing new. It seemed to him that the Bureau was more tightly controlling the flow of information. Zach's focus was on gathering any promising information that could lead to a path to get Peggy back home.

Late that evening, Cody received an encrypted email. The heading states, *"Encryption code to be texted - Best RC."* Cody received half the code on his phone several minutes later, with the promise that the other half would follow. Given that the received code was eight characters long, he assumed the entire code must be 16 characters in length. In Cody's mind, Ruth was going through tight security procedures dealing with the information for his inquiry. Cody, anxious to open the message, started thinking he needed to ask Susie at work tomorrow how many combinations of characters made up a 16-digit security code. Given her IQ, she probably knew the answer off the top of her head; Ruth did not wait too long and sent the 2nd half of the code with a comment - *"reach out if I can help in any way"*.

After applying the security code, the message opened, and Cody had to sit down after reading the details. He was stunned but not shocked by the information Ruth had uncovered and provided for him to read. He knew that at 9 a.m., in his conference room, all five people on the team would also be very anxiously waiting to hear the response he just read. After a sleepless night, Cody contemplated going it alone to avoid putting his team in a perilous situation. Even with Stoney's training, it would be a lot to ask him to back Cody up if they acted on the information received. He sent everyone a text reconfirming the need to meet the next day.

Chapter 26

At 9 a.m. Saturday, everyone—Susie, Karen, Stoney, Q (Carter), and Zach—was seated at the conference table. Cody wanted to be the last to enter so he wouldn't be asked by everyone arriving what the latest news was. Cody was tense, and his team sensed the solemn mood of a person who was always upbeat and jovial.

Cody began by stating that his inquiry, made yesterday, will be discussed and has generated a response. Before I explain my inquiry or the reply, I must state that everyone in this room may be putting themselves in harm's way just by knowing the contents of the email reply I received. Loyalty to me as a friend or boss or both does not allow me the right to put everyone present into a perilous situation. As I stand here, I have no definitive plan or idea of what to do with the information provided. I am asking everyone on the team to consider leaving this room without knowing this information for their safety.

Zach was the first to stand up and say to Cody, We've been through way too much together, and given my personal family involvement, the dynamic duo will take this information, formulate a plan, and get the job done. Stoney said he had faced a lot of bad people and very tough situations, even if the odds against him were not great, but he has never backed down in getting the job done. Cody silently knew Zach and Stoney would be on board until the end. His genuine concern lay with Susie, Carter, and Karen, who were very talented employees with their careers ahead of them. He had to express that thought openly because staying on the team meant making decisions that could jeopardize their well-being.

Looking straight at Zach, Susie said, "If there are only the three of you, referring to Cody, Zach, and Stoney, who can turn on a computer, much less get any information from it?" She added, "I am on board with any plan we come up with to help Peggy."

Karen chimed in, saying the same, Who is doing the legwork to get the information needed to act on what Cody's uncovered? I'm in for the long ride.

Carter was a little more apprehensive, but said that if any of your plans to work correctly require my ability and skills, I also want to help with the solution; I've got to see this through to the finish line with everyone else.

Everyone's sentiment touched Cody. His last comment is that when you know what we're up against, everyone still has an option not to get involved. Zach blurted out to Cody, "Tell us what you asked for and what the response is." Everyone slid to the edge of their chairs, and the room was silent.

Cody indicated that the enhanced picture of the 2nd worker on Kalorama Rd was sent to a resource with access to some of the most sophisticated facial recognition software databases available. My source did get a match with a very high percentage of accuracy. I will read you the body of the reply that I received late last evening:

THE PERSON IN QUESTION did get a 98% match from our database. His name is Ivan Petrov. Age 47 – His association is with Victor Zanoska, the Russian Mafia's principal head. Ivan's status is that of one of five lieutenants who assist Victor in operating the organization. Their territory is the Mid-Atlantic States (VA-MD-PA-W VA-SC-TN-DE & DC). Our sources say they are involved in every criminal activity that provides their organization with substantial income. For any criminal venture they do not run, they receive an override payment to allow someone else to operate in their territory. Victor Zanoska is a well-respected and connected businessman; his daily job in the business world is as a venture capitalist. He lives in Potomac, MD, just outside of Washington, DC. Besides Ivan Petrov, see his top 10 inner circle list below. This is bottomless water full of sharks that can and will kill you. Be careful!! RC

Cody said the crime was extremely well-orchestrated and executed from the outset. He was not shocked by the information he had just read. Given the person of interest, the timing of their video provided solid evidence that the Russian Mafia is running this kidnapping and has Peggy Turner.

He announced again that if anyone in this room has reservations about being involved in formulating a plan to get Peggy back, they can leave the room and walk away. This organization has established a reputation that people do not want to cross or associate with.

Everyone stayed in their seats and uniformly asked what we needed to do to help Peggy Turner. Cody said they needed to acquire as much intel as possible in a very short time frame. When dealing with a snake, always be aware of the head; it's the part that will bite you. The metaphor used by Cody was well understood by the team collectively; the focus had to be on Victor Zanoska, who ran the organization.

Cody asked Susie to use her hacking skills, without leaving any breadcrumbs behind, to obtain background information from law enforcement records – including history, tenure in power, and any legal actions. He then tasked Karen with researching current data, such as whether he plays golf, any hobbies, family size/names, where he lives, any Facebook or Twitter type postings by him or his family, whether his parents are alive or dead, how many siblings, and any other facts that may prove to be helpful.

Cody asked Q to have their best stealth drone with surveillance cameras ready, capable of zooming in from a fair distance. According to the information we received, he resides in Potomac, MD. Please consult with Susie and search for Google satellite images of his property. If necessary, also acquire county records that show the family's plot of land and all adjacent streets.

We need to determine the optimal location to launch a surveillance drone near his home, ensuring it has a nearly zero chance of being detected. To capture daytime video from all angles, Cody asked Q to grab some dinner and kill a little time after a couple of drone passes around the property. I would like to relaunch and capture some video of the property tonight. Be mindful of whose property we are taking pictures of. Ensure the drone can't be traced back to us if it fails mechanically or is detected and shot down.

Stoney, check your sources to see if the military has any history on the organization or intel specifically on Victor. Let me know if your four associates we use for personal security details may be available on short notice. I don't see us kicking down any doors and promoting a shoot-out, but having backup experienced people with firepower may be needed at some point.

Zach, as information develops, we can formulate a plan with the odds in our favor without anyone getting hurt. The unknown is Peggy's current status and when the Mafia will decide what to do with her.

As previously stated, this information must "never" leave this room. If the FBI leaked and the mafia discovered what we knew, we could have become a target.

Cody added that one picture is extremely circumstantial evidence; I am not a lawyer, but I would probably bet it wouldn't hold up in any court. If I were in their position and found out my kidnapping plan had been uncovered, Peggy would be a loose end that needed to be addressed. Cody addressed Zach directly. I speak for everyone on the team, and we will find a way to see that this does not happen. Cody asked if they could regroup late this afternoon with all the information they could uncover to see what direction it pointed them toward.

As the meeting broke up, Zach approached Cody and asked what he had in mind. He said they had been together too long, and he felt Cody had something he was focused on. Cody admitted to Zach that he read him well, but didn't want to make suggestions or discuss any specifics with the team for something that may be impossible. Cody added, Let's see what the intel the team brings to the table on Victor, then we can discuss and weigh our best options. Zach told Cody he was running home to see if there were any new developments and asked him to text the approximate time they expected to get back together.

Chapter 27

Before the meeting broke up, Karen passed Susie a note with Victor's home address. She commented that he did not try to hide where he and his family lived. Karen said Victor probably leads an everyday life to cover up his criminal activities.

With the information on the address from Karen, Susie asked Q to step into her office, and she would get the overhead shots from Google Maps to view. They pulled up a satellite photo showing three houses on a cul-de-sac. Susie determined that Victor's house was the middle property of the three. The lots were enormous, probably running between 8 and 10 acres. Each house was a mansion in size and scope. Q commented that there appeared to be no way to achieve frontal access to the property on a cul-de-sac. Behind each of the three properties ran a creek and wooded tract. Susie shifted to a regular street-type map and saw that the property behind Victor was a small county park bordering both sides of the stream with a parking lot area for about 10 cars. The park showed some walking paths and a tot lot near the entrance. She provided Q with the park's address and indicated he should be able to navigate to the backside of the park through the woods and locate Victor's property from a distance. Q indicated the woods opened up near the creek, which should be adequate for launching and retrieving his drone. Based on Cody's request, Q indicated to Susie that 15 minutes should be enough time to complete the task.

It was pushing 5 p.m. on Saturday when the conference room started to fill up—by 5:15 p.m., everyone was present and anxious to share what they had found.

Susie led off the meeting; Victor Zanoska was born in Saint Petersburg on March 8, 1970, making him 53 years old. Parents Dimitri and Vanvara are still alive and living in Saint Petersburg. I believe the parents are in their early 80s. The family, by Russian standards, was very well-to-do. Susie uncovered documents that indicated the Zanoskas had amassed a sizable fortune in smuggling goods in and out of Saint Petersburg, mostly using the Baltic Sea as their transportation route. Victor was one of five children, with two brothers and two sisters. She said it was difficult to find much information about his siblings, which meant the brothers and sisters had not achieved the same level of success.

Victor exhibited a very high I.Q. Susie indicated that she found no records of Victor attending any schools until he enrolled in Lomonosov Moscow State University, arguably the most prestigious university in Russia. If I had to guess, she said Victor probably had private tutors until he entered college. After university, Victor was required to complete at least one year of military service before reaching the age of 27. His military enrollment appears to have been set up in advance, as he landed on a three-star Colonel General staff in Moscow, tending to administrative matters. His job and responsibilities could not have been grueling, as Victor put in 5 years of military service.

Victor met Elana during his last year of military service, married her, and she remains his wife to this day.

Susie stated that most of the following information was obtained from various law enforcement records, without specifying which agency she accessed for the details. His parents must have been very influential, as Victor returned to St Petersburg and began helping run his family's black market business. From what I can determine, Susie said Victor took control of the entire financial side of their operations. Victor's ability to manage and grow the family business financially was recognized by larger and more powerful crime syndicates in Russia.

One of the larger crime syndicates offered Victor an offer he could not refuse. Victor and Elana moved to Italy, where he would work and learn from the Italian Mafia's inner circle about managing and operating a specific territory. After tutoring, he was sent to the United States at the age of 35 to be second or third in line to run the Russian Mafia's interests out of Washington, DC. Six years later, authorities believe that at age 41, Victor was put in charge of the DC organization, which includes all the Mid-Atlantic states.

Susie said that since his arrival in the U.S., he applied his financial abilities to become a successful venture capitalist and well-respected businessman. With his donations to all the right political pockets and strong ties with the Italian Mafia established during his years in Italy, Victor will be in place until he decides to step down. I accessed some deep financial databases and found accounts where he transfers the same amount each month to his parents in St Petersburg. Victor appears to be a very generous son, paying back his parents some of the investment made in him during his 20s and 30s. I would say the sums sent are sufficient for the parents and all 4 of his siblings to live a very comfortable life back in the motherland.

Susie continued, From what I read, I don't get a warm, cozy feeling toward Victor. This person, taught to rule with an iron hand, uses his intellect to make the best business decisions for his organization. U.S. Authorities named Victor years ago in several criminal lawsuits, but did so as a nuisance to him, never having any concrete evidence to tie him directly to any crime. He keeps himself Teflon-coated so nothing ever sticks to him directly.

Stoney stated he could not uncover any U.S. military-type actions directed against the DC Russian Mafia. If they crossed the lines when running their criminal activity, they did so without someone high enough in the government to bring a covert military action against them. Given what Susie says about his political donations, he probably has enough early warning to back down or take a lower profile. Stoney commented that without the one picture and secured access to an excellent facial recognition database, we would not know who committed the kidnappings. That would put us in the same position as the FBI, which remains in the dark. Victor, for what it's worth, runs a very well-oiled machine.

Karen said she succeeded in getting more current profile information on Victor from the internet. Per Cody's request, she was able to easily get a home address in Potomac, MD, just off River Rd, and send it to Q. She circulated a current picture of Victor taken at a recent non-profit charitable event, where he was honored as a primary benefactor to their non-profit, Victor and his wife Elana had one child, a girl, named Anna. She is currently 15 years old and attends a private academy just south of where they lived off River Road. Victor maintains a very low profile on all the major internet sites, and Elana posts fairly regularly but with plain vanilla information. On the other hand, Anna is a typical teenager who likes to put herself out there, just like her friends do regularly. I think Anna has no knowledge of the Mafia ties and truly believes her dad is a self-made and very successful businessman as a venture capitalist.

Anna has made several comments. Several years ago, she stated that my dad's favorite food is Italian. Another post indicated the family's love for eating at a specific Italian restaurant in Bethesda. One of Anna's more recent posts indicated that, going back to school, I will miss Wednesday's luncheon at Bella Napoli with my dad. Given Susie's information about Victor's time spent in Italy and strong ties with the Italian Mafia, Victor has acquired a liking for good Italian cuisine.

Except for being known to host lavish parties with an "A" list of guests from entertainment and politics, this family maintains a relatively low profile. I believe he is a member of a fairly exclusive country club, but golf does not seem to be that important. I can't identify any regular hobbies, but from current photos, he appears to stay in reasonably good shape. He regularly travels back to Russia, both with and without his family, which would be expected.

Cody knew Susie and Karen had spent much of their time gathering information about Victor's background. He thanked them immensely for the quick turnaround and excellent information.

Chapter 28

Zach reached out to Cody, who had spent the middle part of the day at home; Carly was adjusting slowly, not wanting to leave their house without someone else, which was very understandable. He added it was the second day the FBI had not contacted Alan or me with any updated information. At this point, I have to believe that all the leads the FBI was following, including license plates, cameras, the fountain, and the tunnel, have come up empty. They are waiting for another message in Alan's email to react to. I hate to say it, but we are the only ones who can make a difference for Peggy.

Since Q was still in the field, Cody advised everyone that he had viewed some video feed from Victor's home. Cody also mentioned that he asked Q to get some additional night videos of the property. He said the house was a small mansion, surrounded by an ornate six-foot wall and a gated entrance. Not his expertise, he would defer to Stoney's viewpoints, but one had to expect every modern-day security system to be in place and active. Guards were present but showed a relatively low profile to maintain family-style representation rather than look like a fort heavily guarded 24/7.

Cody specifically addressed Zach, stating he was a kidnapping target until he drove the company car into the Potomac tributary and swam out onto the Airport property. The mafia has his photo and was able to attach a tracker to his car. Given the ransom payment and Carly's release, I think you are off the mafia radar screen as a target.

Cody then asked Susie to please research the ownership of the Italian restaurant in Bethesda and text me with your findings. He added that he felt Victor may be more than a loyal customer.

Cody, to lighten the mood, told the team he wanted to share with you a story about a restaurant in New York City -

Several years ago, I met a girl who lived in New York City. She invited me for a weekend just before Christmas to experience the city with all the holiday decorations. After a day spent walking and touring the town, we wound up in the Little Italy district right after sunset, around 6 o'clock. I asked her if she knew of a restaurant to eat at, and she admitted to never having eaten in Little Italy. I saw a street vendor with a cart roasting chestnuts over a hibachi-type fire. I asked him what the best restaurant in Little Italy is, and his response was "They are all good". I then restated my question to him, saying If your grandmother was turning 75 and you wanted to take her out in Little Italy for dinner, where would you go? He didn't answer but pointed diagonally across the block to one specific restaurant.

Based on the recommendation, we walked the ½ block and went in, and I immediately saw the maitre d' wearing a tuxedo, and the inside decor was fabulous. I advised the maitre d' that we had been touring the city all day and were probably underdressed, but someone in the community had recommended the restaurant as the finest in Little Italy. He responded that the dress code used to be very stringent, but they have since relaxed their requirements, with business casual now taking over. He added that their dining crowd started arriving between 8 and 9 p.m., and he would gladly accommodate us at this early hour. All of you know my love of red wine, so I ordered a relatively expensive Chianti as a token gesture for allowing us to dine there. The wait staff, also in tuxedos, was attentive and highly professional in making us feel at home, even while wearing jeans.

We lost track of time enjoying the exquisite food, not realizing several hours had passed. As the maitre d' said, limousines started pulling up to the restaurant a little after 8 p.m., and every party was dressed in formal wear except for the two gentlemen lingering behind the main party. The two men were seated along the wall close to the main party. I leaned over and asked my date if she knew who owned this restaurant. With a puzzled face, she said she had no idea. I noted that every party arriving was chauffeur-driven, commented on the value of the dresses and jewelry worn, and specifically pointed out the two bodyguards posted near their bosses. My reply to my date was that the Italian Mafia owns this restaurant. Her reaction was that it may be time to leave. I commented that this restaurant was probably the safest place in all of New York City to have dinner. There were perhaps more loaded guns in this place than at the police station.

I planned to tip the maitre d' but knew anything I gave him would be pocket change compared to what he received from the regular customers. I paid him a heartfelt compliment, saying he did not have to take us in, but in doing so, provided us both with a very memorable dinner. The last connection I made involved the chestnut vendor, who was aware that the mafia owned and operated the restaurant. He was too fearful even to speak the restaurant's name, prompting him just to point, then push his chestnut cart down the street.

Having told that story, I think it would benefit us all to check out Bella Napoli. Zach, are you available on a Fail-Safe corporate credit card tomorrow to take Susie for Sunday Brunch in Bethesda? Susie and Zach both blushed a little, knowing they had an open-ended date for when this situation was all over. Cody had just moved up the time frame for their first date to tomorrow. He would have preferred not to ask Zach and do the recon himself, but Kim would never forgive him for breaking their sailing date.

Cody instructed Zach and Susie to pay attention to several details: the parking area, the number of entrances and exits, the bathroom location, the spacing of the dining tables, the windows, and the kitchen. Get a good feel for the place and take some discreet pictures. Please stay away from the $100 bottles of wine – Susie chimed in with a big "Yes, boss", no problem, and I will make a reservation right now. Zach was thrilled to go out with Susie and enjoy a free brunch.

Chapter 29

Stoney, as soon as you review the house video feed from the drone, Cody told him to buzz me on your thoughts as to approaching Victor's property without leaving a string of dead bodies behind. Cody asked Stoney if it was remotely possible to enter the property and get back out undetected. Stoney then assured Cody his four retired associates were available immediately if any plans needed their special talents. Cody believed that at some point, a show of force may be required when dealing with this organization, and until they made some type of formal plan, he would not be sure of the manpower requirements.

Could someone please ask Q for a panoramic view of the area surrounding the house? It would be helpful to better gauge the distances between Victor's place and the two adjacent neighbors, as well as approximately how far the woods are behind his house. Also, ask if the property has any significant elevation changes from front to back or side to side. Cody's last request to Q was to obtain clear facial shots of Elena and Anna if he saw them outside the house. If, for any reason, the drone could not capture a good facial shot of the wife and daughter, he asked Susie to find an internet photo of each person that could be altered, so the background would change, making it difficult to determine where the photo was taken.

Susie, when you're done dining, look deeper into the financial trail for specific account numbers, exact dates, and transaction amounts involving Victor and the funds he sends overseas. Please be sure no fingerprints of ours are left behind when probing around these types of records.

Karen stays focused on Anna when the daughters comment on her postings. Sometimes, a small seed grows into a big tree.

Cody closed the meeting, telling everyone to keep digging. Our target is to start coming up with a feasible plan to move forward by Monday. The clock is ticking, and time is not our friend.

Susie, being the diligent person, sent a text message to Cody that evening, saying she found a building permit request for improvements & betterments for Bella Napoli that required the owner's signature; Elena, Victor's wife, signed it. The actual owner on paper appears to be a shell company; she was unable to trace it to a specific individual, and it was well concealed. Cody passed the information to Zach and advised him that everyone he would be in contact with at the restaurant works for Victor Zanoska. He added a PS to have a good time at brunch, but not to break the budget.

Shaun asked Kim on Friday to review the kidnapping case very closely during her free time on Saturday. Then meet him Sunday morning at the Bureau's headquarters for a sit-down, just the two of them. Kim felt it couldn't take more than a couple of hours and had her travel bag packed with proper boating attire for her 1 o'clock sailing date with Cody.

Kim arrived ½ hour early, but could tell Shaun O'Hara was on at least his second or third cup of coffee. Both with a legal pad in hand and copies of the case file, they had the conference room 100% theirs for the morning. Shaun said he wanted to go through the crime, step by step, and see if they could come up with any angle or scenario that hadn't been addressed. Kim was silent about her 1 p.m. appointment and wanted to complete this as expeditiously as possible.

Shaun started, referencing that noontime or as close to it was the time they wanted to abduct all three family members, with cell phones today and their tracking/GPS programs, having one person go missing early in the day could have alarmed the other targets. The mom and sister were pretty clean snatches, but Zach, with his military training, turned into more than a handful. I expect a taser would have come into play if they had gotten close enough to Zach at whatever place he planned to get lunch. Kim jumped in, saying the family had to be followed for at least a week or two to establish a routine for deciding when to act. The trackers on Zach's car and probably Peggy's were beneficial as they didn't need more than one vehicle to keep tabs on someone's location.

Shaun asked if it made a significant difference in kidnapping 2 or 3 of the family members. What was the impact of losing Zach on the criminals? Kim said the most obvious point to get all three members of the family would be that the ransom demand could be elevated with more lives at risk. She added that the criminals initially set the price at $1 million per person. However, without Zach, they requested $2 million, which was paid instead of a $3 million demand. Shaun's viewpoint was slightly different; losing Zach may have taken some pressure off

Alan Turner, having two members abducted, but not his entire family. He stated they could have easily asked for $3 million for just two members being held.

Shaun told Kim, I've been around a long time and never seen uncut diamonds used or requested to free hostages. Kim replied, believing it was close to pure genius, if you could devise a way to get the uncut stones without getting caught. She added that by requiring this payment method, we now know that when these stones get cut and polished, their value doubles, and they become virtually untraceable. The organization had to feel the water fountain ploy was foolproof enough to execute using this form of payment. Our vehicles equipped with radiation detectors were stationed at the park entrances. However, when the stones passed through the tunnel, which was not near any of the entrances, we never registered a hit.

Shaun threw out the comment. Was that dumb luck on their part, finding the coating on the stones, or did they know in advance? Kim emphatically replied that they knew the stones were coated before payment. With a quizzical look, Shaun asked how she knew that to be true. She cited the debrief session with Stoney in their office. He stated that the first few handfuls of stones made a sound of hitting metal. Once the quantity built up, the stones hit other stones. From that one comment, we concluded the fountain's body was hollow and the stones were being captured in the fountain's base. The drain on the fountain was an oversized PVC plastic pipe, which could not have generated a metallic sound.

The man in the tunnel held a metal bucket or container to gather the stones. Why not use a plastic bucket? It is so much lighter to carry. If one knew they needed to shield against any radiation emission, metal, especially a lead bucket with a cover, would do the job. The criminals couldn't know where we were planning to deploy our detectors and could not afford an emission level high enough to trigger a signal from the tunnel. He stated your logic on the metal bucket makes perfect sense, which points directly to information being leaked to the criminals. Shaun was impressed and said so to Kim. It's why I like working with you, which is the first compliment he ever paid her since becoming his partner.

Kim said our team blew an opportunity when the fountain was removed and hauled out by the exit near our detection equipment. We didn't react quickly when our equipment registered no reading. Shaun jumped in, saying he remembered questioning whether the fountain's metal enclosure was sufficient to degrade any emissions signal. Our technical people replied: "It depended on the type and thickness of the metal making up the fountain." Since Stoney was the only one to get close to the fountain, we had no idea how or what it was made of. During the debriefing session, Stoney warned us that we weren't dealing with a standard-type water fountain.

Shaun said the grass covering of the metal cover had to be in place for weeks before the drop to grow and look natural. How long, Kim asked, do we think the fake fountain sat there with the caution yellow tape wrapped around it? Shaun's reply is probably no more than a week at the most. DC Public Works is not the most aggressive organization in fixing and repairing things. The investment made by the bad guys to build the fountain and then bet your entire kidnapping scheme around using it as the ransom drop could not be jeopardized by leaving it sitting in the park for weeks at a time.

Let's recount the areas we believed the criminals may have screwed up:

1) The fountain, custom-built, but no leads as to who did it

2) Hiring the handyman as a decoy to buy a little time, done by phone and paid in cash, was another dead end

3) license plates with real numbers where no cop would have pulled them over. The VA DMV proved ineffective in determining whether its system had been breached. Kim said there is always the possibility that someone in their organization saw the real truck in Richmond and just jotted down the license plate number

4) Traffic cameras, especially the express lanes, were not helpful; the bottom line is that DC has too much traffic to monitor or search for one or two vehicles. You know the getaway drivers stayed well within the speed limit when transporting the hostages

5) The messages to Alan's email exhibit reflect a very high level of IT expertise to keep us from backtracking to the source. Kim added that one-way communication eliminates any type of negotiation to get a feel of who you're dealing with

6) Searching the tunnel in both directions provided us with nothing useful. Kim said the installation was above ground; the only time one needed to enter the tunnel was to measure the distance from where they parked and then identify the specific manhole for the drop. The second underground trip in the tunnel would have been to secure the ransom payment... No reason for them to leave anything behind, with the limited amount of time spent on their two trips

Shaun grudgingly admitted that unless we get a valid tip or our informant network furnishes us with something to follow, we can only wait for the next message to be received. Shaun and Kim covered some other details with the compartmentalization of the task force. Glancing at her Apple watch, she saw it was a little before noon. Shaun thanked her for using up her Sunday morning; she was exceedingly happy to have an hour to get ready to meet up with Cody for their day on the water.

Chapter 30

Zach drove to Susie's condo in Arlington in his personal BMW M3 sedan; he had bought the car used but kept it in beautiful shape, loving its handling and horsepower. Zach knew Cody's Mustang couldn't keep up with his M-3 without mentioning it to him. The park police had released the company car that had taken the swim, but it still hadn't been dried out or tested by the dealer doing the repairs. He was in no rush to get it back, knowing there would probably be ongoing electrical issues caused by the vehicle being underwater for a few hours.

Susie was ready to go, wearing a bright summer-type floral dress, hair styled in very soft curls falling to shoulder length, showing enough cleavage to have a very sexy look that would turn most guys' heads. Susie commented on Zach's appearance, saying that he looked different. He said he took Cody's advice and wanted to maintain a low profile in public. Cody and Zach both knew the mafia had some excellent pictures of Zach that they could use in their kidnapping plans. Over the past week, he let his beard grow into a 2-3 day stubble, a style commonly worn by guys in their 20s. He mentioned being past due for a regular haircut and had let it grow well over his ears. He had never used it before, but he applied some hair gel to slick his back for today.

He told Susie that man-buns, long hair, were out of the equation for him; somewhere you had to draw the line.

Zach was sporting new, well-cut jeans with an embroidered white shirt worn outside his pants, topped off with a lightweight cotton blue blazer and brown leather deck shoes with no socks. She had to ask him where he acquired the round, lightly rose-tinted sunglasses he was wearing. He did admit going into his sister's and Carly's rooms and snatching them off her bureau to wear for the day. Susie flashed a big smile and said she could handle the slightly Elton John look, but was happy he didn't throw in some flamboyant clothing. During the drive to the restaurant, they talked about each other's interests and shared a common bond about enjoying great food. One thing they both admitted, during the drive, was that neither was involved in any type of current relationship. Susie was very comforted to know Zach was not dating anyone. She commented that she looked forward to brunch and was very excited about their reconnaissance assignment together.

They arrived slightly before their reservation; they saw the restaurant on the first floor of a mid-rise office building. Susie had told Zach that the restaurant's website advised their customers to park in the building's underground facility, and the restaurant would validate their ticket for $10 toward the cost of parking. The parking garage was automated, with no attendant, and accepted credit card transactions only for payment. The garage closed at 11 p.m. daily. The garage had three levels, but, being Sunday, parking spaces were plentiful.

They noted that the one elevator only served the parking garage's three levels and dropped them off in the lobby of the office building. On the right side of the building's lobby were two elevators that served the upper floors of the office building. Zach hit the up button, and when the elevator door opened, he saw the building had nine floors above the lobby level. There was no lockout on the building's elevators, so they rode them up to the ninth floor, then stopped twice on two lower floors. They saw an office building with several vacant spaces, most likely due to the COVID period, when everyone was working from home. The restaurant entrance was on the left side of the lobby, but since they were early, they decided to stroll around the block.

As they walked out onto the street, they noticed the restaurant had a second entrance on the main street, just a short distance from the office building lobby entrance. In their stroll around the block, Zach commented on the limited street parking and that all spaces were marked as Pay-to-Park. The area was typical of downtown Bethesda, with office-type buildings, retail shops, restaurants, nail salons, and various other commercial ventures on the street level.

They used the street entrance of the restaurant and were warmly greeted by the maître d', who was stationed halfway between the two entrances. Considering the warm welcome, Susie felt they were appropriately dressed for brunch. Zach commented to the maître d' that it was their first time eating at Bella Napoli, but the restaurant had come with glowing recommendations from several close friends. Susie, not to waste the moment, said to the maître d' that they were celebrating their 6 months to the day of being together as a couple. Zach supplied a quick wink behind his rose-colored glasses, which made Susie smile. The maître d' was very accommodating and sat them at a corner table, which afforded a little more privacy than sitting in the more open dining room. Zach and Susie were impressed with the decor and felt that the vibe was that of an upscale, white-tablecloth restaurant. The server introduced himself as Josh and brought the menus and wine list. Zach played on Susie's comment, indicating this was their first time dining here, and we're looking forward to a fabulous brunch. After reviewing the menu, Zach said he was thrilled Cody was picking up the tab.

The prices truly supported the upscale appearance, and bottles of wine started at around $75.The brunch entrees range from $35 to $55 per plate. When Josh returned, Zach asked for recommendations and any specials of the day. After taking their wine and meal order, he asked Josh if he had been on the staff for very long. Josh indicated that almost all the staff, from the head chef to sous chefs, servers, bartenders, and busing persons, had been together since the current owner renovated and reopened the restaurant some 7-8 years ago. He went on to say that the owners treat them very reasonably and couldn't think of another restaurant with a compensation plan that could match theirs.

Several trips by each of them to the restrooms provided a good feel for the layout between the bar area, entrances, and two dining room sections. The kitchen was in the back and appeared to have at least one rear exit leading back into the office building. During dessert, Zach told Josh that the food quality and every course were excellent. Josh bragged a little, saying the restaurant was under review for a possible one-star Michelin rating. He then asked Josh about the glassed-in private dining area behind the maître d' stand, which appeared to be able to host upwards of 10 people; he wondered if it was available to book for a family-type function. Josh indicated the space was not offered to the public but was only used by the owners or guests. Susie noted the space was vacant today, even though the restaurant was probably at max capacity during the brunch hour.

Providing a Fail-Safe corporate AmEx card and adding a very nice 25% gratuity for Josh onto the $300 lunch bill, he thought this should get Cody's attention. This dining experience surely topped off a great start on their first date. They were both looking forward to sharing their opinions with the team tomorrow. Zach, not wanting to waste a perfect day off, asked Suise if she was interested in heading down to the newly renovated wharf area in DC and maybe catching some live music at The Hamilton. Susie didn't miss a beat in replying, Lead on, Elton, which prompted another wink from behind his rose-colored glasses.

Chapter 31

Having wrapped up her Sunday morning briefing session with Shaun, Kim was happily on her way to the Washington Sailing Marina, located off the GW Parkway, immediately south of Reagan National Airport. She had used the ladies' room at the bureau to change into a bright yellow bikini with a white sundress. She also had a giant floppy straw hat with an accenting yellow headband to match her swimsuit. Shoes were an issue, and she did not know what to wear on a boat, so she decided on stylish flip-flops for the sailing date. Cody, anxious to get out on the water, saw her car pulling into the parking lot and walked out to greet her. Seeing her in a dress for the 1st time, he commented that her outfit was perfect. Being an avid sailor, he repeated that the marine weather forecast was for westerly winds ranging around ten mph, temperature hitting 80 degrees, and zero chance of rain. He said it was a perfect day to go sailing.

As they boarded Cody's boat, he explained to Kim that it was a Cal-27 built in the early 1970s, weighing about 5500 lbs, and had a fixed lead keel that required 4 ½ feet of water or would run aground in the river. He added that the tide changes from low to high tide every six hours or four times a day. To avoid that, we need to pay attention to the depth meter, which shows how much water is under the boat. The chances of sticking it into the muddy bottom of the Potomac River were very slim, as long as we pay attention to the depth gauge. Kim admitted that growing up in a small town in Ohio never presented any opportunity to learn or go sailing. Cody loved to coach people on the basics of sailing, hoping that would give them a foundation for a very pleasurable hobby to pursue and enjoy.

Before leaving the dock, Cody went below and came up with a Washington Nationals baseball cap. He advised Kim that the floppy hat was great looking but almost assuredly would blow off her head and wind up in the river. Then they would have to execute a man-overboard drill to rescue the wet hat. Kim accepted the apparel change but said it was not as stylish.

With Cody at the helm, they easily motored out of the marina to the river's main channel, where the water was noticeably deeper. Cody had steered the boat into the wind, telling Kim to hold the boat in this position while he hoisted the mainsail up the mast. The Cal was equipped with a tiller attached to the rudder for steering instead of having a wheel. He had Kim hold the tiller and advised her that the boat would turn to port, or to the left, when she pushed the tiller to starboard, or to the right. The steering was the opposite of a wheel; push right to go left and move left to go right.

The Potomac River runs in a north/south direction, he explained. Heading north was not an option as their mast was 37 feet high and would not clear under the 14th Street Bridge, which was the main roadway, I-395, into Washington, DC. So, they turned the boat south, following the dredged channel in the center of the river, keeping the boat in the deeper water.

They shut the outboard engine down, tilted it out of the water to reduce drag, and unfurled the jib headsail. With the westerly wind on the boat's beam, the Cal responded with minimal heel, and the instrument showed 4.5 to 5 knots of boat speed. Kim couldn't believe how quietly the boat glided through the water effortlessly. She instantly realized the calming effect of being on a sailboat underway.

Cody shared his itinerary for the day. They would shortly pass Old Towne Alexandria on the starboard side, then add to its right side – they could see the park where they had their picnic lunch, then proceed under the Woodrow Wilson Bridge, which links Virginia to Maryland. We'll pass MGM Grand Casino and National Harbor with their Capital (Observation) Ferris Wheel on our port side. Easy to remember, "port" and "left" both have four letters. The next point of interest will be Fort Washington on the Maryland side, which was built in 1809 to defend the Nation's Capital from water attack and remained active until World War II. The last scenic place we'll sail by is Mount Vernon, George Washington's estate. By seeing it from the river, you'll know why the father of our country chose this property, because it commands such a beautiful vista.

Our final destination is to head into the Occoquan River and drop anchor for a late lunch in Belmont Bay. We should arrive in under two hours, given the favorable winds. Cody told Kim to go below and check out the Cal. he'd loved the boat and had invested a fair sum of money to rehab the vessel into almost new condition. He chose this boat because it was very stable, especially if the winds or storms popped up, and was the perfect size for sailing on the Potomac. He asked Kim to check the cooler for assorted drinks and to find a bag of snack items he had left out. Below deck, the boat's center area had bench-type seats with a small table that could be folded down. In the stern area, with no inboard engine, Cody had stored some large nylon bags, which must have held additional sails. She noticed that the front of the boat was the only sleeping area and was large enough to accommodate only two people. Lastly, thank god the ship was equipped with a small marine toilet, saving one from jumping into the river when nature called.

Kim returned on deck, leaving the sundress below, still wearing the Nats baseball cap, holding two bottles of water and a bag of pretzels. Cody was nearly speechless when he saw Kim in her bright yellow bikini. He remembered their picnic lunch, where she mentioned that her life was training for the FBI, and her downtime was always spent in the gym. Cody blushingly said to Kim, Wow, all that time you spend working out has produced some beautiful results. Kim replied that the bathing suit was new and she had very few, if any, chances to show off the results of her gym time. Cody's only thought was *that this day went from great to off-the-charts.*

To stay off any work-related topics, she asked Cody where he got his passion for sailing. Cody told her that after leaving the Army, he linked up with some college buddies still living in the DC metro area. One of his friends had a 1/3 interest in a sailboat that they raced most weekends out of Annapolis, where the Naval Academy was located. Cody indicated the Army provides no hands-on sailing training like the Navy and asked how he could help race a sailboat. His friend explained they always needed "rail-meat," which were persons during a race sitting on the outside rail of the boat to provide balance, allowing the boat to obtain better speed. Cody signed on to race and, besides being the rail meat, watched and learned what it took to make a sailboat go competitively fast in all wind conditions. After two seasons of racing with the same crew, they were highly competitive and usually placed in the top three boats in their class.

Cody indicated that, with ramping up my company, I had to cut back on my racing commitments to only crewing 3-4 of the big regattas a year. Acquiring and restoring the Cal-27 allows me to leave my office and be out on the water in less than 15 minutes. I can single-handedly sail the Cal, but would much rather have a crewmate sporting a yellow bikini aboard. He then spent the next hour letting Kim steer the boat and coaching her on how and why the sails needed to be trimmed in the shifting wind. She was an excellent student and showed a good light touch on the tiller to keep the boat at an optimum angle to the wind.

As they approached Belmont Bay, Cody took the helm and tilted the small outboard engine back into the water. He started the engine and steered the boat directly into the wind, allowing them to furled in the jib sail. Then he had Kim release the halyard and drop the main sail, which they both secured with sail ties around the boom. Watching the depth meter, they motor near the shoreline into six feet of water away from all the boat traffic in the river for their afternoon lunch. Cody went below, grabbed an oversized beach towel, and threw it up on deck. He then told Kim to work on her tan while he got lunch together.

About 20 minutes later, Cody announced lunch was served and walked up from the cabin with a tray of goodies. Setting them in the cockpit, he returned for the plastic wine glasses, plates, napkins, utensils, and a chilled Chardonnay.

With the tiller lashed upright and out of the way, one bench in the cockpit served as the serving table, where the food was laid out, allowing them to sit opposite on the other bench. The menu consisted of fresh crab salad, hummus and pita bread, smoked salmon, brie and sharp cheddar cheese, a mixture of Italian olives, cherry tomatoes, and carrot and celery sticks. Kim asked if they expected Cody's race buddies to show up with all the food being served. Cody reminded her that the only crew he wanted to be with today was sitting beside him.

Cody announced they were missing one item and quickly ducked below deck and retrieved a portable Bose Surround Bluetooth speaker. He linked into a playlist from his phone of some of the best jazz musicians of all time, starting with the Dave Brubeck Quartet. They spent the next hour sipping an excellent Napa Valley Chardonnay and picking through the assorted food items. The conversation was easygoing, and both could tell the karma between them was intensifying. After they said they could not eat another bite, Cody offered to pack up the leftovers, knowing where everything was to go.

Cody knew that in the early stages of any relationship, it always felt very awkward to touch the other person, not wanting to feel or experience any rejection. As soon as he climbed out of the companionway, he told Kim they had not shared a hug since meeting for their picnic in the park. She stood up, opened her arms, and they embraced for an endless amount of time. Cody whispered in her ear that they had two dessert options: a chilled chocolate mousse in the cooler or to go below and have another hug. Kim whispered back, "The chocolate mousse shouldn't go bad and can be enjoyed later." Taking his hand, they entered the cabin and exchanged another hug, which turned into a kiss that neither wanted to end. Kim moved to the V-berth, pulling Cody in tow, and said to him, I may be a little rusty when it comes to romance. Cody stepped back, looked at her from head to toe, and said I can't see one spot of rust anywhere on that beautiful body. The yellow bikini and Cody's clothes were gently removed, and the dessert lasted longer than the main course.

The sail back was delightful, with little conversation, and we just sat close to each other and enjoyed the Potomac River's beauty. Returning to the marina at dusk, neither wanted the evening to end. However, the reality was that Kim knew she had to be at the Bureau by 6 a.m., and Cody had committed to the team to provide an update and formulate decisions on a course of action. The last hug in the marina parking lot was electric; both felt every date thereafter would be something special. As Kim was backing out of her parking spot and recounting the day, Cody appeared and knocked on the driver's side window; she thought something of hers must have been left behind when she rolled down the window. Cody handed her a bag with ice and a container of chocolate mousse; she had to chuckle.

Chapter 32

At 9 a.m. sharp, the team was in the conference room to update on any new information and try to decide what course of action might secure Peggy's release. Zach said that Alan had not received any new messages or instructions, which left his mother's situation in limbo. Everyone on the team somewhat agreed this was good news, feeling the kidnappers weren't sure how to handle the situation, dealing with Peggy, and providing them some time to formulate a plan.

Zach recounted their visit to Bella Napoli in Bethesda, with Susie taking the chair beside him. Zach asked Susie to share her thoughts or opinions from their brunch. He recounted that Bella Napoli was indeed owned and operated by Victor Zanoska, based on Susie finding the wife's signature on a building permit application. Zach explained the location on the street level of the mid-rise office building. Susie explained the underground 3-level parking lot with a single-service elevator to reach the lobby area. They both recapped the automated teller feature and the closing time at 11 p.m. Susie mentioned their stroll around the block and the limited street parking available. They mentioned the elevator ride to the top floor and commented on the vacancy rate on several lower floors.

Zach and Susie both shared the same opinion that Bella Napoli was Victor's private way to enjoy quality Italian wine and food in a venue he controlled. Zach shared Josh's comments, the waiter's, that the staff never turned over, which is highly unusual in the restaurant business. Susie added the details of the glass private dining area, which was going unused on a hectic day for the restaurant. It was only used by the owners or guests and not available to the general public. Zach's reluctance to disclose their spending indicated that the prices were "high-end," but the quality supported the cost, and Bella Napoli pursued a one-star Michelin rating. They showed some pictures secretly taken of the restaurant's layout, with its two entrances and an apparent third exit through the kitchen area.

Cody was eager to obtain details from Carter/Q regarding the drone surveillance footage taken in the late afternoon and evening at Victor's mansion in Potomac, MD.

Q indicated he downloaded the video to Stoney's PC for his input. Q said the house is in a high-end subdivision where every lot must be at least 8 to 10 acres. The home sits well back off the street. The two neighboring dwellings and mansions were a fair distance on the left and right of Victor's property, with nothing in the back except a grove of mature trees. This gave me a good perimeter to operate the drone, using high-resolution with a zoom lens to provide decent footage.

The main house property is gated with a stucco-type wall, I estimate at 7-8 feet high, surrounding all the dwellings. Besides the driveway entrance, each of the other three walls has an entry/ exit decorative wrought iron-type door. Besides the main house, the six-car garage appears to have living quarters above, which could house security or maintenance personnel. There is a scaled-down guest house in the same architectural style as the main house, which may have up to 4 or 6 bedrooms. The guest house is situated about 50 yards from the main dwelling. The beautiful in-ground pool is behind the main house, with an adjacent small pool house. The balance of the property has manicured gardens and plants everywhere.

Video taken in the evening clearly showed the master bedroom in the center of the dwelling on the 2nd floor with a massive balcony overlooking the entire back of the property. If I had to guess, the master suite might take 1,500 to 2,000 sq ft. Per your request, Cody, we did get some clear photos of the entire family. Elana was home when Anna was driven back from school. Victor showed up an hour later, and the family dined together that evening on the back patio. I will defer to Stoney about what he saw when viewing the video.

Stoney's first comment, considering who we are dealing with and that this property is his family's home, is that one has to expect every state-of-the-art security system device to be in place and monitored 24/7. The principal cars used are two full-sized black Mercedes sedans. Both vehicles appear to be the model with extra armor reinforcement and bulletproof glass. On several occasions, we observed vehicles coming and going, always accompanied by a driver and another security person in the passenger seat. The family of three could comfortably sit in the rear seat of those vehicles and travel together. I would expect that on any special trips or meetings, the 2nd vehicle would follow with additional security personnel.

Stoney added: It looks to me like the on-site security people kept a reasonably low profile. Determining precisely how many are on the property at any one time was challenging. I could always observe a pattern of one security person walking the premises. There has to be a master security room; all the monitoring screens are located, probably in the main house's basement. If I had to bet, detection devices range right to the property limits in all directions, north, south, east, and west. It must drive them crazy when a deer, fox, or other animal trips their systems. Inside the wall, I guarantee there are no blind spots, and the family knows not to stroll out into the gardens after a particular time. He said marching into any entrances would turn into a shootout like Virgil Earp had at the OK Corral in Tombstone. Everyone of any importance and with money favors an interior safe room to evacuate to when danger is detected. Once an alarm goes off, trying to breach any of these types of rooms, once they are located, can be very difficult, if not impossible. Lastly, I would expect the local police response time, given the neighborhood, to be a top priority and done quickly when an alarm is triggered.

Two landing areas are coming in by parachute: the flat roof on the west wing side of the main house, which may or may not have monitors, or, surprisingly, the swimming pool. However, a small target to hit typically has no detection system until you exit the water onto the pool deck. Remember that once you choose to parachute in, you must plan and find a reasonable way out.

Stoney felt that with some additional surveillance, the easiest target may be the 15-year-old daughter while at the private school during the day. Even if she had a security person babysitting her, they could be neutralized, and the girl could be taken. Cody stepped up and said Victor would use every legal and illegal resource to get his daughter back, including making Peggy a target. Cody added that if Anna did not know her dad's criminal connections, if we abducted her to use as leverage, Victor would never stop looking to find and punish the people who took his daughter. He added that when you grab a tiger by its tail, the teeth and claws still pose a big problem and must be dealt with!

Karen's additional internet research on Victor's parents or siblings did not provide any new information beyond what was previously discussed. She said that all family ties to Victor appear to be back in Russia, which is not a country we could easily enter or operate in, especially given our limited timeframe.

Cody stood up and said he would like to share his thoughts on what we know now. The Russian Mafia has Peggy Turner. It's safe to say the FBI does not have this information and may have leaked details back to the mob. We have an unknown timeline for trying to secure Peggy's release. Zach knew Cody was about to reveal his plan of action, which he had been contemplating for days.

I always felt we must follow the old proverb—An Eye for an Eye; Cody stated that, from what was uncovered and discussed, he believed there was only one option to pursue to get Peggy back:

"Our team must find a way to kidnap Victor Zanoska!"

Before I continue and share my thoughts, I need two questions answered:

My first question to Susie was: Can you hack a building's operational computer system, control the elevators to open and close, and specify which floor they are on? Susie immediately replied that it would be effortless if the elevator systems were computer-controlled.

The 2nd Question to Stoney: While Zach and I were in Army intelligence, we knew special forces groups had access to a canister containing a nerve agent that incapacitates anyone inhaling the vapor. If true, can you get your hands on one or two canisters on very short notice? Stoney said they had access to such a device when a mission required a person or persons who had to be neutralized quickly, resulting in no residual harm. Cody said they needed it by tomorrow regarding access and the timeframe. Stoney noted that if it is required, he will make it happen.

CODY SAID HE'D NOW like to share his thoughts on how to kidnap Victor Zanoska. Based on the positive replies from Susie and Stoney, I propose the following plan:

Cody cited Karen's discovery of a social media comment from their daughter, Anna, expressing her desire to have missed Wednesday's lunch with her father. We must take a leap of faith that these lunches will still happen, and in two days, on Wednesday, Victor will attend the next one. Based on Zach and Susie's intel about Bella Napoli, we expect Victor's driver to use the parking garage to access the restaurant. When Victor enters the garage service elevator, we need to disperse the nerve agent, rendering everyone inside incapacitated. We know the garage has three floors serviced by the elevator. We arrive early and block off the 3rd level ramp with cones and a sign, indicating that maintenance operations are being done. Victor and his party would enter the elevator Susie controls on the 1st or 2nd floor, lock the doors shut, and disperse the nerve agent to neutralize everyone inside. Then Susie sends the elevator to the 3rd level, where we remove just Victor. Our end goal is to swap Victor for Peggy, and while he is our guest, we need to convince him not to take any retribution against us after the swap is done.

OPEN FOR DISCUSSION: Zach said the plan is brilliant, but it's based on two major assumptions – Victor will show up on Wednesday for lunch. Also, Stoney can deliver a nerve agent to be used, and we will figure out a way to disperse it in a closed elevator. Cody said the quicker we move, the better our chance of getting Peggy back. If he doesn't show up, two days and some serious planning will have been wasted. But if we succeed with Victor, we can almost guarantee Peggy will return safely.

Q leaned over and asked Stoney if you could draw or describe how the canister operates. I should be available to design and build a device with a trigger mechanism that activates and funnels the agent through a hose back into the elevator compartment. Stoney added that the results should take less than 20 seconds in a small, confined space. Stoney grabbed a legal pad and drew out to approximate scale a canister that looked the size of a beer can with a trigger mechanism on the top for Q to use.

Chapter 33

Zach said, Let's start a checklist right now on everything that has to happen to pull this off– Everyone on the team began shouting out items that would be critical:

1. Susie has to find out who owns or manages the building and hack into the operating system to control an elevator
2. Send someone out to check if the elevator has a ceiling access panel that can be used to load and retrieve the nerve agent.
3. The same person is visiting the garage with a plan to block the 3rd-level ramp.
4. Renting a van and making fake decals with a maintenance company name
5. Making some fake license plates with real numbers from another vehicle
6. Secure communications devices so everyone can talk to each other
7. Military grade tasers if the nerve agent does not do a 100% job
8. Someone is watching Victor's car if his driver does not

go to lunch

9. Someone in the restaurant in case Victor arrives by the street entrance, but leaves by the garage elevator

10. Construction-type vests and hard hats to appear as maintenance people

11. Where to take and hold Victor? How many people are needed to watch him?

12. How do they plan to communicate with the Mafia to make a swap

13. Ways to approach Victor so that he does not invoke some type of retribution

14. What if other persons enter the elevator with Victor and his security person

15. How to be sure no trace or evidence is left behind, ventilating the elevator

Cody took the lead, emphasizing that all the team's input was needed, and other items would be addressed when we fine-tune the plan the next day. He added that every possible contingency could be addressed if we had two weeks. As it is, Wednesday may provide an opportunity that doesn't come around again.

Cody had sketched some notes and read them to the team. Right now, let's go forward with these assignments:

Zach, go to the Bella Napoli garage and check the elevator for a ceiling roof panel. Be sure to bring a step stool and put the elevator on hold while examining the roof panel. Determine the best way to secure the ramp area to prevent parking on the third level. Then, obtain a car count on each parking level to assess whether blocking the third level would disrupt tenants during midday.

On your way back, visit any retail store that sells cell phones and select a phone with at least 24 hours of talk time. Pick up six of these disposal-burner phones. We may need them to communicate with Victor's organization once, then trash them. Be sure to pay cash for them.

Karen, could you rent us a standard white cargo van today? Then, use our 3-D printer to create 6-inch letters - 2 sets–with a message like "AA Maintenance Co." and a phone number from one of the burner phones Zach is picking up. Take an intern with you and also secure a mid-size SUV that Stoney and any members of his team can use on Wednesday –Go by Home Depot and buy five high-quality respirators rated for chemical usage, six orange construction cones, four contractor vests and hard hats, light weight chain in 6, 9,12, and 15 ft lengths with four good padlocks, Ryobi battery operated floor fan at least 20 inch, Box of zip ties at least 12 and 15 inches, Duct tape, the best brand made. Need two medium-duty tarps (10 ft x 10 ft), a Whiteboard, or sign boards that can stand up independently. Heavy-duty Febreze-type spray and disinfecting wipes for the elevator car – A foam rubber mat used for camping that fits inside the van – Box of extra-large latex-type gloves – six pairs of tight-fitting safety goggles. Get two 12X12 inch signs with suction cups attached, saying "Out-Of-Order" - Use Stairway for Lobby." We will attach these signs to the 1st and 2nd-floor elevator doors when the unit is locked on the 3rd level.

Susie, use the building address to access the building's operational system. If you get in and are successful, call Zach if he is on-site and run an elevator test. Next, hack the VA DMV to obtain a real license plate number for the exact year and model of the van we rent, and then have Karen 3-D print some fake license plates.

See if you can find Elana Zanoska's cell phone number. For starters, try the backdoor into Verizon and T-Mobile. We may need to contact her at some point.

Carter/ Q should consult with Stoney for the best description of the canister we may be dealing with, and then start to engineer a device that can be triggered remotely inside the elevator. Also, I want a box for Victor's phone that guarantees it does not emit any GPS-type tractor signal. We may need to remove the phone from the box later and use it to validate messages sent to his organization. Last item, Q, please provide a frequency jammer with a broad range. I want it in the van and operating after we load Victor. High-profile individuals have reportedly had chips embedded under their skin for tracking purposes. As a precaution, this device will be on the entire time Victor is in our possession.

Stoney – You and Susie have the keys to unlock this plan. Get the Q canister ASAP; we will need eight sets of secure communications devices, microphones, and earbuds. The last item is to get four military-grade tasers as a backup if required. Recruit two of your retired team members and brief them on the basics of our plan so they know we are crossing the line into a criminal offense. They'll need to be here tomorrow for the team meeting. We will need them on Wednesday to help with guard duty on Victor. Cody told Stoney that a 2-4 day commitment should suffice if everything goes smoothly.

I am sure everyone is thinking, What's Cody going to do? The answer is to put my feet up on my desk and crack open a cold beer. After the laughter settled, Cody explained that he had a place in mind outside of Madison, VA, near Lake Anna, remote and far off Interstate 95, South of Washington, DC. This is where we would keep Victor while we negotiate a swap. When we gather tomorrow morning, I will have scripted an exact timetable of events, like orchestrating a ballet, that requires perfect timing for the performance to be pulled off. If any of you come up with other must-do items, get them to me ASAP so the plan can be amended as needed.

Let's roll. It will be a hectic day, and the next 48 hours will pass quickly.

Cody went back to his office and called his Dad. Ben was a professor at the University of Virginia in Charlottesville, VA. Ben was always happy to hear from Cody and get updates on Fail-Safe's progress and his success as the CEO of a growing company. Cody thought it best not to expose Ben to everything happening, given the potential danger level of their plan. So after some family chit-chat, Cody asked his Dad for a big favor– He would like, if it's available, to use Ben's cabin or what the family referred to as the "lake house", near Lake Anna, VA He didn't like lying. Still, he had little choice, telling his dad that he had met a woman and, after several dates, the relationship had blossomed, and they wanted to spend some quality time together.

If no one plans to use it, he will be down this Wednesday for 3-5 days. His dad said their schedule had them committed to being in Charlottesville for the next couple of weeks. Cody thanked him and said he knew where the spare key was kept and how to turn everything on and off. In closing, he asked his Dad to ensure no family shows up unannounced to check the new girlfriend out! His Dad committed that there would be no uninvited guests and asked how serious this new person was in his life. He didn't have to lie when he said Kim was something very special – Cody hung up knowing they had a place to use if they successfully snatched Victor off the grid. His next task was to monitor everyone doing their jobs today and draft a detailed itinerary starting Wednesday morning.

Karen was one of the first to provide Cody with an update; she had called around and found a local Enterprise Car Rental office that also carries commercial vans. With a Fail-Safe corporate credit card and two interns, she rented a white panel van and a Hyundai Santa Fe SUV. The interns drove the vehicles back to the office, and she headed to Home Depot with her shopping list. An hour later, she arrived at the office parking garage and unloaded her purchases into the van. She contacted Susie and requested that she search the VA DMV for a valid plate number on a 2022 Chevy Express 2500 white cargo van and a 2023 Hyundai Santa Fe SE, which was also white. Susie said she would return with the license plate numbers in 30 minutes so they could use the 3-D printer to generate the fake plates.

Susie's first task after the meeting ended was researching the property management company for the Bethesda office building that housed Bella Napoli. She knew that without the ability to control the elevator, their plan would fail before it started. Finding the property manager was public knowledge for anyone renting space in the building. She then used her dark skills to hack into their computer system and see the exact link used by the management company to operate all the building systems, including the elevator. She dialed Zach's cell number and found he was stuck in traffic, but indicated to give him 20 minutes, and he would be parked on the 3rd level of the garage.

When Zach buzzed Susie back, she saw the elevator was programmed to always reset and return to the lobby floor. Without anyone pushing buttons, Susie moved the elevator down to level 3. With Zach on the line, she asked him to press for the lobby, which he did, and the elevator door closed. Susie immediately put it on hold – Zach confirmed from inside the elevator that pushing any buttons didn't cause any more movement, and the door would not open. The last thing Zach asked was if he tried the red emergency button, could she prevent it from sounding any alarm? She replied and told him to push the red button; Zach did without any alarm going off. He knew the first big hurdle was behind them. He asked Susie to let Cody know the results and said he would be heading back after inspecting the ceiling panel of the elevator.

Susie shared the positive news with Cody, explaining the test results from the run they had just conducted with Zach. Cody was excited knowing they had a green light to keep moving forward, leaving Stoney to make his connection as the next big hurdle. He asked her to be thorough and ensure no trace of her actions remained in the property manager's system. She commented, "I didn't get 3 degrees in computer science from Stanford University for nothing."

True to his word, Zach was back in Cody's office in just over an hour. Earlier that morning, Cody advised everyone on staff that he would cover lunch. A local deli dropped off every type of sandwich imaginable, with chips and assorted drinks. They grabbed some food and returned to Cody's office, closing the door, given what they needed to discuss. Zach reviewed the elevator test with Susie and said that part of the plan would work perfectly.

With his three-tier step stool, he could access the maintenance hatch built into the ceiling of the elevator car. No lock, just a simple handle mechanism to release it and lift it. Zach said the cavity above the elevator ceiling was pretty open, except for the cables and pulleys located directly in the center. The hatch door measured 28 X 28 inches. He would provide these details to Q to incorporate into building his device to hold and disperse the agent. The interior height of the car was 7 ½ ft, and required them to pack the step stool on Wednesday.

Zach explained to Cody that entering and exiting the 3rd parking level was simply controlled by arrows painted on the floor for directions. He suggested using traffic cones to block access and parking the van near the entrance ramp. He counted 33 parking spaces on the 3rd level, with only three used today. He walked up the ramp to count parked cars on the upper levels and saw 26 spaces taken on level one and 11 used spaces on level two. Zach noted that the restaurant had posted signs for 14 spaces on level two for their customers, though he doubted anyone would enforce who parks in the restaurant spaces. Zach reminded Cody that he and Susie had ventured to the upper floors of the office building and found several vacant spaces for lease. He told Cody that as long as they acted professionally as maintenance people, they shouldn't cause any issues blocking the 3rd level of the garage for the entire morning. After finishing his sandwich, Zach said his next stop was at Walmart to get the burner phones.

Cody advised Zach of the availability of the Lake house as a place to park Victor for a couple of days. Zach had been there numerous times for Cody's family get-togethers over the past few years. He commented it would be perfect given its quiet location because the property the house sat on was almost 10 acres of land. As Zach walked out the door, his parting comment to Cody was that the dominoes were lining up and starting to fall over very nicely. Let's hope Stoney still has pull with his old military buddies.

Susie had indeed also hacked into the VA Department of Motor Vehicles. She ran a search engine on the rental cars' year, make, model, and color, and obtained in-force license plate numbers for the identical vehicles. She quickly texted Karen with the characters for the plates and then put the office 3-D printer to work—one more item to cross off their checklist.

Chapter 34

Stoney came back after Fail-Safe was closed for the day. All the employees had headed home except for the team. Everyone knew the importance of Stoney getting back in touch with currently enlisted special ops people who would be willing to get the items needed to pull off this plan to kidnap the head of the Russian Mafia. Cody invited Stoney into his office; if the news was bad and Stoney could not acquire what they needed, he wanted to present it to the team tomorrow morning and advise them that Stoney had tried his best. Tasers may be their only other option. Cody knew that dealing with armed and trained men, tasers would be a perilous proposition.

Stoney started with: Do you want good or bad news first? Cody responded I have always been an optimist, beginning with the good news. Well...I have the tasers and communications devices in hand; they are stored in reasonably large quantities and will never be missed. The bad news is that the nerve gas has become a tricky item; due to its potent nature, it must be requested in writing, leaving a chain of custody paper trail. Stoney said to Cody, I am sure military intelligence was a small and tight-knit community, but special ops personnel, active or retired, are truly blood brothers for life.

Stoney stated that my contact requests two nerve gas canisters for tomorrow's rush-scheduled training mission. If the request is approved, he plans to run a secretive mission scenario and use only one of the two canisters. The big "IF" depends on his superiors signing off on the request, which I should know by morning. The best-case scenario for us may be tomorrow at midday. Cody told Stoney, 'I realize you probably called in every favor in the book. I speak for Zach and everyone on the team; we will deal with the results either way it goes.'

Stoney informed Cody that two retired squad members would be attending tomorrow's detailed briefing and would remain available for as long as needed. The two guys showing up tomorrow are Bones (who had incurred more injuries during their special ops than anyone else) and 'V" which is short for Viper; no explanation is needed.

Cody thought quickly and told Stoney that, to hedge against the uncertain outcome if the canister could not be secured, they should plan B – dealing with the talent and training you three guys have- and consider the tasers as a backup to secure Victor. Stoney chuckled and said whatever was needed to get the job done, and then felt much better hearing there was a possible option number two. Cody closed by commending Stoney for a great effort today and saying he valued him as a trusted employee. Stoney just nodded and said a drink was waiting for him somewhere. He hoped everything else they needed was coming together.

Cody got hold of Q and advised him that the canister may be unavailable. He wanted Q to have a prototype ready in case they got their hands on the nerve agent. Q explained to Cody that, based on what Stony had drawn up, it was a simple device with an electromagnetic piston that pulled the pin and dispersed the agent. A cell phone would be wired to trigger the piston. The box holding everything would be sealed, forcing the agent through a tube into the elevator. He had advised Zach that he would need to drill a 2-inch circular hole in the access panel hatch door for the tube to fit into. Q told Zach he would give him a 2-inch rubber cap plug to cover the hole once the box was removed. Q liked his design, but until he had the physical item in hand, he had no idea what modifications might be needed. Cody told Q to call it a night and that he would see him tomorrow morning.

Tuesday morning found everyone assembled in the conference room. Cody introduced Bones and V to the team, stating they had been briefed by Stoney and were committed to being available until the job was done. Cody commented that it was probably the largest grouping held in this conference room. He reminded everyone that what they were going to try to do tomorrow was criminal in the eyes of the law, but necessary for the following reasons:

Cody stated If we turned over our video to the FBI, it would only provide very circumstantial evidence as to who committed the kidnapping. This could well trigger the organization to kill Peggy Turner to close that exposure and take their chances in court on someone proving they were responsible for kidnapping Carly. If we do nothing, Peggy is still a hostage, and fate will solely be determined by the persons holding her.

No one in the room had any reservations about what needed to be done over the next several days. . .

He opened the discussion with an update on his family's lake house, located about an hour and a half south of Washington, DC, not far off Interstate 95.

Zach, Karen, Susie, and Q provided an update on the progress made, purchases, and custom-built items in Q's department. After meeting with Stoney and learning that the nerve agent canister's acquisition was in question, Cody informed everyone that Stoney had submitted his request and was awaiting confirmation on whether the item could be acquired by the end of the day. Stoney and I have discussed a backup plan, possibly using tasers if the nerve gas cannot be acquired. Cody, staying positive, said to Q, Be ready if we obtain the canister to finish and test your dispersal device, and make sure it's operational for tomorrow. Q replied that it only needs some fine-tuning and will deliver the results when used.

Cody explained he had scripted assignments and a timeline of events for tomorrow, Wednesday, in Bethesda. Reading from his notepad:

Zach, Stoney, and I will drive the van to the parking garage, arriving when it opens at 7 a.m. We will post a signboard stating that the 3rd level is closed for maintenance until 3 p.m. and will cone off the entrance ramp. If anyone questions us, we advise them that we are waiting for power washing equipment to clean the 3rd level so that we can restripe the parking spaces.

Susie will move the elevator to level 3 and lock it off as soon as we secure the level. That early morning should present little to no traffic coming into the garage. Zach and Stoney will drill the vent tube hole and install the device canister in the space above the maintenance hatch. Once installed, Susie will be notified to put the elevator back into full service, for only the 1st and 2nd levels of the garage. Stoney has indicated that this gas agent will put you under for a solid hour, once inhaled by anyone inside.

Bones and V will drive the SUV, arriving by 10 a.m., and park on the second level. Cody indicated that we should expect Victor to arrive between noon and 1 p.m., which means the first parking level may have limited spaces. Victor's driver will not risk parking where his Mercedes will get dinged up, which most likely puts him on the 2nd level of the garage. Bone's or V, one of you must cover the 1st level elevator, just in case it's used. The other person then covers the 2nd level. One of you must communicate with Susie the second Victor enters the elevator, and the door closes. She will then send the elevator down to the 3rd level and keep the door closed. Then Q will trigger the device in the ceiling to fog the elevator car. Bones and V must then attach the Out-of-Order signs on the 1st and 2nd level elevator exterior doors. Bones and V will come down to the 3rd level, and one of you will post on the entrance by our cones to be sure we are not interrupted. The other person will assist us in removing persons from the elevator and cleaning it. I estimate that clearing and ventilating the elevator on the 3rd level, wiping it down, and returning it for service should take no more than 7 to 9 minutes. Once the job is completed, Bones or V must pull the signs off the doors on the 1st and 2nd levels. At this point, we should be driving our two vehicles out of the garage.

Karen, Zach indicated there were several public benches near the restaurant. Please pack your lunch and laptop, and choose a spot to view traffic in both directions. Looks like a secretary during her lunch hour while surfing the web. Arrive by 11:30 a.m. and walk around the area to find two good spots. Be on station by 11:45 a.m. and then move at 12:30 p.m. to your second spot. This way, you will not be seen loitering for an hour and a half in the same position. Victor should be in a black Mercedes with a driver. Any heads up to all of us that his car is approaching, even if we get only 30 seconds' advance notice, will be of great value. Of course, you'll be fitted with a communication mic and earbud. I recommend using Uber for your trip there and back, so parking isn't an issue.

Susie and Q, be aware that Stoney has indicated his communication gear has a several-mile range. However, he has stated that being underground may have a slight impact. At 7 a.m., we can communicate by cell phone to set up the elevator. After that, both of you head to Bethesda, mid-morning, after rush hour, and research some coffee shops in the area with excellent Wi-Fi so your laptop can link into the building's operating system. Q has the phone number to trigger the canister. The timing is critical; when Victor and anyone with him enter the elevator, they will feel movement, thinking they are going up to the lobby. When, in fact, the first jolt will send them down to the third level, Stoney has said the gas is relatively instantaneous, but we have to allow an average person to hold their breath for about a minute. Susie will hold the door shut for 1 minute..

Bones or V, whichever one of you IDs the party entering the elevator, tell us after the door closes how many persons and the makeup between male/female. Here are the pictures of the players: Victor, Elana, his wife, Anna, his daughter, and Ivan, his right-hand lieutenant. The other individual, either Bone or Zach, who fails to identify the persons entering the elevator, comes down to the 3rd level to assist in clearing and cleaning the elevator. The other person will cover the ramp until we are ready to leave. The person making the ID will have just over a minute while the elevator door is locked to get down to the 3rd level and grab a respirator, vest, and hard hat. We will position two persons on each side of the elevator door at an acute angle and have tasers ready to fire. Let's agree now: going from left to right, I'll take person one on the left, Stoney will cover person two, Zach will take the 3rd, and either Bones or V will take the fourth, Stoney let's get a couple of cans of good mace as another backup contingency, really can't expect more than four persons max. to deal with. If the door opens and we find bodies on the floor, we need to start the battery fan on high and get the elevator car ventilated before wiping it down.

The van will be relocated from the ramp entrance to the front of the elevator at 11:45 a.m. – Zach and I will get Victor, zip tie his hands and feet, and load him in the van after searching for his phone and any weapons. His phone will be placed in a secure lockbox, and the frequency jammer Q has provided will be activated to eliminate any tracking devices in or on Victor's phone or body. We'll place him on the foam rubber mat for his ride to the lake house. Zach will drive, and I will monitor Victor when he wakes up to inform him why he was kidnapped.

Stoney, Bones, and V have several alternatives: Hopefully, the car's driver, as a bodyguard for Victor, goes to lunch with the main party. If that is the case, you retrieve the car keys, drive the Mercedes down to the 3rd level, and load everyone comfortably into the car. We'll leave only the cones behind to block the 3rd level, allowing time for Sleeping Beauty to awaken. Given Victor's position, there is no way the police will be contacted by his security people when they awaken. I plan to use Victor's phone to contact one of his lieutenants once we're on the I-495 Beltway around DC. Leave a voice message and advise them that Victor's life depends solely on Peggy Turner being alive and well. Expecting his phone to be locked, we'll try his thumbprint to open the phone and search his contact list. As a backup, Susie, please let me know today if you can secure Elana's cell phone number.

Stoney, as soon as you feel the elevator has been ventilated, wipe it down and use the room spray to mask any odor. Be sure to remove Q's box and plug the vent hole. Double-check the area, and then the three of you take the SUV to head to the lake house. Let's leave the fake plates in place until both vehicles are at the lake house.

This part gets a little tricky. What if the driver stays in the car during lunch? We wind up with multiple bodies on the 3rd level, with nowhere to put them. We bought two tarps and could conceal the persons under the tarps in one corner of the garage. This presents a couple of options: 1) leave them there until they wake up, or the driver comes looking. A bystander may stumble upon them and call the police. We then spark an investigation we don't need or want. The last option is for us to approach the driver and tell him where he can find his drugged companions.

Stoney said the tarp poses too much risk to someone finding 2 or 3 bodies, not knowing if they are dead or alive. 911 calls would be made, and police would be there before anyone woke up. If the FBI got involved, it might be a long shot if they made a connection to Turner's kidnapping. Given the pictures of Victor's

Mercedes, it most likely has bulletproof windows. The 3 of us, Bones, V, and I, wearing the construction vest and hard hats, should not feel threatened by the driver at a distance. I will approach the car, indicating I need to speak with him. Bones and V will reposition to take covering angles if required. If he hasn't already started to lower the window, I'll knock on it and say I need to speak to him about moving his car. Once the window is down, I'll put my 9 mm to his head and explain briefly that his pals are alive and well by showing him my phone picture of the people on the 3rd level. Tell him to roll up his window and drive there to retrieve them. If he gets out of the car or rolls down his window again, my two fellow workers will shoot him dead where he sits. That should resolve our problem reasonably quickly!

Chapter 35

Cody said that with your guys' skill set, this should work with minimum risk and eliminate several potential problems.

There are several last contingencies I want to address:

1. Victor gets in the elevator with his wife, daughter, and probably one security person
2. Victor, his wife Elana, and one security person enter the elevator
3. Victor gets in with his people, but 1 or 2 citizens also enter the elevator

Situation One: In my opinion, we do not use the chemical on three people, two of whom are women. My reason is that with a woman present, it is more likely that firing weapons in a confined space will not be an option. In this scenario, we would avoid venting the gas from the elevator, making our timetable slightly quicker. Stoney and either Bones or V aim their weapons at them and immediately taser the security person and haul him out with zip ties on his feet and hands.

Situation Two: Similar to Situation One, this should present little to no potential for gunplay or injury. We show force with our weapons when the door opens. We load Victor in the van and take the women's phones to remove any chance of them taking photos or calling for backup. Zip-tie the guard for our security. Then we pull Elana aside and explain Victor is being held because his organization is holding a family member hostage, and a swap will be made.

Situation Three gets tricky: With bystanders at risk, we must gas the elevator car to put everyone out of commission. Cody addressed Stoney, V, and Bones, saying, "I hope your past training included stealing a vehicle." We borrow someone's car from level one, drive it to level three, and pick up the bystanders. By leaving the cones in place, with a recovery time of approximately one hour, we should be ok with them not being found. Police will be called, but no one will have pertinent information to provide to the authorities. As to Victor's security, we'll stick with using their car or tipping off the driver if he remains in his vehicle.

Zach and I leave as planned with Victor. In situations 1 & 2, we have live hostages. Bones and V watch them and apply zip ties where needed. Stoney retrieves the device box from the elevator ceiling. If the security

person for Victor is his car driver, and we zip-tie him,
then we need the car key fob and give it to Elana.

For any other combination of persons involved, we stick
with the basic plan and use the nerve gas to incapacitate
everyone in the elevator.

Questions or comments: No one spoke up, but everyone
nodded approval and understood their roles that had to be
executed on Wednesday. Cody lastly reminded everyone that
their entire plan was based on a teenager's post on her internet
page. If Victor does not show up for lunch, they would have to
find another weak link in his travel schedule or find out when he
plans to eat again at Bella Napoli.

Cody asked Stoney and Q to keep him updated on the
canister acquisition and the device's readiness for use tomorrow.
He asked Stoney to pass out the communication devices to
everyone so they could learn to operate them correctly. He
instructed Stoney to demonstrate to Zach and himself how to
arm and fire the tasers in case the gas device failed. Cody then
announced a quick get-together of the team, knowing from
Stoney if he had acquired the canister and gotten it to Q so that
the team could go over their plan one final time.

Early that afternoon, Stoney showed up with Bones and V
and a reasonably big smile across his face as they all walked into
Cody's office. Just came from the basement, and dropped off
one U.S. military-grade nerve agent canister to Q; this stuff can
immobilize anything that breathes it into their system. Cody
responded that if Victor didn't disappoint us, the last piece of the
puzzle would now be in place. Cody asks them to stick around

and let Q play with his prototype design, and then he'll round everyone up for a final update and briefing.

Q buzzed Cody and, like a proud parent, said he wanted to show off the final product. Cody walked through the building and said, "Conference room in 10 minutes." It's not surprising that Zach was hanging out in Susie's office.

With the team seated around the table, Q put a white plastic box in the center for everyone to view. The box was made of durable marine plastic and approximately 18 inches long by 12 inches high and 12 inches wide. At one end, a 3-foot black flexi hose extended. Q lifted the cover and showed off an olive green canister, looking like an oversized hand grenade, with the trigger ring connected to a steel rod and motor. The motor was connected to wires going to one of the burner cell phones Zach had picked up at Walmart.

Acting as the professor, Q explained that when the phone rang, its battery powered the electromagnetic motor pulling the steel rod affixed to the ring pin that triggers the gas release. He went on to say that since they had only one canister, he tested it with a live grenade and blew up half his shop in the basement. Cody was the only person who didn't think Q was a good comedian, playing for a laugh. Cody asked Q to meet with Zach and Stoney to demonstrate how to seal the box and power up the cell phone when it's in place.

Cody asked if the van had been loaded with everything they had purchased. Karen said the van, as requested, was now AA Maintenance Co., with a phone number advertised that would go directly to voicemail on one of the burner phones. The voicemail was recorded to say the mailbox was full; please call back later. The white signboard they purchased stated in red letters, "**CLOSED - Maintenance Repairs**". Cones and all the other miscellaneous items were readily available and stored in the van. Both the van and the SUV had new fake license plates that were attached with double-sided tape. A good tug would remove the counterfeit plates and expose the real ones assigned to the rental company. She added they would find box lunches and drinks for everyone before the fireworks started.

Cody went over the options of using gas or tasers, and everyone's responsibilities before, during, and after they kidnapped Victor. Cody's mind was trained to think of every advantage in any situation. He said to Karen, 'When you arrive a little early and have your places to sit and watch the traffic, please go into the restaurant and ask them what their dinner hours are for serving.' According to Zach, the maitre d" stand is directly in front of the private glass dining room. Please note if any tables have been set in the private room to accommodate someone for lunch. Specifically, count the place setting and advise us on what you saw. It might indicate if Victor will show up and how many may be in his party.

Cody's last request was for Karen and Susie to provide one unused credit card to Stoney and himself. Since the garage uses credit card payment only, each card would be used to get the van and SUV in and out of the facility. Once we leave the garage, please call your credit card companies to report that your cards were stolen that morning from Susie's vehicle. Cody added I don't see us triggering any police involvement, but if it happens, they would be checking all credit card transactions from Wednesday. Zach said Cody could try to cover all angles and would probably make an excellent criminal. One could sense the nervous energy as the meeting broke up, knowing a good night's sleep would be a little more difficult tonight.

Chapter 36

Cody and Zach were in the van, headed to Bethesda at 6:15 on Wednesday morning. Washington, DC, a white-collar city, was hitting peak rush hour for commuters between 7:15 and 9 a.m. The 45-minute drive time should put them there early enough to grab a coffee and be among the first to enter the parking garage. Entering right on time, Cody set up the cones and maintenance sign while Zach called Susie and asked her to send down the elevator and lock it off. When the door opened, Zach had the white box in hand with his portable drill, step stool, and 2-inch bit to cut the hole in the elevator ceiling panel. He knew time was limited, not to tie up the elevator as other people started entering and parking in the garage. Cody didn't time Zach but felt it took him less than 2–3 minutes to complete his task and had Susie release the elevator, locking out only the 3rd level from access. Zach commented to Cody that the black pipe and hole looked like a ventilation opening and would not cause anyone looking up any concern.

The first step of their journey had gone exceptionally well. Cody and Zach had time to kill, so they inventoried every item in the van and made sure it was readily available when needed. They took turns walking around with tape measures and clipboards, looking as busy as possible and keeping a watch for anyone approaching the third level.

Susie called around 9:30 a.m. and said Q and that she was in transit to Bethesda. They had located a combination coffee bar and bookstore several blocks from the parking garage. They planned to be in place by 11 a.m. This facility advertised excellent wi-fi service. Susie mentioned they would buy a few books, run up a nice tab, and have no issues being there for several hours. She also indicated they would run a communication check once they secured a table, but knew the distance was close enough not to be a problem.

Stoney, Bones, and V were the next to call. They said they picked up the white SUV and had everything they felt was needed to support the plan. Cody could only guess with their training and experience that every type of small arms weapon was probably stored in the back of the Hyundai. . . They told Cody they would drive straight to the parking garage and plan to park on the second level. Bones said he would be the recon for the 1st level when needed. He would choose a spot to observe the elevator traffic without being noticed by people driving in the garage.

Karen was the last to check in and said her Uber driver should drop her off just after 11 a.m. This would give her time to find two locations to sit and watch the traffic. A slight change of plan was made, advising Karen to link up with Susie and Q to ride back to the office. Since no one knew when they would be done and leaving Bethesda, there was no reason for her to sit and wait for an Uber ride back.

Stoney, Bones, and V parked in a far corner of the 2nd level, which provided them with a good line of sight to the elevator and quick access to the ramp leading to the 3rd level. They put their communication gear under their clothing, and Stoney hailed Zach and Cody. The reply was loud and clear– Stoney and V walked down the ramp and put on construction vests and hard hats, which matched well with their old jeans, work boots, and denim shirts. Zach walked up the ramp to the second level and their SUV, and position himself to cover the elevator. Cody advised them that the canister box was armed and in place. Tasers were on everyone's belt under their vest and ready to go if needed. The taser's range was 20 feet, shooting its two-needle prongs into someone, then dispensing 50,000 volts, which would stun any human being. Bones walked down to join them and said he had the perfect spot in one corner of the 1st level, where cars couldn't park due to the building's sprinkler pipes and pump being located there.

Susie and Q came over the earbuds, checked the communication gear, and indicated they were in place for the duration. Susie told Cody the Wi-Fi was off the charts and that her laptop was linked to the building's operations system. Q said he was not used to secure communication equipment, but heard everyone's conversation and was ready when the canister was needed. Cody replied to Q that Bones or Zach would be the ones to confirm Victor's arrival and should be able to identify the number and makeup of the party walking to the elevator. He also reminded everyone of the deviation from their plan, specifically not to use the gas if Victor, accompanied by one security person and one or two females, entered the elevator. As an alternative to the nerve agent, they would taser the security person and hold Victor and the women at gunpoint.

Cody restated to Q, "If you disperse the gas, advise us and run the one-minute and fifteen-second clock so we know when the elevator door will be open." Everyone on the communication equipment acknowledged they understood.

Karen was the last to announce her arrival, and everyone was happy to hear she was coming, clearly over the communications device. She began her walk around and planned to report back around 11:30 a.m. after attempting to enter the restaurant with fake questions about the dinner hour. She said the main street runs east-west, and she has two excellent spots across the street from each other to view all the traffic flow.

Cody said to Stoney You have run more operations than I can count. Are we missing anything, or do we need to make one final adjustment to ensure this goes smoothly? Stoney commended Cody as the team leader and said that, given the compressed time frame, we are in good shape with what you put together. He went on to say, No matter how good you are, shit still happens sometimes, and everyone needs to react and respond quickly if it does. They all triple-checked everything from zip ties to tasers, to small caliber weapons, to mace, to respirators, to safety goggles, to latex gloves. Then Stoney announced we were ready to rock & roll and hoped like hell Victor was having Italian food for lunch.

Karen was the first to come back on through the earbuds, saying she had spoken with the maître d' and that he seemed to appreciate her having her blouse unbuttoned about halfway down. The way men stare at cleavage is impressive, and it did buy me a few more minutes of conversation. I hate to report that the restaurant was chaotic, with waiters and busboys running everywhere, trying to prepare for the lunch crowd. The glass dining room had not been set up for any party. She wanted to end on a positive note, mentioning that it probably only takes a few minutes of lead time to put everything in place if Victor is coming for lunch. I am heading to my first bench with a laptop and lunch. Soney replied to Karen, Thanks for the effort, and remember to button up!

Bones was next with an update, saying about 75% of the first level was filled with cars. When someone shows up, another person in their vehicle is on the way out. Zach chimed in, saying the second level was pretty wide open and less than 25% full. He said that the cones are apparent enough, and no one should approach the third level, given the number of open parking spaces.

Cody had moved their van near the aisle in front of the elevator with the side cargo door open. Respirators were lined up with safety goggles, a portable fan, and cleaning supplies. Cody ensured that everyone had gloves on once they arrived to eliminate any fingerprints left behind. The clock seemed to be ticking slowly, and Cody knew everyone was anxious for something to happen. He considered risking Karen's visit to the restaurant again, but she might miss seeing Victor's car, so he decided against asking her.

At 12:30 p.m., Karen said her 45 minutes had passed, and she was crossing the street to another bench about a half block from the restaurant. She added that her new line of sight on traffic traveling in either direction was still excellent. Susie said she and Q were doing fine and saw no issues staying in the coffee shop/bookstore for as long as needed. Zach, to break some tension, came on saying he had never been a father, but this apprehension of whether Victor is going to show or not has to be worse than waiting for the baby to pop out. Karen replied to Zach's comment, "Men will never truly know that feeling".

Chapter 37

With the clock approaching 1 p.m., Karen cupped her hand over the mic piece and announced, I see a black Mercedes, two cars back, waiting for the light to turn green with their right blinker on. There is no place to turn right after the light except for the parking garage entrance. She added that she could not determine how many people were in the car due to the distance and tint of the windows. With excitement in her voice, Karen said the car had made the turn into the garage and had stopped for the parking ticket.

Bones chimed in, saying he had the Mercedes in sight and could confirm two people up front, but couldn't determine if anyone was in the backseat. The Mercedes smoothly made the turn for the 2nd level of the garage. Bones told Zach Coming your way - can't wait to see who exits the car.

Zach announced they are parking near the end row, away from most other vehicles on this level. When they exit the car, it will be about a 100+ foot walk to the elevator, giving me a solid view of them. Zach's following comment to everyone was "Holy Shit!"- positive ID on Victor Zanoska and Ivan Petrov exiting from the Mercedes back seat. The two up front have to be the bodyguards, both wearing light sports coats covering guns being carried in hip holsters. I confirm only four occupants; no one is left in the vehicle. Cody cut in and asked Zach to ID the driver; he wanted to know who was holding the Mercedes key fob. Zach replied that the bodyguard wearing the light tan sports coat was driving.

Zach gave Susie and Q a countdown in time as the foursome approached the elevator. Susie said she has operational control of the elevator, and Q added the canister's phone number was loaded on speed dial. As soon as the door closes, it will be activated. Zach jumped in, saying the door was opening, no one was exiting the elevator, it was empty, and then said they were inside with the door closing. Susie told Q, sitting beside her, to make the call and trigger the device. Susie held the elevator briefly before sending it down to the 3rd level.

Bones announced that the Out of Order/Use Stairway sign was posted on the exterior of the 1st-level elevator door. Zach said, "Ditto; the same sign is also attached to the 2nd-level elevator door." Both men stated they'd be down to the 3rd level and in position before Susie popped the door open.

Susie counted down every 10 seconds to the 75 seconds the doors would remain closed, allowing the nerve agent to incapacitate the four men inside. Stoney had the left side, and V had the right side, with Cody providing backup. Everyone had their respirators, latex gloves, and goggles in place. Bones was near the ramp entrance to be sure no one could interrupt them when the elevator door opened. Their van was parked in the aisle, blocking anyone from seeing the elevator opening.

Stoney and V, in one hand, each held a 9mm Glock pistol with a suppressor; their other hand had a military-grade taser, armed and ready to be fired. Cody and Zach knew that with

Stoney and V training, they would take the lead on what to do when the door opened. He had their two tasers ready, knowing the four inside the elevator had to be subdued instantly if the gas agent was not 100% effective.

Susie's countdown was **10-9-8-7-6-5-4-3-2-1** door opening. Stoney was the first to shout, confirming that all four were down and out. As Susie locked the door in the open position, Cody could see that the two bodyguards knew something was happening; they were in the center of the elevator car with their pistols drawn. Stoney went in first, removing the two weapons from the drugged bodyguards. He commented to Cody and Zach that the two handguns were U.S. military-issued based on the metal colorization and type of aiming sites. He went on to comment that both weapons appeared to be brand new. Stoney said to Cody, he wondered what military base had been targeted by the mafia to get their hands on these quality handguns.

Victor was slumped in the right corner of the elevator where the button panel was located. V indicated the bodyguard probably shoved him aside to avoid exposing him when the door opened. Ivan Petrov was on the opposite side of the elevator car, crumpled up in the corner, so he would also not be in the line of fire.

Zach had the battery fan ready and operating before anyone was removed. Cody and Zach, as planned, carried Victor to the van. His hands and feet were zip-tied. Zach searched Victor and emptied his pockets, placing his cell phone in a special lead-lined box made by Q. This would ensure no tracking signal could identify the phone's location. Zach also turned on Q's box, blocking any transmitter possibly embedded under Victor's skin.

Victor was then loaded into the van onto the rubber camping mat for his journey to the lake house.

Stoney and V had removed the other three, and they were positioned leaning against the wall out of sight for the time being.

Susie was running the clock and announced that 3 minutes had passed since they entered the elevator. Awaiting confirmation to reinstate it for the 1st and 2nd levels.

Cody said into his mic for Bones to get the Mercedes key fob from the guy wearing the tan sport coat and bring the car down to the 3rd level. Then V can help you load all three into the Mercedes rear seat. Zip-tie their hands, limiting their mobility until they find a way to cut the plastic ties. Leave the front windows halfway down and park the car in the far corner of the 3rd level. With the blackened back windows, no one should be able to see them inside the vehicle and raise any questions. When the sleeping beauties awaken, they won't call the police for help.

Zach had used the step stool to remove the device from the elevator's ceiling and pushed in the 2-inch rubber plug to cover the hole they drilled. Cody and Zach began by wiping down the elevator's surfaces, removing any traces of the chemicals used, and then sprayed the deodorizer to mask the smell. Once the three mafia men were tucked away in the back seat of their vehicle, Bones went back on watch duty while the other four finished up the cleansing work.

Susie announced that 7 minutes had elapsed since they took control of the elevator. Cody told her to wait one more minute and then return it to service. He also instructed Bones to head up the ramp and remove the Out-of-Order signs from the 2nd and 1st-level exterior elevator doors.

Cody told Zach it was time to leave with Victor and asked Zach to drive and program his phone for driving directions to the family's lake house. Cody estimated the driving time to be about 2 hours, as they should avoid rush hour traffic. He told Zach he had to get off an email to Q for a task he wanted V to do tonight. Cody indicated he would be happy to drive the 2nd hour because he was familiar with the way there.

Bones moved the cones as the van headed for the garage exit. Cody spoke into his mic and asked V to meet them at the coffee shop, then ride back with Susie, Karen, and Q to the office. Bones and Stoney will take their rented SUV and head directly to the lake house to provide additional security. Cody said he would send Q an encrypted email with instructions on a task he wanted to be done tonight by both Q and V – they both heard the request and acknowledged back to Cody that they'd look for his instructions.

Stoney told Bones to get their SUV off the 2nd level and bring it down to the 3rd level to load up the remaining items, like the portable fan and some cleaning materials. He told Susie they were leaving in 30 seconds, and the spray disinfectant that was used left the elevators with a very pleasing scent. Susie chimed in, stating the mission was completed in under nine minutes. She added that the elevator was being returned to regular operation and was accessible to all floors. Since no other vehicles but the Mercedes were on level 3, they felt the chance of anyone exiting the elevator was minimal.

Stoney left the cones in place to deter traffic from parking on the 3rd level. The cones had no markings, were purchased at Home Depot, and couldn't be traced back to them. Leaving them allowed a safety margin for the mafia men to awaken and leave the garage without knowing precisely what had happened. Once the Mercedes left the garage, the only item the team left behind besides the orange cones was the rubber plug in the elevator's ceiling. Stoney's last thought, driving their white SUV through the exit gate at the garage, was that Victor did not get to enjoy whatever was on the menu today!

Chapter 38

Zach was focused on driving within the speed limit and avoiding any circumstances that could lead to an accident. Given the cargo tied up in the back of the van, it would be challenging to explain the situation to any policemen who stopped them for a traffic incident.

Cody took Victor's phone out of the secure box and told Zach, "I hope it's an encrypted iPhone that can be opened using a thumbprint." He announced it looked like the latest model iPhone and rolled Victor, who was still out from the nerve gas, onto his stomach because his hands were zip-tied behind his back. He pressed the phone screen onto Victor's right thumbprint and told Zach he had opened the phone. Cody then searched his recent call menu and found his wife's, Elana's, cell number and Ivan Petrov's phone number. Cody didn't care what other secrets the phone might hold, but those two numbers were the means they would use to communicate their demands.

Cody told Zach he was sending a text message to Ivan, knowing it wouldn't be read for another hour or so, until they all woke up and could drive out of the garage. Cody read his message out loud to Zach, asking if he needed to say anything else:

Victor is safe and sound, and his continued well-being will depend on Peggy Turner being alive and well. Our instructions will be sent to your phone and must be followed precisely. There will be NO negotiations. Do not reply to Victor's phone; it will be offline. Peggy Turner must be advised today that she will be released within the next several days and made ready for exchange.

Zach told Cody he was on board with the wording and liked the demand to advise his mother of her pending release. Cody hit send, powered down the phone, and placed it back in the secure box Q had built. Cody told Zach that he had been formulating a plan to handle Victor playing a little mental game with him the next day. I advised him of what would happen to him when he was released. Cody's goal was to ensure the team's safety after the exchange with Victor, seeking any retribution or harm against the team.. Zach replied he couldn't wait to see what tricks Cody had up his sleeve to accomplish that.

Cody spent the next 15 minutes composing a secure email to Q with instructions for him and V to follow on a job he wanted to be done that night. Another email was sent to Susie, requesting that she send the best quality pictures of the facial shots of Victor's wife and daughter. Use Photoshop to make the image look like it was taken from several feet away. Then he asked Susie to add a tiny, red dot to each photo, making it subtle yet visible. Cody asked Susie to attach them as a PDF to his email address.

A quick text message also went to Stoney's phone, asking him to stop on the way down for some basic provisions for the five of them. He also requested Stoney's approximate ETA at the lake house so they could know when their vehicle should be approaching the property.

Susie drove Karen, Q, and V back to their office in Alexandria. Everyone was euphoric after knowing their plan was executed flawlessly with Victor in their possession. No one needed to say that the odds of getting Peggy Turner back were now very much in their favor. Susie stated that Cody had not expressed the exact next steps to be taken, but felt, knowing him, that he had a plan ready to execute. She instructed everyone in the car to be prepared to respond and assist in any way possible over the next few days until Peggy was safely back with them.

Q mentioned he and V were expecting an email upon their return with some instructions from Cody on a task that needed to be done this evening. He added it felt great to be proactive rather than wait for the criminals' messages to pop up, making more demands.

Karen's only concern was that when Victor awoke, he would probably not be pleasant and would make all kinds of demands for his release. V indicated that with Stoney and Bones babysitting Victor, he would not cause any trouble to the team.

After getting a quick bite to eat, Q took V to his basement facility and fired up his computer. He pulled up Cody's email, and he and V read it together.

We have sent Ivan a text stating that Victor will be held by us until an exchange for Peggy Turner is arranged. Not 100% sure yet of the best way to handle the exchange, but have some ideas to pursue and iron out –

Cody then wrote: I want to send a message to Victor and his organization tonight with both your help. Q, please pull the daytime and evening video of Victor's mansion and let V watch it to become familiar with the property's layout. Explain to V the design of the park and wooded area that backs up to Victor's property, where you were located when flying our drones.

I'd like you to drop V off at the park after dark. I am sure you can't leave or park a vehicle after sunset at the park. Please use the communication gear from today to stay within range of each other. If you can obtain a sniper rifle (believe you may have several weapons at your disposal), work your way to the tree line behind Victor's house. You'll need to climb a tree to take a shot over the perimeter wall, which appears to be about 8-9 feet high.

The video shows that the master bedroom occupies a good portion of the second floor at the rear of the house. If you can confirm this, I would like you to wait until Elana, Victor's wife, is in that bedroom. Select a target to shoot that will explode upon impact by one shot – for example, a lamp, mirror, or glass item. Etc. After taking the shot, immediately work out of the woods, have Q pick you up, and head home. Text me ASAP the word **"done"** when you take the shot, and Elana was present in the room, or text **"done/done"** if she was a no-show in the bedroom and took the shot without her presence. My preference would be to have her witness the event..."*Be careful; we've come too far to make mistakes and expose ourselves.*" — Cody

V looked at Q and said he needed to run home and gear up for tonight, and would meet him back at the office in an hour or so. Q's only thought: What was Cody's endgame on putting one rifle slug into Victor's home?

After completing a couple of tasks, Cody offered to drive the rest of the way, saying he would be more than willing. Zach replied that Victor should be coming around in about half an hour, and he would rather Cody deal with him when he awoke.

Zach added that, given what his organization did in taking Carly and Peggy and coming after him, when Victor woke up, he would like to put his hands around his neck and squeeze hard.

Chapter 39

Cody understood where his friend was coming from and jumped into the van's passenger seat. To lighten the mood, Cody told Zach he would share his fondest memory of the family's lake house, which involved the initials T.S. Zach said he was always up for hearing a good story about Cody's past.

Cody started by saying his dad bought the lake house property for a family summer getaway when the University of Virginia was out of session and he wasn't teaching. The drive to Lake Anna was just about one hour from Charlottesville, which made it an easy commute. My dad, Ben, was getting a flat tire repaired at a time back then, almost all car tires had tubes in them. At the repair shop, there was a stack of tubes in the corner, and my dad inquired if they were any good. He was told the repair shop patched tire tubes with holes made by nails, but any with a slight tear in the tube couldn't be used on a car again. Dad saw a deal and asked if they could be patched just to use as a float in a river or lake. The shop person said they could and asked Dad if he wanted larger truck tubes or car size. Since the price was right, Ben took four larger truck tubes for the lake house and four-car tubes to float down the Rivanna River that runs through Charlottesville.

Cody continued the story by saying that when he needed to select a college, he had no interest in the University of Virginia, where his dad was a professor. He wanted to get out on his own, so he chose Virginia Tech, located in Blacksburg, VA. VA Tech is Virginia's other premier state university and was an arch-rival to UVA. Didn't make old Ben happy to possibly have a "Hokie" graduate from VA Tech in the family. Tech offers an excellent ROTC plan, allowing him to become an officer in the military after graduation.

He then explained to Zach that the summer after his sophomore year, he was back home in Charlottesville and met Sharon, a UVA student needing additional summer credits to graduate the following year. After several dates, Sharon was very excited when Cody mentioned the family's lake house as a possible weekend getaway. Picking a weekend when Ben and the rest of his family had commitments was the perfect time to get away for a couple of days, knowing Sharon and he would have the place to themselves.

One Saturday morning on a beautiful summer day, the forecast was sunny, in the low 80s with a westerly breeze. After they arrived at the lake house and had unpacked, Cody said Let's hit the lake. The water temperature this time of year should be bathtub-like. Sharon changed into a day-glow green bikini, which didn't cover much. Cody headed to the shed and found one of the truck tubes fully inflated. Launching off the dock, sitting on opposite sides of the tube, and using their hands, they paddled out into the lake. After swimming and trying to dive off the large truck tube, they took a break to enjoy the sun. Cody felt something on his leg, thinking fish were nibbling, and found Sharon's foot wandering up his leg, working her toes under his swimsuit. His reaction was like lighting a fuse on a stick of dynamite. Cody pulled Sharon off the tube so they were both in the water, facing each other inside the tube's inner circle. He said it only took a few seconds to remove both their bathing suits. Truck tubes have a valve stem to fill them with air on the inside, which is about 4 inches long—turned out to be the perfect place to hang both their bathing suits. Given the height of the tube around them, they were hidden from view, in the middle of a lake under a sunny sky, very naked. After getting very frisky, they kind of figured out the best way to hold onto the inside of the tube, keep their head above water, and have sex.

After drifting for a while, Cody noticed a small powerboat heading their way and thought we might have company, so he suggested we slip our suits back on. Several minutes later, an older white-haired man with a couple of fishing poles pulled up to them in a small skiff-type boat. He said he was done fishing for the day and saw the tube floating in the lake. Do you know how far out in the lake you've been pushed by the breeze? Cody then realized the lake house was just a speck in the distance. The fisherman threw them a line, hitch it to your tube, I'll tow you in. Just need you to point me in the right direction. With big smiles, Sharon and Cody happily accepted the offer to get towed back to Cody's family's house.

Upon reaching their dock, Cody untied the tube and introduced themselves, saying This is Sharon, and I am Cody and thanked him for rescuing them and towing them home.

Cody offered to run to the house and get the fisherman a few beers for his return boat ride home. The old guy said his name was Clive, and he had a cooler full of beer and two keeper fish he planned to grill for dinner. As he cast off from their dock, his parting comment was, "It seems you two young ones enjoyed the water today." Sharon and Cody both blushed, thinking, How did he know?

Cody finished the story by saying he dated Sharon all summer until college started in September. Whenever they wanted to return to the lake house, one person just had to tell the other, "It's time for some T.S... T.S. stands for Tube Sex.

Cody said the lake house would take on another memory if we successfully swap Victor for Peggy. Zach was more infatuated with underwater sex and asked Cody, once the ordeal was over, how about doing a double date at the lake house? Cody replied that T.S. is only for the younger generation, and he'll take a pillow-top mattress in a comfy bed over a truck tube floating in the water any day.

Chapter 40

Cody could see Victor stirring in the back of the van. He unbuckled, went back in the van, and kneeled beside him; with his hands bound behind his back and his ankles secured, he posed no threat to Zach or himself. Within the next couple of minutes, Victor's eyes fluttered open and started to come into focus. Seeing an unfamiliar face, Victor reacted by asking, "Where am I and why can't I move my arms and legs?" Cody did not immediately reply, seeing as Victor might have recalled what had happened in the garage elevator. Victor, trying to move his arms and legs, realized he was bound and being transported in a van. His mind seemed to be putting the puzzle together, realizing the elevator had somehow been a trap.

Victor immediately went into a rant, shouting Do you know who I am and what I can do to you? At this point, Cody leaned close to Victor's ear and said, We know exactly who you are; you are bound up and receiving the same treatment as Peggy and Carly Turner. If you say another word unless I ask you a direct question, Cody unclipped the taser from his belt and showed it to Victor, I will hit you with 50,000 volts of electricity, which I expect you'll find very unpleasant. Victor closed his eyes and digested the information, knowing he was being held hostage.

Cody returned to the passenger seat and advised Zach that they would not hear from their cargo until they unloaded him at the lake house. Cody glanced at the mapping program, giving them driving directions, and saw they had approximately 45 minutes until their arrival. Zach saw Cody holding up his taser in his rearview mirror and knew Victor didn't want any part of being zapped.

At the same time Victor was coming around, Ivan and one bodyguard woke up in the back seat of the black Mercedes. The other bodyguard must have inhaled more of the nerve gas agent and was still out cold and not moving. Their hands bound in front of them with several zip ties, they started looking for something sharp in the vehicle to cut the plastic ties. After looking through the glove box and center console, they couldn't locate anything sharp enough to cut off the ties. The one awake bodyguard saw the key fob in the cup holder and told Ivan he could drive the car with his hands bound together. He added they should get out of the garage, not knowing if any police would respond to what happened in the elevator.

Ivan agreed, found his phone still in his pants pocket, and climbed into the passenger seat. Opening his phone to call Victor, he saw Cody's text message sent from Victor's phone and understood precisely what had happened and why. Ivan told the driver to go straight to Victor's house; he needed to speak with Elana. The next hurdle the driver faced was that, with his hands bound together, he couldn't retrieve his wallet from his back pocket to get a credit card to pay for the garage. Ivan had to get out the driver's wallet and card from the passenger seat, but the driver couldn't reach the credit card slot to insert the card. With bound hands, Ivan had to climb out from the passenger side of the car, grab the card, and make the payment while keeping his hands under his sports coat. So, someone passing by wouldn't find it odd that someone had their hands tied together in a public parking garage.

On the short drive to Victor's house, Ivan had no idea how much of the business side of their criminal operations Victor conveyed to his wife. He decided not to show Elana the text message sent from Victor's phone. He would tell her Victor had been abducted, provide brief details about the elevator, and that he received a text message from Victor's phone saying he was safe and would be returning home in a couple of days, and not to worry.

Ivan called the security detail at Victor's house and instructed them to provide a knife or scissors as soon as they drove through the gate. The second bodyguard had just woken up in the back seat and was firing off a dozen questions about what was happening in Russian. He asked Ivan to cut the ties holding his hands. Ivan held up his hands, showing the back-seat bodyguard he was in the same position, and then told him in Russian not to say another word.

Cody told Zach that Stoney and Bones would arrive at the lake house about 45 minutes to an hour behind them. He leaned over and spoke to Zach quietly, saying they should leave Victor bound up with only two of them, and Zach was watching over him. Cody indicated he would go into the house, decide which bedroom to hold Victor in, and remove any items that could be used as weapons against them. Cody added the chains and locks in the back of the van to secure Victor to some permanent or heavy items in the house that can't be easily moved. We'll need to set up a watch schedule so one of the four of us has him in sight 24/7 until this ends.

Half an hour later, they pulled into the driveway and parked next to the lake house. Cody jumped out of the van, found the spare house key under the front steps, and surveyed the best room to hold Victor. The lake house was a rambler style, one level with four bedrooms and three bathrooms. The house was close to 35 years old but had been renovated some 8-9 years ago by his dad into an open great room, custom kitchen with a huge center island, hardwood floors throughout, and a beautiful deck and screen porch facing the lake.

Cody focused immediately on the 3rd bedroom, which shared a Jack & Jill bathroom with the 2nd bedroom. The standout feature was an antique wrought iron bed frame, likely weighing around 400 pounds. It was bolted with fasteners that could not be removed without a unique tool. It is the perfect item to chain Victor to, allowing him bathroom access, and to keep him chained to the bed frame. Knowing the longest chain they purchased was 20 feet long, Cody got a tape measure from the kitchen and figured out where Victor would reach if he were attached to the iron bed frame. He removed all items within reach and felt their four bodyguards would be OK for a few days. His last thought was to avoid a confrontation inside the house that might damage some of the beautiful renovations his mom and dad had done. He didn't want to explain what caused the damage or get his checkbook out to restore anything that had just been damaged.

Cody went out to the van, opened the side door, and checked Victor's ties binding his feet and hands. He then told Zach everything seemed secure, but he still wanted to take no chances. He pulled Zach aside to show him where he planned to keep Victor and to get his opinion on the room, in case he had missed anything. Taking zero risk, Cody put the 20-foot chain tightly around Victor's waist, attached it with a padlock, and then locked the other end of the chain to the van's back door. If Victor somehow figured out how to break the plastic ties, he wasn't breaking the chain or padlock.

Zach came into the house and looked at it from a prison viewpoint, and how anyone would try to escape. They discussed several scenarios, but always came back to the fact that one of the four of them had to be watching Victor 24/7, with a taser ready to fire. The house had too many windows and doors for someone to use as exits, and it was impossible to secure all of them. Victor was their sole means of getting Peggy released.

Cody and Zach returned to the van to help Victor get into a sitting position and cut the ties binding his feet. Cody told Victor he would be taken inside and chained to an iron bed frame. His hands would be untied, and he would have access to a bathroom, chair, and bed. Several other security people would be arriving very shortly with food and water. He stated that if he caused any trouble, they would all be armed with tasers and use them without hesitation. He said to Victor that if a taser had to be used, then the remainder of his captivity would be spent on the bed with his hands and feet bound with chains and locks. Hopefully, he added that this could be over in several days. He told Victor they would be calling Elana that night using a burner phone on speaker mode, and his conversation would be scripted in advance so that no coded words or secret messages could be relayed.

Lastly, he mentioned that they would meet tomorrow morning to discuss the necessary steps for his release. Cody looked directly into Victor's eyes with a menacing stare and asked if he understood the situation. Victor did not answer except to nod his head yes. They escorted Victor inside the house, Cody taking his arm, and Zach followed about 10 feet behind with a taser in hand. Victor was led into the 3rd bedroom, and Cody double-checked that the chain around his waist was still snug and secure. He then wrapped the chain around the 3-inch iron bedpost at the foot of the bed and attached a sturdy-looking padlock. He said the chain would allow him to use the bathroom, and the bedroom door would remain propped open day and night.

With Cody standing at the doorway, Victor lay in bed, staring up at the ceiling. Zach had entered the kitchen, gotten a glass of water, and found a box of crackers in the pantry. He brought the items in and set them on the small table next to the chair in the bedroom. Zach advised Victor that dinner would be made when the additional security people arrived with some food. He added that dinner would not rate a Michelin star.

Cody didn't trust Victor for one second based on his history and his organization's reputation. However, Cody knew that in his dealings with Victor, he needed to lay a framework that convinced him he was dealing with someone not to be taken lightly or double-crossed. Cody did not want to get Peggy back and have his team or him look over their shoulders for years to see if Victor had dispatched one of his men to cause them harm.

Chapter 41

Stoney and Bones pulled in with the rented white SUV an hour later. With Zach playing watchdog over Victor, Cody went outside and briefed them on the ride down, which was uneventful, and how they had Victor secured inside. He ran by Stoney and Bones a shift schedule starting at 9 p.m., based on two hours on, 6 hours off until 9 a.m. the following day. Stoney and Bones offered to cover the 12 hours between themselves. Still, Cody said he wanted everyone rested and fresh and thanked them for the offer.

The food provisions bought were basic meals that were easy to make and clean up. After everything was unpacked, beds were assigned: Zach took the master bedroom, Bones took the fourth bedroom, Stoney took the second bedroom connected to Victor's bedroom, and Cody crashed on the sofa pull-out in the TV room.

Stoney told Cody that when he picked up the canister, he had told his counterparts still on active duty that he might be babysitting a safe house. Out of the back of the SUV, he pulled four infrared red, battery-operated lasers and reflectors. That, once activated, would provide a perimeter around the house if anyone approached. He planned to set them up about 50 to 75 yards away from the dwelling, giving them about 30 seconds' warning of anyone who may have tripped the beam. He told Cody he was hoping the area didn't have a huge deer population, causing a lot of false alarms.

Stoney expected that anyone approaching who would be a threat would lean toward between 3 and 4 a.m. Most animals were not up and about in these hours. He instructed Cody to inform Zach that if the alarm were triggered, Bones and he would exit the house to deal with the threat outside. You and Zach must remain inside to guard Victor and not become targets by leaving the house. Be mindful if you're walking around outside; don't venture more than 50 yards or half a football field to avoid breaking the beams. He recommended leaving the system alarmed day and night unless it became a problem with false alarms during the day.

Cody then asked Stoney and Bones if they could take Victor for walks around the house several times a day to get him some exercise. He indicated that both of you are better trained than Zach or me if Victor were to act up in any way.

Cody said to everyone that keeping their weapons readily available would be prudent, but not inside the house. Victor's only means to deal with the four of us would be to get his hands on a loaded firearm. Cody mentioned that a storage box adjacent to the back door, which held firewood, could be empty. He added that a large flower planter box was unused on the front porch. Stoney said, Bones, and he would check both locations and walk the house's perimeter to see if anything else was helpful. He agreed with Cody that weapons inside the house could be a problem they didn't want to deal with.

Cody shared the email sent to Q and V about their little mission tonight to Victor's house. He told everyone that his goal for the next 12 hours was to convince Victor that there would be no ill will between them once the swap was done. Stoney said if your plan is not 100% successful, I have a sniper rifle that is close to 100% accurate at 1000 yards. Cody said I'll keep that in mind if option one doesn't work.

Why don't I introduce you to Victor? We'll take the chain off, and you two can walk him around the house several times. I need to email Susie and Q about several other matters I need to attend to.

Victor was still on the bed and awake when Cody, Stoney, and Bones walked into the bedroom. Cody said these two gentlemen would be the ones to mind you when we remove the chain to allow you some exercise. We need you alive, but if you consider taking on these two guys, you will become damaged goods. Cody unlocked Victor from the chain and gave the key to Stoney. His last comment to Victor was, Enjoy the fresh air, and don't consider bribing these gentlemen to join your organization; it might cost you several front teeth and a lot of discomfort.

Cody asked Zach to plan a menu for dinner and breakfast tomorrow morning. He grabbed his phone and started typing encrypted emails to Susie and Q.

His encrypted message to Susie read:

Susie: I need you ASAP to obtain a conference call phone number and password to join tonight's session. I plan to provide Elana with the time and numbers to call in to join the conference call via text message. Will use a burner phone from here, allowing a scripted dialog between Victor and his wife. Need confirmation that the chat room call numbers can't be traced back to us and that the burner phone will be destroyed after the call. My other need is to visit a Walmart and purchase three black hoodie sweatshirts in XXL size, which I'll then give to Q to send down with the device he's building for us. Thanks—C

Cody's encrypted message to Q read:

Q: Tomorrow morning, the first thing, please go to a hobby or craft store and buy several pounds of molding clay in a light gray color. Make or get your hands on an object that appears to be a detonation cap that has wires running out of each side. Shape the clay into a block about the size of a large bar of soap, insert the cap, and run wires inside the phone. The finished product has to look like C-4 explosives rigged to a cell phone detonator. Keep the box holding the device relatively small, but ensure it resembles a real-looking bomb. Have V drive it down here tomorrow; you may want to ask his opinion on the looks of the final product. - Tell V not to leave it on the front seat; some trucker driving by may look down and freak out!!! Thanks –C

After walking Victor around for 20 minutes, Victor was chained back in the bedroom, with Cody watching over him. Zach was prepping food for dinner and announced to everyone that it wouldn't be five stars. Bones and Stoney went back outside to set up the four perimeter security laser devices and check that each one was functioning. When they were done, Stoney showed Cody the hand-held monitoring screen that indicated all four active devices were armed and working. He explained that the units were numbered 1 through 4 and would provide a direction from the house if tripped, either North / South / East / West. Next, they emptied the wood storage box in the back of the house and found a tarp that fit nicely over the empty planter on the front porch. They stocked both locations with assorted firearms that could be useful, including several sets of night vision goggles.

Chapter 42

Susie had texted Cody the 800 number for the conference call meeting room with the access code. She confirmed that no one calling in could be traced, and when she acquired the room, it also left no trail.

Q acknowledged Cody's email request for the fake bomb device and said he would send a PDF picture of it to an encrypted email when it's done. If you find it acceptable, he will give it to V to transport to the lake house.

At sunset, Zach had dinner ready and served Victor in the bedroom on the small table beside the chair. Cody indicated he would stand, watch, and get his dinner after the three of you have finished. Victor had taken Cody's instructions not to speak unless addressed and had not uttered one word since being removed from the van.

Q arrived with V at the park located behind Victor's property. It was slightly after sunset, and V was decked out in black camo gear and carrying a rectangular black vinyl case. He also had some paracord that may be useful if he needed to climb a tree. No other vehicles were in the parking lot, making it easier for Q to pull up close to the tree line to drop V off. As Q was turning to leave, V entered the woods and, like magic, disappeared from view. V turned on his communication gear and asked Q if he had heard him. Q said loudly and clearly, advising V that he would cruise around the area to find a place to park and wait. Once there, Q told V he would use the beep function to be sure they were still both in range.

Since it was close to total darkness, V had no problem locating Victor's mansion, given its size and the number of lights illuminating the inside. He found a tree that elevated him higher than the security wall and had sturdy branches to support his weight for as long as he needed this perch. He opened the vinyl case, assembled the sniper rifle and scope, slung it across his back, and shimmed up the tree. Once he located an excellent resting branch that afforded him some back support, he chose another branch to rest his rifle on. The following item to resolve was the distance to the house; using a rangefinder, the display showed he would be dealing with 635 yards. In his favor, the wind was negligible; it would not alter the bullet's trajectory at this distance. The lights in the master bedroom had not yet been turned on, so he couldn't identify a specific target to shatter. He got as comfortable as possible, knowing the waiting might take a while. V told Q that he was in position and to be ready to pick him up. Q acknowledged with an OK, a beep to indicate he was parked and still in communication range.

Just over an hour and a half later, the bedroom lights came on, and Elana opened the double French doors on the bedroom's balcony and slid the screens across to let the night air in but keep the bugs out. V, sighting through the rifle scope, began to survey the room for a suitable target. Given the position of the king-size bed, adjacent to it was a low bureau with a large vase and a beautiful flower arrangement. What made it even better was that the bullet's trajectory would be through the screen door and would not be deflected by the window glass. V notified Q that he'd identified the target, the wife in the room; if nothing changes, he will take a shot in the next couple of minutes. Following message: V spoke to Q, pick him up in 10 minutes, then texted Cody the work was **"done"** and added to the text message that it made a huge impression.

Cody received the text and was very pleased with the results. He waited 15 minutes for Q to get V and vacate the area. Before sending the chat room numbers for their call to Elana, he went in to see Victor, who was reading a book someone had left at the lake house. Cody asked Victor if he would like to speak to his wife and tell her he was OK. He stated their phone would be on speaker, and he could only say what was written down.

The script Cody had written up that he showed to Victor said:

> Hello Elana, this is Victor. I am well and hoping to be home in a couple of days. You are on a speaker phone with others listening
>
> **DO NOT reply to any questions if she asks...**
>
> Please tell me what happened tonight at the house.
>
> **LET her reply and then say:**
>
> I must go now; please do not worry. You are in no danger.

Victor spoke for the first time, saying he would like to reach his wife and follow the script as written. Cody said he would return in 10 minutes to make that call happen. Cody did not trust Victor to have some prearranged word codes with his wife to provide instructions to his organization. Monitoring the call and scripting what was spoken should minimize the risk.

He left the room and texted Elana a message. Victor wants to speak with you in 10 minutes. Call this number and enter this passcode to enter the chat room. Please announce your name when you are in, and we will put Victor on the line to speak with you.

Before returning to Victor's bedroom, Cody told Zach, Stoney, and Bones to post up by the open door and listen in on Victor speaking to his wife, Elana. Cody entered the bedroom, using a burner phone, dialed the chat room number, and entered the master passcode. He put the phone on speaker and reminded Victor that he should only say what was written down, or he would immediately terminate the call and not provide him another opportunity to speak with his wife.

Several minutes later, they heard Elana announce she was in the chat room.

> Victor said, "Hello, Elana, this is Victor; I am well and hoping to be home in a few days."
>
> Elana replied: "Ivan met with me this afternoon and told me about what happened in the elevator at the restaurant. Do you know why this has been done?"
>
> Victor replied. "Please tell me what happened tonight at the house."

Elana said, "I was in our bedroom planning on changing into my night clothes when someone fired a bullet into our bedroom and destroyed the beautiful Waterford crystal vase on the bureau next to our bed."

She shookly asked: "Are Anna and I also in danger?" Was that bullet intended for me?

Victor said, "I must go now. Please do not worry; you both are in no danger."

Cody shut the phone down and threw it to Zach, saying, "Please destroy it and throw the parts into the lake."

Chapter 43

Cody then advised Victor that they would meet tomorrow morning to discuss the details and conclude this situation. With Victor out of hearing range, Stoney said to everyone, including Cody, that it was a great message delivered by V to let Victor sleep on tonight. Then he added, I wonder what Waterford crystal vases go for these days; pretty sure you can't glue those pieces back together.

Q wrapped up the night with a quick text saying that V's evacuation had gone smoothly and they were back home. Plan to send the new device you ordered down there tomorrow.

Early the next morning, Bones watched Victor, and Zach told Cody that Alan had emailed him a message. Given the events yesterday, Zach had put his phone on do-not-disturb, and Alan's voice message to Zach was *"Please check your email; I need to take a business trip to Europe."* The email message he showed Cody read:

The U.S. Government has approved AX Tech Corp to supply small arms to Hungary, a NATO member. These negotiations with the Hungarian military have been ongoing for a while. This would be a significant contract and may open access to other smaller NATO members. Flying out tomorrow, expect the trip to take 3-6 days. Carly has access to my work email and will monitor for any messages. She also has all the contact numbers with the FBI in case anything develops. I'm not familiar with the cell service available there; please use the WhatsApp link to contact me. Alan

Cody advised Zach that they both knew there would be no new developments with Victor in their possession. If everything goes well today, we can try for the exchange tomorrow. What a great WhatsApp message to send to your dad. Your mom has been released and is safely home with Carly and you. After breakfast, I want you to join Victor and me; we'll meet at the kitchen table without the chains on. I have formulated a plan that should be agreeable to him. I find Victor a tough person to read, but if he is the business person from our research, the proposition I plan to present should sound very appealing. I plan on asking Stoney and Bones to be in the kitchen area to add a little intimidation factor, but also give us a layer of security if Victor tries anything.

Cody walked into Victor's bedroom, unlocked his chain, and asked him to join him at the kitchen table. Zach was already seated and waiting for them to sit down. Stoney was by the rear door, and Bones covered the hallway that led to the great room.

Cody addressed Victor, saying he expected him to want to know the answers to two questions: 1) how they knew his organization kidnapped Carly and Peggy Turner, and 2) how they knew he was having lunch at the restaurant he owned in Bethesda yesterday.

Cody went on to say to Victor, We have resources at our disposal that are very far-reaching. The bullet fired last night was also a resource that I wanted you to understand clearly. Cody then produced two pictures and put them in front of Victor. The pictures were enhanced by Susie, and included facial shots of his wife, Elana, and their daughter Anna. Cody did not have to refer to the red dot on each person's head; Victor knew this was a laser beam point for sighting with a rifle. When the trigger was pulled, the bullet would enter the person exactly where the red dot was located. Cody also knew Victor had never seen these exact photos because they were taken from their drone video with some enhancement from Susie's Photoshop skills. Cody then told Victor that the answers to those questions may be provided at some future date if you and I can establish a relationship to include some degree of trust.

The next step caught everyone in the room off guard. Cody passed Victor a slip of paper. He instructed Victor to put the paper in his pocket, explaining that it contains his name and cell phone number to avoid any trouble in identifying him. Cody said, Victor, given the organization you run, I know you're a businessman, not just a thug. The kidnapping netted you $2 million in uncut diamonds that, once polished, will double in value. I don't doubt the expenses to plan, organize, and run this kidnapping were in the $150,000 range. As a businessperson, a gain of over $ 3.8 million is a nice return on investment. Here is what I am offering your organization: keep the ransom payment, and we will make a straight swap on our terms for Peggy Turner, returning you to your family safe and unharmed.

The other assurance I will provide you is that the FBI does not have our information about who was responsible as of today.

If you ever cause my team any problem during and after our negotiations, the FBI will be camped on your doorstep with warrants in hand. If we can get this swap done, I genuinely believe that the FBI training facility in Quantico will teach recruits about the water fountain, the tunnel, and the uncut diamonds on a case that remains unsolved. I shouldn't have to remind you that kidnapping across state lines is a Federal offense without a statute of limitations. The one thing I can assure you is that we have extremely well-documented evidence that proves your organization committed this crime.

As a business person, I believe this offer is as close to a win-win situation as I can propose. I am looking for your agreement and assurances that after this ends, we have no reason to look over our shoulders, wondering if you're there. Victor pulled the paper out of his pocket and said, "Cody Wall, you presented terms I will agree to with the assurance that my organization will not cause anyone on your team any harm down the road. I understand and admire your available resources and your capacity to use force if you feel it is warranted".

Cody knew they had crossed a high hurdle in securing Victor's commitment. He advised Victor that he was still their captive and must remain secured until a trade was completed. He told Victor that they would meet again this afternoon to review how an exchange could occur the next day. Victor seemed more cordial in saying he looked forward to the next meeting. Then he looked across the table and said to Zach, "Your swim to the airport was a loose end that I should have taken more seriously. Your only real flaw seems to be your cooking skills."

After Victor was secured back in his bedroom, Stoney complimented Cody on his Bad-Guy (firing the bullet into the bedroom) and Good-Guy (letting them keep the ransom) approach with Victor. He then asked Cody his thoughts on how the exchange would occur, minimizing any risk, knowing they were dealing with the Russian Mafia. Cody told Stoney to stay tuned to the next meeting later today; I still had some kinks to work out, but one hurdle at a time.

Q sent Cody a text message to check his emails. The device was built, and the picture has been forwarded. Cody immediately opened his email and saw what appeared to be a very well-constructed bomb with a cell phone detonator wired to the explosive. He knew a small block of clay was textured to look like C-4. Cody texted Q back to send the package down with V, ASAP, and told him he had built an excellent replica that hopefully would serve its purpose during our negotiations.

Cody took Zach outside and explained the general parts of his exchange plan. He suggested that Zach take V's car to their office building, leave it there, then reclaim his vehicle and head to Turner's home to stay with Carly. After hearing the details, Zach agreed he would be more helpful at the family's house tomorrow. Cody mentions to Zach that if any part of the exchange has significant problems, you would be removed from any association if you were back home when it happened. He said with V here, we'll have enough bodies to cover Victor and handle the trade for Peggy.

Stoney and Bones walked in with Victor, who appeared more relaxed since the morning meeting. Zach made lunch, and he considered spiking Victor's lunch with some serious hot sauce and pepper flakes to see if that level of seasoning met with his approval. He didn't want to rock the boat, so he made another basic meal for everyone.

V arrived with the device enclosed in a small shoebox. Cody explained to V that Zach needed to return today, as they would be able to use him both today and tomorrow. He replied, "Anyway, I can help, just let me know what needs to be done." Cody pulled V aside and thanked him for the job he did last night at Victor's house.

Cody asked V to touch base with Stoney and review the perimeter laser system and what weapons were stored outside the house. He gave V a recap of the morning meeting and the conference call with Victor's wife last night. With that subtle message you delivered, destroying that crystal vase, Victor seems to be on board and cooperative. V said thanks, but with a stationary target, no wind to speak of, and a reasonable distance, it was pretty easy to execute; V added that waiting in the tree was a pain in the butt, but was happy the shot did the trick.

Chapter 44

After lunch was cleared, Cody unlocked Victor and had everyone meet in the kitchen. Zach, Cody, and Victor sat at the table with the other three spread out around the room. Cody said he wanted to review what must happen to exchange Victor for Peggy.

Cody began by explaining that Victor's phone had been turned off and stored in a secure box that blocks any access to locate the phone. He went on to say that he used Victor's phone after leaving the garage to text a message to Ivan Petrov, stating that an exchange would be made, with Victor for Peggy Turner, and that she would be available today or tomorrow. Victor, in the call to Elena last night, Ivan told her about the elevator and abduction because she had mentioned it. I am guessing she does not know why it was done. Ivan did have my text message on his phone when he woke up in the garage. In my text, I also advised Ivan that all future communications would go through him. Instructions to Ivan need to be sent from Victor. I would like you to send our message after this meeting, using the password you have. The message coming from your cellphone validates it's real. I assure you that only a text will be sent, and no data will be copied from your phone. Cody added that since

I opened your phone using your thumbprint to send the first message, this is where the trust factor starts.

Without going into every detail, we will be back near Washington, DC, tomorrow mid-morning, using a public parking lot. Victor will be riding in our white SUV with me as the driver. Ivan will be instructed to arrive at a designated time and blink his lights several times, as will I. Your car, Victor, will have one driver and Peggy Turner in the back seat. I will exit our vehicle, and so will your driver. We will meet and exchange car keys or fobs. I will get into your vehicle and drive a short distance to another public parking lot. During this short drive, I will verify Peggy Turner is OK physically and mentally. My car with you does not move until the burner phone on the passenger seat of our vehicle receives a call from us with directions to where we left your car. Your driver or you will be given directions on where to drive and how to transfer from our car back to your vehicle. The keys to both cars are to be left in the cup holder. We will have left the area by the time you arrive and make the swap back to your vehicle.

For your organization's protection, a second message will be sent to Ivan to do the following: 30 minutes after the trade, he must generate a message to Alan Turner's work email. We will provide the wording, stating that Peggy Turner has been released and noting where she was dropped off. The FBI will be contacted, but only after we take Peggy Turner to this location will she become familiar with it, especially when she gets debriefed by the FBI later in the day. Peggy will know never to speak of our swap for you that took place in the public lot. Peggy, then, at the release location in your message, can provide factual details of her captivity, including where she was dropped off and the end of the ordeal. Your timely message is crucial to our plan to keep your organization out of the picture. This plan provides little to no risk. The exchange with both of you remaining in the vehicles guarantees no one will see either of you. The second public lot is lightly used, and I expect getting your vehicle back and driving off will not attract any attention.

Cody asked Victor directly, "Victor, do you want to be home tomorrow with your wife and daughter?" If yes, please provide your password to unlock your phone, and we'll generate our messages and set things in motion. Victor asked for a pencil and paper to write down his password and handed it to Cody. He said it was a fair plan and did not expose us to the authorities. He added, "I must trust you only to use my phone to communicate with Ivan."

Cody commented to Victor, You'll note I have not asked you if Peggy Turner is alive and well. If I were in your position, the only answer would be yes, because to answer NO would drastically change what happens to you going forward. Knowing she is not alive, a YES answer would buy you time until the exchange, with the hope of being rescued by your organization. If she is alive and well, you should be able to sleep well tonight knowing you'll be back with your family tomorrow.

After Victor returned and was secured in his bedroom, Cody informed the other four that once he had written the messages to be sent to Ivan, they should meet to review the exact timetable, locations, job assignments, and the plan for executing the trade tomorrow. Cody wrote down the following messages:

First Text Message to Ivan

Ivan: Tomorrow at exactly 9:45 a.m., we will exchange Victor for Peggy Turner. One vehicle with Peggy in the back seat, driven by one person. **NO** exceptions! Take the George Washington Parkway south toward Reagan National Airport. Passing the 14th Bridge ramp to DC, the next right turn is the Roaches Run Parking lot. It is also referred to as the limo or Uber lot, where cars wait for arriving flight passengers. Drive into the lot and blink your lights several times. The vehicle with Victor in the back seat will blink back. Park your vehicle, leave the keys in the cup holder, and have your driver walk toward our vehicle. Our driver will exit our vehicle, leaving the keys in the cup holder, and walk straight to your car. We will leave a disposable phone with Victor. **Do not** move our car until you receive our instructions on the phone left with Victor. We will transfer her to another vehicle once Peggy Turner's condition is verified. Directions will be given for the short drive to where your vehicle was left. You will drive there as instructed and transfer Victor back to your car. Leaving our vehicle unlocked with the keys in the cup holder.

Second Text Message to Ivan

Exactly at 10:15 a.m., you will use the same format to send Alan Turner's work email the following message—

Peggy Turner has been released. She was dropped off in Old Towne Alexandria at the Masonic National

Memorial and instructed not to leave the premises. We have decided not to seek an additional payment for her release. This will be our final communication.

Cody took Zach out on the front porch and had him read both messages. I'd like you to take V's car to drive back to the office as we discussed. Please take Victor's phone to send both messages en route during your return. Put Victor's phone on my desk when you get to the office. We may need it once more. Leave V's car in our garage, pick yours up, and head home to be with Carly. When this message hits Alan's work email inbox tomorrow at 10:15 a.m., you immediately call my cell requesting that I pick Peggy up after reading the whole message. Then, I will wait a few minutes to call Kim, read her the message, and advise her that I am on my way to get Peggy. Mention to her that, depending on Peggy's condition, both mentally and physically, you would like the FBI to be considerate and schedule a meeting for tomorrow morning.

Being at home with Alan overseas is the perfect position, with no way to link you to Peggy's release. To cover yourself, call and send Alan a message, and be sure to CC Beverly, his assistant, on Peggy's release.

On your way back, pull off at the first highway rest stop. Take Victor's phone out of the box, use his password to open the phone, and text these two messages to Ivan. Once done, power the phone off and store it in the box. If they can run a trace of that phone, it will only lead to a rest stop on I-95 North. I will get the phone back to Victor tomorrow.

Chapter 45

Cody asked Zach to watch Victor while he spoke to Stoney, Bones, and V. He gathered the team out on the boat dock while Zach watched Victor. Cody re-read the text messages Zach would send to Ivan on his way back to Alexandria. He then said he would like to review the full details of his plan with them to facilitate the swap.

Victor will be loaded in the van with his hands bound, Bones will handle driving, and Stoney will be assigned to watch Victor. I will also ride in the van and plan to have a couple of chats with Victor en route. There are several wrinkles I am putting in the plan that he is not aware of. You will follow us in the rental SUV. I want to get to my office before the traffic becomes unbearable. We'll leave at 5:30 a.m. tomorrow, heading to my parking garage in Old Towne Alexandria. We should arrive in 2 ½ hours, or around 8 a.m.

I want everyone to put on their communication gear so that if anything changes, we can address it and confirm that everyone understands. We'll keep the gear on throughout the morning until the job is completed.

Once at the garage, V will take the car Zach dropped off and head to the Uber lot on the southbound side of the GW

Parkway. Come armed if the situation changes and the Mafia shows up with more players than the one driver; you become our security blanket.

Cody said he would drive the white SUV with Victor in the back seat. He planned to be in the Uber lot 15 minutes early, facing the entrance to the parking lot. If my instructions are followed, one car and one driver will enter with Peggy Turner in the back seat. Blinking headlights will identify their car, and I will blink back.

Their driver will exit their car, I will exit our vehicle, and we'll swap places. A burner phone will be left in our vehicle, allowing us to communicate with Victor. Stoney will drive the white van, and Bones will take my Mustang. South of the airport, turn onto Daingerfield Island. It is also called the Washington Sailing Marina, where I keep my sailboat. As soon as you exit the parkway, turn left into the first parking lot. I will drive their car with Peggy from the limo lot to meet you, and it should take 2-3 minutes to get there. We'll transfer Peggy into our van. Stoney and Bones will bring the van with Peggy on board and head to the Masonic Memorial in Old Towne. There will be several black hoodie sweatshirts to minimize your identity when you drop Peggy off at the Masonic Memorial. My expectation is that exterior CCTV cameras are monitoring the property. Drop Peggy off; open the van's side door without exiting our vehicle. This should provide a film on the drop-off without exposing any of you individually.

I will coach Peggy on how to act once she gets there. Drive a circle-type route and make your way back to my office garage. Be mindful of your arrival time at the Masonic Memorial; try to time it as close to 10:10 a.m. as possible. Also, drive up the hilly driveway near the Masonic building when you drop her off. I will be nearby in my Mustang once Zach calls me with the email information he received that was sent to Alan's laptop, describing Peggy's release. I plan to wait a few minutes and then arrive at the Memorial around 10:20 a.m. to pick her up. From there, I expect to drive straight to the Turners' home with Peggy. This will allow me a second chance to coach her on her release before the FBI interviews her.

Cody told V he needed him to stay in place at the limo lot and verify our SUV does not move until we confirm Peggy's okay. After calling the phone left in our SUV and providing directions to Daingerfield Island to retrieve their car, you can exit the Roaches Run parking lot and head southbound toward Alexandria. There is a left-turn lane from the southbound side to turn into Daingerfield. V, please follow our car when it leaves the limo lot with Victor on board. Keep us posted on the communication gear and what they do once they leave the parking lot, so we know our instructions are followed.

Does anyone have questions or comments about what needs to happen tomorrow? I will discuss the few wrinkles with Victor during our return drive and review them in our parking garage before we head out to make the exchange. Everyone in this group is top-notch and professional. We need to be on target today to execute this plan. Cody knew he didn't need to repeat anyone's assignment to complete this.

Zach headed out in V's Toyota Corolla. His only thought was that V could not be a car guy and drive such a plain vanilla ride. His other idea was never to mention his first thought about the Corolla. V was not a person you wanted to get on his bad side at any time for any reason. Zach did pull off at a rest stop near Fredericksburg, VA, on his way north on I-95. He took Victor's iPhone out of the security box, powered it up, and was very happy to see Victor was a man of his word when the password provided opened the screen. He unraveled the paper Cody had written down his text messages, typed in the first one to Ivan, hit send, and saw the delivery icon pop. He then entered the second message with Cody's instruction, and it was also acknowledged as delivered. Zach felt Cody would like to know if both messages were sent and received, so he sent a quick text message with that information. The phone was powered down and placed back in the box, making its movements untraceable.

Cody went into Victor's bedroom and advised him that the plan was to make the trade tomorrow morning. He said they were getting him up at 4:30 a.m., having toast and coffee, and heading back to DC on the road. He would be riding in the van with him because they needed to agree on a few other items they would discuss on the ride back. Cody told Victor, "I believe that we have reached at least a mutual respect.". For this reason, "your hands will be bound in front of you but not your feet". This may allow you to be slightly more comfortable during the ride back.

Zach arrived at Cody's office and ventured upstairs to see Susie, Karen, and Q. They were all very anxious to get updated on Victor's demeanor and how close they were to making the exchange for Peggy. Zach had everyone crowd into Susie's office with the door shut and went over the highlights of the past 24 hours. He mostly detailed the morning meeting with Victor when Cody handed Victor a piece of paper with his name and phone number, which elicited a couple of gasps from everyone. He described Cody putting a scenario together: 1) to leave the authorities out, 2) they keep the ransom, and 3) a straight exchange of Victor for Peggy, which Victor agreed to. The most crucial point was Cody getting Victor to commit to this being a straight business transaction, and Victor's organization would never take any repercussions against anyone on his team. Everyone in the room felt great relief knowing their collective efforts should not cause them any harm in the future.

The mood in the room became very upbeat, especially when Zach said if all goes well, the exchange will be made tomorrow morning. Cody's garage will become our staging area tomorrow. Cody would like everyone here by 8 a.m. You may not be needed, but if he tweaks his plan, additional help may be required. The finish line to get my mother back is very close. As everyone left the room, Susie pulled Zach back into her office and hugged and kissed him. She whispered If all goes well, our next date should be spectacular! Zach told her about heading home so that she could process the drop-off message to Alan's email, so the FBI would believe the same format was used when Carly was released.

Zach was floating in the air, wondering what special date he could arrange to WOW Susie. He was happy to get into his BMW, leave V.'s Corolla in the garage, and head out to his family's home. So as not to surprise her, he texted Carly that he would be there in 30–40 minutes and was looking forward to having dinner with her if she didn't have a big date. Carly saw Zach's car coming up the driveway and ran out to see him. Her first question was where he had disappeared over the past few days. He apologized to her, explaining that he had been staying at his condo and spending most of his time with Cody. After receiving Alan's email about his overseas trip, he wanted to come home and keep her company. She jokingly said she wouldn't mind hanging out with Cody. Zach knew his sister had always had a crush on Cody, but he was confident his buddy would never cross the line to date his little sister. Zach told her that, unfortunately, Cody seems to be attracted to Kim Ross, the FBI agent handling their case. Carly quickly replied that he must be thinking that women who are packing a gun must be sexy.

Zach asked Carly about monitoring Alan's emails; she said the company's IT person had set her phone up with prompts to tell her when an email arrived. She said their dad received far too many emails to manage, but none from the kidnappers. He said his sister, with her phone linked in, Let's go out and get some Mexican food with a margarita to wash it down. He knew they could go to the little Mexican restaurant in McLean's small strip shopping center, which is entirely family-run. He said the dad and daughter do all the cooking, the mom will greet you at the door, and the son is the principal waiter. She replied that I could be ready in 30 minutes and thanked him for coming home. It was challenging not to tell her; there was an excellent chance they would have dinner with their mother tomorrow night.

Chapter 46

Cody texted Zach, asking him to call and discuss several things tonight, noting that nothing was urgent. After Carly and Zach got back to the family's house from dinner, Zach told Carly that Cody had texted him and he needed to give him a call back. On her way upstairs to change, Carly told Zach to pass on her best when he spoke to Cody. Sensing Cody's message was subtle and conveyed the opposite of urgency. Zach took a stroll out to the garden, which provided him with total privacy, and placed the call.

Cody answered on the first ring and asked Zach if he was available to discuss tomorrow. Zach replied that he was sitting in the garden and said, "What's up?" Cody expressed his concern that, upon completing the exchange, he would have only a few minutes to inform Peggy that the team would transfer her to the Masonic Memorial. He would arrive some 10 minutes later in his Mustang to pick her up and drive her home. On the drive home, I will need to coach Peggy on what to say to the FBI about the drop-off in the parking lot. I think the best approach would be to share some half-truths with Peggy about our role in securing her release. We should agree to inform Peggy that the FBI has no leads on the crime; through research and old military contacts, you and I have identified the responsible organization. We believed that if this information were shared with the FBI, the criminals might react aggressively if approached by authorities, potentially leading to serious consequences for you. That would close a loose end, and the criminals could take their chances with good lawyers in a courtroom to beat the charges.

We stick with the story that you and I approached the criminal organization on our own, trading our promise not to divulge our evidence to the FBI in return for requiring them to release you to us immediately. We needed a very public place where you could swap cars without being seen, ensuring you were safely back with us. If the FBI were told exactly what happened, we would possibly be in legal trouble for withholding our information on the kidnapping crime. When Carly was released, the criminals used a white van and dropped off your daughter at a small park in Old Towne. To mimic what was done with Carly, we asked you to drop by our white van at the Masonic Memorial.

He told Zach, I think it's best if no one knows precisely what took place except for our team. I would like Peggy to share all her experiences with Carly, except for how she was released at the limo/Uber lot. Be mindful that Victor may not be our best friend, but we certainly don't want him to become our enemy if any of this were to become public. Zach was on board with this approach, knowing his mom would be curious at some point about how they solved the crime. He already knew his reply to her would be, *"I am grateful and blessed to have you home safe and sound."*

Everyone but Victor was awake and dressed at 3:30 a.m. With a flashlight in hand, Bones disarmed the four perimeter laser detectors and stored them in their SUV. Stoney retrieved the cache of weapons from the front and back of the house. He had to lower the SUV's rear seat to create enough storage space. All the food items, except for small breakfast items, were packed and loaded. Bedsheets and towels were piled in the laundry room. Cody knew he would contact a local cleaning service to come out and tidy up the whole house before his family's next visit. Everything else, like personal possessions, would be put in the van. Cody thought that one day, when it didn't matter if everything worked out, he would be at the lake house sharing a glass of wine with his dad and telling him an unbelievable story.

Cody had provided Victor with some of his old sweatpants and sweatshirts, which he kept in one of the bedroom closets. He gave them to Victor to wear after showering last night. His original clothes were put in a paper bag to be returned during the exchange. With everyone pitching in, the lake house served its purpose well and would keep its secrets of the past several days. They left the lake house a few minutes before 5:30 a.m., heading north to Alexandria.

Chapter 47

Staying within the speed limit, the drive back was uneventful, except for the commuter traffic building as they got to the DC area. Knowing the roads well, Cody approached Victor, who was sitting on the floor in the back of the van, with about 30 minutes left in the drive. Cody was very open, knowing Bones and Stoney could hear his comments.

Cody told Victor that he had several issues to discuss with him. The first concern was the agreement between the two of them. He read the exact 1st message that was texted to Ivan Petrov yesterday afternoon. He asked Victor what IF Ivan wanted to be a savior in your eyes, showed up with six cars and a dozen guns at our meeting place, and believed he could get you back safe and secure? My problem is that Ivan has not been a party to our agreement. My other concern is that Peggy Turner is not sitting in the back of your car when I open the door.

Cody took out Q's box, opened it, and showed it to Victor, asking him what he saw inside it. Victor said it appeared to be C-4 explosives wired to a cell phone detonator. Cody replied to him, You are 100% correct. What if I told you to safeguard and address both my concerns? This device can be placed under the rear seat of the car you're in. When the exchange occurs, if our instructions are ignored, and a show of force by your organization occurs, or Peggy Turner is not in your vehicle, a call will be made to this device under your seat. A chain will be secured to you and around the child seat anchors when you're placed in the back seat. Any thoughts of running from the vehicle will be eliminated. When your driver opens the door, sees you're okay, and all hell breaks loose, you may have 10-15 seconds to defuse the situation, or our only option may be to activate the device you're looking at. If your driver plans to speed off with you because Peggy Turner is not in the backseat of your vehicle, the explosion on the parkway will clog traffic for the remainder of the day.

Before we try to resolve this problem, let me share problem two. We plan to protect your organization from the authorities. Cody read the second message sent to Ivan, dealing with the release email sent to Alan Turner's laptop at an exact time. Suppose this email is not followed to the letter. In that case, the FBI will see inconsistencies in Peggy's release and not back off until they know exactly what happened. Using the white van you are now riding, we will take Peggy to the Masonic Memorial exactly on time. This will mirror the same way you dropped off Carly Turner. If Ivan does not feel this is important and deviates from our request, your organization risks a potentially high level of exposure to this crime.

I can speak for my part of the agreement; we will execute as promised because our sole goal is to get Peggy Turner back. If your people have an endgame in mind, your life may hang in the balance.

We will arrive shortly in Alexandria and enter a secure garage, where we will be staging for the exchange. You must convince me that our win-win agreement is ironclad and that the trade will go precisely as planned within our timeline. If there is any doubt when we leave the garage, I will have no choice but to place this device under your seat as a motivational tool to encourage you to use your authority to complete this exchange as requested. Give me your thoughts once we are in the garage.

Stoney and Bones looked at each other without having to say it; Cody Wall was the real deal in playing hardball when negotiating. They knew their team could spend years in prison if this exchange went sideways. Any potential gunplay that could erupt in a very crowded parking lot would result in numerous bystanders getting hurt or killed. Stoney leaned over and whispered in Bones's ear, "Where the hell did Cody get his hands on a small block of C-4?"

Arriving at the underground garage at 7:45 a.m., Cody punched in his code; the gate opened long enough for the van and SUV to enter. The first order was to unload the weapons and miscellaneous equipment from both vehicles. They left the fake license plates in place and only removed them when they returned the rental cars.

Cody told V to use his car and head to the limo/Uber lot near Reagan National Airport. Check your communication device and see if it has the range to reach us here. Keep us updated; I will have the SUV with Victor in the back seat parked in the lot by 9:30 a.m.

Victor asked Cody if his phone was available. Cody replied that he could get it in a few minutes, knowing it was sitting on his desk upstairs. Cody asked him what he planned to do to resolve the two problems he discussed earlier. Victor started by saying it was indeed very beneficial to both of them for the trade to go without any issues, and the email sent at the time was requested. Victor said he plans to call Ivan from his phone because we are still about 2 hours out from the 9:45 a.m. meeting time. I will put the phone on speaker mode so you can hear my request. Cody prompted that there would be no discussion in Russian during the call. After I am done, Victor said you may decide if you still need your motivational tool under the car's rear seat. Cody took the elevator up to his office, said a couple of quick hellos, grabbed the box that held Victor's phone off his desk, and took the elevator back down to the garage.

Victor saw the special box, and Cody opened it, handing Victor his phone. Victor asked if the box was custom-made to block his phone's GPS tracking, and Cody replied, "Bingo."

Victor dialed Ivan's number; he saw the incoming call was from Victor's phone and picked up immediately. Ivan first thought the people who abducted Victor would be on the line. When Victor said hello to Ivan, Ivan asked Victor if he was okay. "*I am well, and you are in speaker mode,*" Victor replied, and continued, "Please listen to what I am about to say: *I want you to drive my Mercedes with Peggy Turner in the back seat; she should not be restrained.*" *You will be on time as instructed. No one in our organization should be within 10 miles of the meeting location. I understand that making this exchange exactly as requested is in our best interest. I have given my word that there will be no outside interference. Ensure that someone sends the release message exactly within the noted time. There will be no excuses for not doing your job as instructed. Do you understand completely and have everything in place to comply?*"

Ivan knew from Victor's tone that he was not under any duress and that if he screwed this up, he was a walking dead man.

His answer to Victor was that there would be no problems on our end, and he looked forward to driving him home. Victor hung up and handed Cody his phone back.

Cody informed Victor that his call and Ivan's reply were sufficient to confirm the exchange and subsequent drop-off at the Masonic Memorial would proceed as planned. We will not install the device under the seat of our car. I do appreciate your solutions to my two problems. As I repeatedly said, "If we are successful today, it will benefit both of us."

Stoney is in the van, and Bones is driving Cody's Mustang. They head to the Daingerfield Island parking area to wait for Victor's car with Peggy to arrive. Cody and Victor, in the rental Hyundai SUV, followed shortly behind, timing their short drive to arrive at the Uber lot at 9:30 a.m. Cody got on the comms and asked V if the parking lot activity was unusual. V immediately replied that the routine is the same: planes are landing from the north and flying right by us exactly 15 to 18 minutes later; most of this lot empties when people are off their aircraft and booking Ubers. Then, a trickle occurs as new Uber drivers arrive for the next plane's landing. Currently, there are enough parking spots for everyone. Cody asked Stoney if he and Bones were in place and got a reply that they were ready to *rock & roll*.

Chapter 48

Cody arrived on time, saw where V had parked, secured a parking space on the other side of the lot, and slightly passed him. This way, he thought that when he and Ivan walked toward each other, they should pass directly in front of V. Never can be too safe. With 15 minutes to spare, Cody handed Victor a burner phone and instructed him to wait until he called, explaining that it should not take more than 10 minutes from the time they left the lot. Cody advised that he would give him the okay to drive south on the parkway, past the airport, and make the only left turn marked Daingerfield Island. The distance from here to there is less than 2 miles. A small parking lot is on your left, and your Mercedes will be waiting for you with the key fob in the cup holder. Please transfer vehicles and leave our keys where they are in the cup holder. Peggy will be going to the Masonic Memorial in our van and will be dropped off when you arrive. Cody asked if he had any questions; Victor replied that he understood the procedures and would follow them as requested.

At 9:44 a.m., V announced that a black Mercedes, not an Uber ride, was entering the parking lot. Cody saw the vehicle blink its lights three times. Cody replied with three blinks to show where he was located. Ivan parked the Mercedes on V's side of the lot, about ten spaces above V's car.

Cody told Victor it was time to make the exchange and hoped they could meet in the future in a less stressful situation. Victor acknowledged him and said he felt their paths would cross again. Cody got out and started walking toward the Mercedes; Ivan also exited his vehicle and approached from the opposite direction. They did make eye contact, but no words or gestures were exchanged; this was strictly business.

Cody opened the driver's door and saw Peggy Turner looking confused until she saw Cody's face. Cody immediately said into his mic that Peggy was wearing a big, radiant smile in the vehicle. She was a little startled to see her son's best friend telling her the ordeal was over, and she was safe and would soon be home. As Cody climbed into the driver's seat, she reached from behind with tears running down her cheeks to hug him. He told Peggy they only had several minutes as he drove out of the lot to listen carefully to what he had to say. I will drop you off in a few minutes, and two people who work for me will take you in a white van to the GW Masonic Memorial Temple in Old Towne and drop you off at the entrance to the building. Please find a bench or stand somewhere outside where I can see you. I will arrive in my white Mustang 10 minutes after they drop you off. Take in the surroundings, focus on some details, and consider how you feel. This is where you'll tell the authorities that, at some point, the people who kidnapped you dropped you off from a white van. We are mirroring the drop-off that was used by the kidnappers when they released Carly. Your daughter is safe and sound at your home. I will explain everything in more detail once I pick you up and we start the drive to your home in Great Falls.

Cody pulled up next to their white van, opened Peggy's door, and introduced her to Stoney and Bones. These two handsome men are going to drive you to the Masonic Memorial. They will open the van's side door, and you'll exit and walk to a convenient place to wait for me to arrive. You must leave right now to stay within our timeline. Cody saw they both wore black hoodie sweatshirts, which would hide them enough from any cameras. Before they closed the door, Cody grabbed the box with the fake C-4 explosive lying in the back of the van. Bones told him as they drove out that his Mustang keys were in the cup holder and pointed to his car, parked about 100 yards away.

Cody dialed up the burner phone in the SUV, and Victor answered. Cody told him to follow the directions; his Mercedes was the only one in the parking lot. He informed V via comms that when Ivan turned left off the parkway to the parking lot and continued straight to his office, he would keep an eye on the Mercedes. He got several things from his Mustang, walked over, and placed them in the Mercedes' back seat. He hurried back to his car, knowing Zach would be calling in 10 minutes or so to advise of the incoming email message on Peggy's release. It would only take him 5 -6 minutes to get to the Masonic Memorial for the pick-up.

Cody saw Ivan driving their white SUV into the entrance of Daingerfield Island, heading straight to where the Mercedes was parked. Victor jumped out of his SUV, opened the rear door of his Mercedes, and froze in place. The box containing the C-4 explosive device was sitting in the middle of his back seat. At that very second, a phone inside the box rang, and Victor's only thought before he died was that Cody Wall had double-crossed him. The phone continued to ring, playing a Russian lullaby, which Victor knew; he reached into the box and picked up his cell phone. Cody said hello to Victor and told him he wanted to return his phone and the bag with his clothes. Victor said he thought their relationship would end with a big Boom! Cody said that since he provided Victor with his cell phone number, he figured it was only fair to have Victor's number stored in his phone's contacts. When the phone was in his possession, he copied the number to verify if it worked.

Cody said the only other advice I can give you now is that everyone abides by their commitments and agreements. When you return to Bella Napoli to eat, take the stairs; it may be the safer route. Victor stood there, happy he wasn't blown to bits. He thought Cody Wall was a son-of-a-bitch but had a good sense of humor. Victor told Ivan to head home, and as he climbed into the Mercedes, a car horn beeped twice. Victor looked toward the exit and saw Cody wave to him as his white Mustang drove out onto the parkway.

Zach's call came in on Cody's phone several minutes later, right at the requested time. Cody told Zach that he had stopped by the store this morning and picked up the item he wanted. Zach immediately knew what this coded message meant; Peggy was released and probably waiting to be picked up at the Memorial. Zach read the email message excitedly and asked Cody to drop everything since he was so close and pick up his mom. He added that Cody seems to be the family's Uber driver in bringing stray family members home.

Cody replied on my way; I will call back when I get there, adding, 'Let us hope this is not some hoax to give us false hope, in case the FBI is monitoring the call.'

Stoney told Peggy they would pull up near the entrance and open the side door just enough for her to slip out. They would pull up their hoods to hide their faces, knowing this facility has exterior security cameras. He said to her, "Become an actress, look very relieved, stay in one place, and wait for Cody to show up, remembering you have not seen him today." Peggy said she enjoyed a little drama after being cooped up for several weeks.

Chapter 49

As the van pulled in, Stoney said it was show time, as Bones slid open the side door, and Peggy left the van. She did not see any benches to sit on, but spotted a grass walkway that took her away from the entrance to an area on the building's east side that provided a gorgeous view of Old Town Alexandria.

The George Washington Masonic Memorial sits on a hillside, possibly the highest point in Alexandria. Where she was facing, one could see the Potomac River. She took Stoney's advice, soaked up the sun on her face, took deep breaths of fresh air, and enjoyed the wind blowing through her hair. She saw cars winding through the long entranceway from her vantage point to visit the Memorial. Her being here was like getting a second chance to live her life. Knowing Carly was released and safe provided her with the comfort to enjoy the sunshine.

It didn't seem long, but she spotted Cody's white Mustang driving up the entrance road. She wanted to wave and run to see him, but knew she must remain calm and let him find her. Cody played his part; he saw Peggy on the east side overlook, parked his car, and wandered around the entrance briefly. As he expanded his search, he walked the same grass path, shouted her name at the appropriate time, and ran directly toward her.

He threw his arms open to give her a big hug. He whispered in her ear; this was a welcoming hug, and she was doing great. She said freedom had a new meaning and was blessed to see him. Cody had his cell phone out and told her he was calling Zach to confirm she had been released and appeared in good shape. He told Peggy, Just follow me, our next stop will be your home. Zach took the call and played his part, thanking Cody for the quick response to the Memorial and confirming his mom had been released from her captivity.

As Cody drove down the Memorial's winding driveway, he took Peggy's hand and said, "Everything from this point forward will be just fine. I know you have a million questions, and I'll try my best to explain what happened this morning." Peggy tilted her seat back, holding Cody's hand, and said, Knowing you and Zach, it's probably a whopper of a story.

Cody first asked if she knew Carly was also taken; Peggy said she did and explained that the same white dry-erase boards and pictures of Carly holding the same sign were used. Cody asked if she knew Carly had been released a week ago. She was not positive, but the change in the guarding routine, along with her maternal instincts, told her Carly was no longer there. Her only thought was that she needed more money to get released. Cody told her that Carly and Zach anxiously awaited her arrival at their family home. Alan had no idea when your captivity would end and flew to Europe yesterday for a big business deal involving a NATO country. I'm sure Zach will reach out to him and provide the great news.

Cody said what I am going to tell you must never be repeated. I don't want to sound dramatic, but a small group of people has put in a tremendous effort to get you here today. If anyone finds out how this happened, their lives could be at risk.

Cody explained that Alan called the FBI immediately, using his defense/military contacts as leverage. As you're aware, it's all about the money. She said the only way she kept her sanctity was when they wrote on the board, by her captors, a ransom demand was being made.

Cody said, "I can tell you this was professionally planned and executed." As of today, the FBI has no clue who is responsible. I expect that the authorities will never solve this case.

Zach and I assembled a small group to explore how we could assist. We stumbled upon a lead that we believed was the person who committed the kidnapping. Our problem during the ransom payment was that a message from the kidnappers referred to something they should not have known. The FBI thinks they may have an employee who is possibly being paid by the criminals who leaked this information. We discussed sharing our information with the authorities, but if there were a leak, that would have put your life at risk. The bad guys knew they covered their trail well, but you were still a loose end after Carly was released. If they were caught with you still in their custody, the case would be solid, and people would go to jail for a lengthy time.

Our information was only a lead and insufficient in a court of law to convict anyone of this crime. Your release was our sole focus, with no strings attached. We decided to approach this organization and tell them we knew they committed the kidnapping and had the evidence to prove it, which was a bluff if you ever played poker. That got enough attention from these criminals to convince our team that we had the proper organization that planned and executed the kidnappings.

We decided to broker a deal with this organization; they keep the ransom paid to date, release you, and we never contact the FBI with what we know. They accepted those terms, which resulted in the vehicle switch today and your release. Knowing the FBI will interview you as they did Carly, they are desperate to find any type of lead in this case. For this reason, we had to mirror Carly's release using a white van, dropping you off at a public place. When you're required to describe the men who transported you and dropped you off, provide their description, indicating they were the same guards who held you captive and then transported you to the Memorial. The 20 minutes spent switching vehicles before meeting at the Memorial should be forgotten and never mentioned to anyone, including Alan and Carly.

Peggy said, "I will be forever grateful to all of you, but I am unable to express my sincere feelings openly." I knew there would be some resolution with the two of you involved, but I could have never dreamed up this scenario.

Chapter 50

Cody called Susie to remind her to send someone to return the rental SUV to the office; she told him it had already been done.

After hanging up with Susie to lighten the mood, Cody told Peggy something amazing had come out of all this ordeal. He said his office conference room had become their "think tank." His IT person, who holds multiple degrees in computer science, is also very single and attractive. I would venture to say your Zach has developed more than a crush after only one date, for which I paid their $300 brunch bill. If I were a betting man, my wager would be that your arriving safely home will free up everyone's time, and we might see the two flowers start to bloom. Peggy responded that at the right time, I will use my motherly ways to find out what direction this may be headed...

Cody advised Peggy to chat with Carly and share their kidnapping experiences before being interviewed by the FBI. Cody's instincts were that he believed both of them were held at the same facility. It would make little sense to set up two separate facilities for the criminals to keep their hostages. Carly was debriefed without being able to provide the FBI with any substantial clues to the location or identity of the persons involved.

Everything can be discussed, including the drop-off at the Memorial. In my opinion, with your safe return, this becomes a victimless crime. The harm now becomes the money or the ransom paid. By the way, Alan checked with his insurance broker and verified AX Tech's corporate insurance policy covered family members for kidnapping. The limits in the policy were sufficient to cover the ransom payment. If there were ever a conviction and recovery, the actual loss would be the insurance company getting reimbursed.

Peggy saw that they weren't far from her house. She looked at Cody and said I am curious about what Carly and I are worth on the open market. Cody chuckled at her question and said the ransom payment for you both was two million dollars in uncut diamonds. That represents close to 1000 stones. The retail market value would double to approximately four million when the stones are cut and polished. When she heard the figure, Peggy commented that I should feel flattered because I was worth that kind of money. As they pulled into the driveway, Cody squeezed her hand and said to Peggy You are priceless!

Carly and Zach sat on the mansion's front porch and hurried to the driveway as Cody parked his Mustang. Zach opened the passenger door as Peggy stepped out, but neither said anything. A group hug between the three seemed never to end, and the tears flowed. Cody wished the team were here to see and feel the emotion of reuniting this family. His eyes also watered up at this touching moment.

Zach said they had set up a light lunch on the back patio, since it was a beautiful day that became even more exceptional with their mom returning home. As they started enjoying the simple lunch, Cody asked Zach if he had contacted the FBI this morning. Zach indicated that he called and spoke with Agent Kim Ross immediately after contacting Cody, requesting him to head over to the Masonic Memorial to verify if Peggy had indeed been released. When Cody confirmed he had Peggy with him, he called Kim back to share the great news. She had asked if her partner, Shaun O'Hara, and she could come out to their house and sit down with Peggy to record her account of the kidnapping. Zach said his mother requested that the FBI allow the remainder of the day to be spent with family, and if they could schedule tomorrow morning to come out and conduct their interview.

Peggy said it was very kind of Zach to consider allowing her to return to an everyday life, even after a small adjustment period. She said it would be fine for the FBI to come by tomorrow and take her statement. Zach texted Kim, confirming that 9 a.m. at their home would work. Within a few minutes, he received Kim's text message that Shaun and she were looking forward to meeting and interviewing Peggy.

Cody then asked Zach if he had reached Alan with the news. Zach said he immediately tried to call his dad, but his call went straight to voicemail. I read the message we received from the criminals into his voicemail. Then, I asked him to contact me as soon as possible. Alan did indicate he had no idea of the cell service availability where he was going. As a backup, Zach said he sent a WhatsApp message to his dad, CC to Beverly, after Cody confirmed he had picked up Peggy.

Zach said that Alan is not the best person to monitor his voicemail, check text messages, or even open a WhatsApp link.

Alan's attitude toward technology led him to hire a competent assistant to handle matters and keep him updated.

The rest of the lunch was spent on very light topics about future trips, places to see, and what would be exciting things to do that none of them had ever done. The one that got everyone's attention was Carly suggesting that the entire family, including Cody, must be included in a skydiving experience. Zach said Cody and he had parachuted as part of their Army training, but he had never tried falling freely through the air.

Peggy commented that she didn't know Carly had that daredevil attitude and wanted to jump out of an airplane. Carly replied that she might have second thoughts when the plane took off, but doing it as a family adventure would be all the motivation she needed. Carly added that we seem to be given a new lease on life, so we may want to explore some different things.

Cody jumped in, saying he knew that until anyone got certified to skydive, they had to jump in tandem, attached to an instructor. He asked the other three if they knew why jumping tandem was mandatory. Everyone shook their heads, unable to see the reason why. Cody answered his question, explaining that the companies running skydiving jumps couldn't trust anyone to pull the ripcord and open the parachute at the right moment. If someone had a panic attack while free-falling and didn't pull the cord, it would not end well. Peggy said it sounded more like a young person's adventure until Zach reminded her that former President George H.W. Bush had made jumps into his early 80s. Peggy said, "When Alan returns, let's get his input and see who wants to jump out of a perfect airplane to soar with the birds."

As lunch ended, Peggy asked Carly if she could share her experience of being interviewed by the FBI. It would provide her with some insight before tomorrow's meeting. Carly said she would be happy to do so and added that Shaun, the senior FBI agent, has a no-nonsense type A personality, and Kim Ross, the junior agent, was a delightful young lady who seemed very caring. Cody had not shared his new relationship with Kim with anyone, feeling it would just complicate the kidnapping ordeal that everyone had been focused on. Now that Peggy was home and appeared physically and mentally sound, he would share the news of his relationship with Kim in several days. May even ask Zach and Susie to join them on a double date somewhere.

Chapter 51

Cody said he had several business commitments and was returning to Alexandria. Hugs were exchanged with Peggy and Carly, and then Zach offered to walk Cody out to his car. When they reached the driveway, Zach asked if there had been any issues with the transfer. Cody gave him a short recap of the exchange and commitment made by phone to Victor to get it done without any interference. Stoney advised him that the drop-off at the Masonic Memorial went smoothly. They pulled near the entrance and slid the van's side door just enough to allow Peggy to exit, not exposing themselves to any exterior cameras.

Cody said he found Peggy looking over Old Towne from the overlook area of the Masonic Memorial. He told Zach on the ride to their home that he had time to convey to his mom that the FBI was ineffective to date. Peggy fully understands that we obtained evidence to ID the organization responsible and used it to secure her release. She is fully aware that you are aware of the details in negotiating her release, whereas Carly is not. Provided the interview with Shaun and Kim tomorrow doesn't raise any red flags, we should be able to put this behind us, with the only damage being the insurance company taking the financial hit.

Zach asked Cody if he would swing by before the FBI showed up in the morning. He indicated that with Carly around, he didn't think Peggy would bring up any of the morning events with him. That may happen when he and his mom are alone somewhere. I expect the FBI won't let us sit in their debrief session. I will advise Peggy that you will be here in the morning for moral support before the meeting, implying she could pull you aside if she has any issues to discuss. Cody said to expect him around 8 a.m. and have a good cup of dark roast coffee ready. He also told Zach that he wanted to get the team together in a few days for their debrief meeting and share some well-deserved congratulations from us. Zach said the office conference room was the only secure place to chat openly. Let's think about scheduling late afternoon when the cocktail hour is appropriate, and we can toast our success. Cody replied - "Good thought; I'll stock up on some beverages and keep you posted."

Cody, probably due to his Army training, was never late to any appointment or meeting. At 8 a.m., he was driving into Turner's driveway, knowing Peggy's interview was the last major hurdle in dealing with the FBI.

Zach knew Cody's timely habits and was waiting on the front porch. He had a mug and a carafe of coffee, closer to espresso or motor oil because it was black and strong. Zach said the ladies were having a light breakfast in the kitchen before the FBI showed up. Cody pulled up a rocking chair and asked how the evening went with Peggy being home. Zach indicated the night was uneventful, which was positive; Carly and Peggy spent some time recounting their experience while being held hostage. Cody said he recommended that Peggy have that conversation so her facts and talking points would mirror what Carly had already disclosed to Kim and Shaun.

Cody told Zach he intended to ask Shaun if they could sit in the background and listen to Peggy recount her experiences. This would allow them to gauge if anything was said that could steer them toward Victor. Cody inquired if Alan had responded to Zach's voice message or WhatsApp text. Zach said that, having worked for my dad for years, he gets tunnel vision when negotiating a big contract. I'm not surprised if the talks hit some speed bumps, and he's not checking anything until he gets the deal done. As they were headed toward the kitchen, he asked Zach what brand of coffee they used because it was excellent. Zach replied I made it, especially for you, and you don't want to know how it got there.

Carly and Peggy were clearing their dishes when Cody walked in and hugged them each. He asked Peggy if she was ready to be interrogated by the FBI for several grueling hours. Peggy looked surprised by his comment until he said Just kidding, they are both lovely people. He asked Peggy if she would be uncomfortable if Zach and he were in the room during the debrief session, assuming it was OK with the agents. Peggy indicated that if the FBI allowed them to listen, she was okay with them being there. Carly showed no interest in attending the meeting and said she would be in her room if needed before or after the interview.

Shaun and Kim arrived in the standard FBI black Suburban. Cody saw them pulling in and wondered how much taxpayer dollars were spent to get a fleet of Suburbans for the FBI. He knew they were all modified with powerful engines, probably bulletproof glass, and specially made compartments to hold various weapons.

Cody had not spoken to or seen Kim since their recent sailing adventure. Cody walked to greet them both, and when Shaun went to get his briefcase out of the rear seat, Cody flashed a big wink to Kim, which she promptly acknowledged. She winked back and added a big smile. Cody walked with them to the study, where Peggy and Zach were waiting, and introduced the two agents to Peggy. Kim said the Bureau was very excited yesterday to get the news of the email received and the subsequent release of Mrs. Turner.

Before starting our interview, let me update you on the release yesterday. Yesterday afternoon, we sent a team to the Masonic Memorial to interview employees who had worked that day and to view any camera security footage. As with Carly, a white van did enter the premises a few minutes before the 10:15 a.m. message was released to Alan's email. The van proceeded through the parking lot and turned around so the passenger side faced the entrance. The driver was purposely seated back from the windshield and appeared to be wearing dark clothing and a hooded sweatshirt. The Masonic Memorial's cameras were of poor quality, resulting in a grainy picture. The side van door was open just enough to let Peggy exit the vehicle. The people inside the van never exposed themselves to the cameras. We captured the first three characters of the rear license plate. Our data search revealed nearly a thousand vehicles with the same three-digit combination. Applying filters to what we believed was the make, model, and color narrowed it down to only two possibilities. We believe the license plates that could have been on the van yesterday were real registered numbers and accounted for by the owners yesterday. We know three white vans were involved because of the timing of Peggy, Carly, and Zach's approach and subsequent escape. The van following Zach was the only one without an ID on its license plates, and it was most likely the one used to drop Peggy at the Memorial.

As the gracious hostess, Peggy offered everyone tea, coffee, or juice before we started her interview. Everyone declined and indicated they were ready to record her statement. Zach took the lead and directly asked Shaun, the senior agent, if it was okay for Cody and me to stay in the study to hear the recount of Peggy's experience. Shaun thought about it and replied, "As long as you do not interrupt or ask any questions, I see no issue with both of you hearing her statement."

Zach and Cody both got up from the meeting table in the study and moved back to the two chairs stationed in the corner of the room. Zach flashed Cody a thumbs-up signal, indicating their ability to listen to Peggy's debrief would either validate that the FBI would have no new leads to follow or some detail they may have to address later with Victor personally.

As expected, Shaun would take charge and announce it to everyone. He wanted Peggy to provide every detail of the time she was held captive. They would not interrupt her unless clarification of a particular point were necessary. The statement would be recorded so they could play it back at Bureau headquarters for other agents to listen and provide input.

Peggy started by explaining that she worked as a volunteer at a nonprofit organization for half a day every Tuesday. She parked in the same garage adjacent to the office building that housed the non-profit's headquarters. Around noon, she left the office and walked to her car for the drive home. I remember using the car key's remote to open the driver's door. A white van was parked next to my car, on the driver's side. I thought there seemed to be ample parking spaces, so why did the contractor park next to me and possibly ding my car? I saw no one in the van, as the rear windows were heavily tinted. As I was about to open my door, I heard the van's side door abruptly slide open; two arms wrapped around me and lifted me off the ground. A second person then pulled a black hood over my head and held their hand over my mouth to stifle any screams for help. I was placed on some type of foam or rubber mat lying down, and my hands and feet were secured tightly enough that I knew escaping was not an option. During this ordeal, not one word was spoken. I did not see if a third person was in the van, but we were pulling out as I was being bound, so I expected there were three people involved: two who apprehended me and one driver.

Shaun asked if she remembered dropping her keys and whether she had her purse or cell phone on her. Peggy said she didn't remember what happened to her car keys, but knew she had unlocked the car. As for the purse, I was dressed in very casual clothes and had my phone in a small bag slung over my shoulder. I hadn't thought of it until you mentioned it, but my purse, wallet, and phone were never returned to me after I was released. All that stuff can be easily replaced, but what need did they have to keep those items?

Peggy said the drive was stop-and-go as they navigated the city streets. She could only guess it took about 15 minutes to get on some type of highway where the van's speed remained constant. I admit to being scared to death, having no idea why anyone would abduct me in broad daylight. I stayed perfectly still for the duration of the ride. My sense of time is not the best; I can't even guess how long we were on the highway before pulling off and then starting and stopping again on secondary roads for a while.

Kim asked if Peggy had noticed any distinctive sounds or noises while being transported. She replied that the only thing she heard was the usual traffic noise from cars passing by. When we reached our final destination, my feet were unbound, the hood was still in place, and my hands were still secured. Two people took me by my arms and walked me into a house or building to a specific room, where they removed the hood and cut the plastic ties around my hands. The two men wore black ski-type masks and were dressed identically in all-black clothing from head to toe, and never spoke. The room had one double-sized bed, a chair, and a table in the corner. The one window was blacked out, and off to the side was a small bathroom with a sink, shower, and toilet. Once in the room, I noticed a white dry-erase board with a marker pen, but its purpose eluded me until later, when I discovered it was used for communication after the two men left. I immediately tried to open the window; I did not try to escape, but to see where we were. The window was sealed shut, and I could not force it open.

Peggy continued to recount that I was brought a food tray a short time later. The guard wrote a message on a whiteboard, instructing me to write down if I needed anything, and pointed to the corner of the ceiling where a camera with a blinking red light was located. It was evidence that I was being monitored while being held captive. After the person left, I went into the bathroom and saw no camera, knowing this small, windowless room was my only place to have any privacy.

When my food tray was picked up, I was asked to hold a sign before me so they could take my picture. I did as instructed and had my picture taken, and then I held up my signboard, asking for anything to read or look at. Whenever I was approached, two men were present: one stood at the door entrance, and the other stepped into the room to leave or pick up an item. The standard procedure was a knock on the door, followed by a pause of about 10 seconds before someone entered my room. About 10 minutes after my written request, several books and magazines were left for me to read. Shaun asked if any magazines had a delivery label showing an address. Peggy said there were no markings on the many books and magazines she read, saying she probably had read each one 3 or 4 times during her captivity. If there were any mailing labels, they had been removed, or the pages were torn out.

Before the dinner meal was served, one person knocked on my door and entered my room with a picture and a written message. The picture was of Carly holding the same sign I was provided earlier in the day. The message, as I recall, stated: We are holding your daughter captive. You both will be held until our ransom demands are met. Do not cause us any trouble, or Carly will be punished and may never be released.

I knew instantly that my abduction was driven by money and felt that if I caused no problems, it would be just a matter of time before Carly and I would be released. I know from watching crime dramas on TV that some people who get kidnapped get killed so the criminals can cover their tracks. These types of thoughts also weigh on you as each day passes.

On the second day, I was given fundamental clothing: sweatpants, a sweatshirt, and cotton underwear. My clothes were taken and provided back to me to wear during the release. I did make two written requests that morning when my breakfast was brought to me. First, I requested to see and speak with Carly, and the second request was to be able to walk outside and get some exercise. I received a simple head shake for "No" on both items.

Our captives appeared to work in the same teams based on simple observations. Their build and size were very similar; I didn't notice any marks, like tattoos, because they were always covered in black clothing and wore ski masks. The only person I noted was left-handed when he picked up anything.

The daily routine did change slightly without any notice or reason. As a mother, I had an instinct or feeling that they were no longer holding Carly. What reinforced that belief was when they bound my hands and took me outside for the first time. We were being held in a two-story house in a very densely wooded area. I could see no neighbors or other structures in any direction. There appeared to be only one driveway in and out of the property. I noted the two white vans parked down the driveway with duct tape over their license plates. Two security guards, one on each arm, walked me in circles around the house, kind of like doing laps in a racecar.

Shaun interrupted, asking if the house had any numbers posted or if I had seen a mailbox with numbers. Peggy replied that she saw no numbers or mailboxes. She added that she never heard any vehicle noise, wherever the main road was, so it had to be a fair distance from the house. She said the walks were allowed only once a day and lasted about 20 minutes.

The other thing that caught my attention was that only two blacked-out windows were on the first level. One was near the front door on the left side, and the other was on the opposite side, near the back of the house where I was kept. The house was average in size, with a white exterior and a black roof. There was one storage-type shed about 100 feet from the main house. It was a place where someone wanted to escape and have privacy. I had to believe Carly was in the front room because when I entered the house, we walked down a hallway to a door on the left side toward the rear of the structure. I doubt they would have let me outside if Carly were still on the premises.

As days passed, no one indicated how or when I might be released. This period was unnerving, and I began to anticipate the worst. The night before my release, after dinner was provided, my original clothes were brought in, and the whiteboard message said, ' You will dress and be transported tomorrow morning. ' When the van gets to the chosen place, you will exit the vehicle and remain in place until someone retrieves you. As you can imagine, sleeping that night was pretty difficult. I had dressed and was waiting when they walked into my room and promptly bound my hands, but not my feet. Placed the same black hood over my head and escorted me to the van. The same foam or rubber mat was still there, and I was told to lie down.

The van mainly drove on a highway; once we started to stop and go, I felt we must be getting close to my final destination. I was helped up and managed to stand as well as I could inside a cargo van. The ties around my hands were removed, and the next thing I knew, the side door was open only a foot or so; they had me facing out the door, yanked off the hood from behind, and kind of shoved me out the door. I immediately recognized the Masonic Memorial and gazed at its peak, where the bright sunlight shone. When I turned around, the van was already out of sight, heading down the hill. Several people were either leaving or coming to visit. I saw a grassy path on the left side of the building, followed it around, and went to a spot with a beautiful vista overlooking Old Town. I felt the sun on my face and the wind blowing through my hair, and I said a prayer, thanking God for being alive. I never moved until I noticed Cody approaching me. I felt I had survived a terrible ordeal but was now finally safe. We hugged, and tears of joy flowed down my face.

Shaun told Peggy that her story and experience were similar to what Carly had shared after her release. He stated that her observation of the dark windows and the belief that Carly was no longer there were probably accurate.

Kim asked if any reference was made besides the first notice that a second ransom was to be demanded or was being demanded. We had expected to receive another ransom demand for your release after the first payment. Peggy said she never saw another reference to ransom after the first day she was held.

Kim told Peggy, "We are incredibly grateful for your safe release, but we would like to know or understand the motivation for not asking for more money." Peggy replied that she had no idea why the decision was made, but tried very hard to be a model captive while being held.

Shaun openly admitted they had very little to go on in trying to get closer to this case and put the criminals in jail for a long time. Since neither of you suffered bodily injury, the crime focuses on recovering the ransom paid. The statute for prosecuting kidnapping involves crossing state lines, which occurred in this case involving Maryland and Washington, D.C., and remains in effect. Shaun added that if it takes 20 years, we can still find and bring the criminals to justice.

Chapter 52

Kim felt obligated to advise everyone that she and Shaun were being reassigned to the domestic terrorism division. There is a genuine threat to the Washington, DC, area involving rail transportation. Recent freight train derailments in various parts of our country involved some that dispersed very toxic chemicals into the local atmosphere, which have provided terrorists with new means to attack our country. She specifically addressed Cody. I know your business and residence are in Old Towne Alexandria, and we have identified a potential target zone for a possible massive derailment.

She continued that an old rail spur line used to deliver coal to the power plant in the north section of Old Towne was shut down years ago, but was never secured or sealed off. Anyone can easily drive a vehicle right up to active train tracks from this spur line, detonate a bomb at the right time, and derail a freight train pulling chemical tankers. The DC area could be toxic enough to shut our government down for months or possibly years. Cody's only thought in processing the information just disclosed by Kim was that if the FBI knew a specific weak point in the rail system, they could do one of two things: 1) Monitor this area with the intent to negate any terrorist attack and apprehend the criminals or 2) Seal the area to make it impossible to access in causing any type of train derailment. Cody knew he would approach Kim to get more specifics on the threat level and what action or direction the FBI planned to take to address this situation. Either way, this terrorism assignment would be a very high priority for the Bureau in the coming weeks or months.

Cody and Zach were thrilled to hear Shaun's statements, which were very close to an admission that the FBI had no suspects to pursue or apprehend. With the agent's reassignment, they would be focused on more important matters, and he couldn't see any new information that could surface that would be sufficient to get them involved again in the kidnapping case.

Shaun closed the meeting by asking Carly or Peggy to note any facts from their captivity that could aid the investigation. Please contact either of them immediately. Zach stepped forward and said that, with Alan overseas on business, they would still monitor his emails for a time. He added that he saw no reason for the criminals to reach out to them again, given that Peggy was being released. To lighten the mood, Zach said they could still try to kidnap me, but they probably knew I was not worth what was paid for Carly and Peggy. That got a few laughs from everyone but Shaun, who had not exhibited a real sense of humor from the start.

Cody and Zach walked out with Shaun and Kim to their government SUV. Zach had engaged Shaun with several questions, which allowed Cody to whisper to Kim, "I need a date for this Saturday night. I am planning to go to the best French restaurant in all of metro DC, L'Auberge Chez Francois in Great Falls." Can you help me find someone because I hate dining alone? Kim whispers back. The person standing next to you may be available and have a fondness for French food. Cody replied, saying to expect a text message later today. As they approached the car, Cody asked in a normal voice for Shaun and Zach to hear, "How real was the terrorism threat for the DC metro area?" Kim replied, "It is shaping up to be an 8 out of 10." She said that's all I can comment on right now, adding it's a severe problem and potentially very damaging.

As Zach and Cody enter the house, Peggy tells them Carly has left to meet some friends in DC for lunch. The three of them sat on the front porch, and Peggy asked the two of them what they thought of the interview. Cody jumped in first and told Peggy she should audition for the Broadway theater. He commented on her recollection and delivery, which were informative and very sincere. The description of the Masonic Memorial drop-off was perfect and believable, but furnished no trail for the FBI to pursue. Zach added that this discussion between the three of them should never be brought up again for the time being. He felt that if several months passed without any action from the authorities, the case may be labeled unsolved. Peggy said these words are from my heart - *"You guys together found a resolution to a nightmare, and I will always be forever grateful to you both."*

Cody hugged Peggy goodbye and told Zach about a wrap-up meeting with the team tomorrow afternoon at the office. On the way home, I will pick up some beverages at the Virginia ABC store. Zach replied, Text me the time, and I'll be there. Cody arrived back at his office and took care of some basic housekeeping. Advised Karen to clean the rented SUV and van and remove any trace of their use. He thought the car rental company would be very pleased when they returned the two vehicles in pristine condition. Cody also asked Karen to destroy both sets of fake license plates. Get a cleaning crew to the lake house immediately," he would text her, listing several companies that their family had used in the past.

Cody then sent Stoney a message about the meeting, inviting Bones and V to attend, but not wanting to impose on their time. He also said they should return any equipment they had borrowed from the government and report any expenses or out-of-pocket costs to let him know the amount, and he would arrange for them to be reimbursed.

Susie and Q were also messaged about the afternoon meeting and asked if they knew of any loose ends to get them tied up by tomorrow. The last notice he sent was a text to Zach, informing him of a 3 p.m. meeting in the conference room for debriefing and Happy Hour with beverages. Cody headed to his local gym for a good workout, backed up by an early dinner and hopefully the best night's sleep he's logged in the past several weeks.

Stoney called Cody in the morning, advising that Bones and V would take a pass on the meeting, but when the next adventure turned up, count them in on whatever was planned. Cody asked Stoney what he could do as a token gesture for Bones and V to show his appreciation for being an integral part of the plan to get Peggy back safely. Stoney told Cody he would think about it, but knew they would decline anything offered if he asked either of them directly. He said that when my brothers are called on and tasked with making a "wrong" into a "right," they will always be there and do what it takes to get the job done.

Chapter 53

At 3 p.m., all the team members, Susie, Q, Karen, Stoney, Zach, and Cody, had secured a beverage of choice and were seated around the conference room table.

Cody told everyone we have a guest who will call at 4 p.m. to discuss our adventure. Zach said that, except for Bones and V, who are not here with us this afternoon, the only people who know what happened are in this room. Cody said that the caller is not Bones or V, and this person does have intricate knowledge of what we did. This left everyone a little mystified about who the caller was and somewhat concerned that their secrets might be exposed.

The one item that seemed odd to be sitting in the middle of the conference table was the box and the fake C-4 bomb connected to the cell phone detonator Q had assembled. Cody said before updating everyone on Peggy's release, he wanted to share a story about the device sitting in the middle of the table.

Cody explained to the team that he had to wrestle with a serious problem as everyone sipped their cocktail. *What IF Peggy Turner had been harmed or killed? Turning Victor over without Peggy in return had to be addressed. My only solution was to have Q create a fake bomb that looks real and present my problem to*

Victor. When Victor saw the device, he immediately believed it was real C-4 explosives. I advised him that this device would be placed under the seat of our vehicle, which would be used to transport him to where the swap was to take place. I also told him he would be chained to the child seat anchors in our SUV and could not exit the car without us providing the key.

IF Peggy Turner were not alive and well in their vehicle, we would either take Victor back or call the cell phone connected to the explosive. It was a mental bluff, but one that left Victor few options. Victor was allowed his cell phone and made a call to his 1st Lieutenant, which I listened to. This conversation convinced me that Peggy would be in their vehicle, and his organization was not planning any subversive actions. For this reason, the bomb device was not used and subsequently stored in the back of our van.

After the exchange, I drove Victor's Mercedes with Peggy in the back seat to the sailing marina parking lot. This is where Stoney was to get Peggy into our van and take her to the Masonic Memorial. During the transfer of Peggy to the van, I noticed the box holding the fake bomb device you were all looking at. When Stoney exited the marina with Peggy, I took the liberty of placing the box in the middle of Victor's rear seat in the Mercedes. Zach said this is becoming a good story.

Cody replied to Zach: Sit tight and fasten your seatbelt; it improves. I got into my Mustang, parked a couple of hundred feet from the Mercedes. Within a few minutes, as we instructed, Ivan pulled into the parking lot with our white SUV and Victor in the back seat. As soon as Ivan parked next to their vehicle, Victor bounced out of the car and opened the rear door of the Mercedes to head home. He freezes when he sees the box on the back seat, knowing it holds our bomb. At that moment, I dialed a number that made a phone ring inside the box, and I guarantee he thought he had taken his last breath. When the phone kept ringing, he realized it was his cell phone's ringtone. He had to lift the box lid and answer the phone. I told him I was returning his phone and was pleased we could complete our business transaction to everyone's benefit. To express my sincerity, I drove past him in my Mustang, beeped the horn, and gave him a big wave. I would have liked to have had Victor's blood pressure monitored when he opened the car door. It would have been off the charts.

Susie, Q, and Karen all gasped at the possibility of upsetting the head of the Russian Mafia. Q said you poked a Russian bear with a very pointed stick. Stoney and Zach got it and started to laugh out loud. Stoney told Cody, "You sent a very humorous message to Victor, but with a much deeper meaning: don't mess with us, or the next time you'll never hear the second ring tone."

Cody got a little philosophical and stated, *"When you're in a chess match with someone who is probably better than you, put them immediately on the defense, the reason being they will focus on how not to lose rather than looking for a way to win. . . "*

Cody drew an analogy to putting a puzzle together; you see the picture on the box, but what will it take to complete the puzzle to match it? He said everyone present had to contribute to make their plan work.

I want to provide a brief recap of everything that had to happen or be accomplished to secure Peggy Turner's release:

Let's start with Zach not getting kidnapped -He provided us with the motivation to help him get his sister and mother back.

Zach was our lifeline for information on the messages delivered to Alan and advised us of the FBI's input from briefing the family.

Q's drones gave us aerial video of the ransom drop and the nerve agent dispersal device.

Susie provided maps and details of the city's tunnel system

Karen's research on Victor and his family gave us the restaurant and lunch date

Stoney gave us access to trained people, the agent used in the elevator, and communication devices

Zach ID'd the vehicle used to retrieve the diamonds and provided us with one picture, which led us to Victor

Words can't express my gratitude for the effort you all put in and the ultimate risk you took when the decision was made to kidnap Victor. Raise your glasses and toast to a herculean job well done by our team. **"CHEERS, or should we say Nostrovia?"**

Cody announced it was approaching 4 p.m. and their guest speaker would call his cell phone. To his surprise, Cody said that this person had called him this morning and asked if Zach was with him, and he could listen in. I advised this person that we would be together this afternoon, and we scheduled the call for 4 p.m. Since nothing was conveyed to me this morning regarding the nature or intent of the call, your guess is as good as mine. Everyone was puzzled when dealing with a mysterious person tied to the Turner kidnapping.

Chapter 54

Cody's phone rang at precisely 4 p.m. He asked the person if he could put them on speaker mode and listen to the response. It was acceptable to them, and they replied that the person had assurances that the call was not being recorded. Cody announced to everyone that Victor Zanoska was on the line and had something to say to them as he turned on the speaker of his cell phone. Cody informed Victor that Zach was present, along with several other individuals who played a key role in finding a solution to release Peggy Turner.

Victor said he was okay, knowing that everyone present had broken numerous laws, and it was best never to share their knowledge with anyone. Victor asked Zach if he had a pencil and a notepad; Zach grabbed one off the table and replied Yes, he had both items ready. Victor told Zach to write down the following numbers: 37 left / two turns to 11 right / one turn to 21 left, and ½ turn right to 3. You now have the combination to the office safe in your dad's study. I expect there are some papers in there for you to read. Zach told everyone that the floor safe in Alan's study was over 100 years old and that it had been given to him by their insurance broker when the agency relocated their offices. The safe was very old and ornate, and the broker didn't want to pay to move it, which must have weighed well over 1,000 pounds. The safe is a showpiece of custom craftsmanship, but I understand the combination was misplaced many years ago. Victor replied I know nothing of its operation and just served as the messenger. This statement triggers murmurs in the room, implying that Victor has obtained personal information from Alan Turner.

Victor openly asked everyone for their attention for the next 10 minutes, as he had something to share. He started by saying, "You are about to hear a fairy tale or a nice bedtime story." This made the team all slide their chairs closer to the table and lean in to hear what the head of the Russian Mafia was about to say.

Victor started by saying that about seven years ago, I was contacted by a particular government organization. We all know those three clandestine letters from this agency. Before I arrived in Washington, DC, the locals told me that when one drove north on the George Washington Parkway, the exit past the City of McLean was posted as The Farm Bureau at Langley, VA. There is no need to mention their initials; you all know the government agency.

This agency requested my presence for a meeting at The W Hotel, which is ironically just a block from the White House. A suite had been secured, sparing no expense, as American taxpayers were footing the bill. Alan Turner and I, plus two people from the Farm Bureau, attended the meeting. It was all very cordial, with drinks, food, and small talk before getting to business.

One agent indicated that AX Tech Corp, owned by Alan Turner, had secured a government contract to supply, warehouse, and distribute small arms to every military branch in the United States.

The Farm Bureau representative said there are times when the U.S. needs to support and promote our democratic values overseas. This must be accomplished with minimal knowledge and involvement of our government. The people benefiting from our support sometimes become friends one day and enemies the next.

It was proposed that AX Tech establish an account with Langley, complete with sufficient layers to ensure legitimacy and legality for the distribution of small arms, tailored to the agency's specific needs. Mr Zanoska represents an organization that, with Langley's help, will have a secured and bonded warehouse facility located at Dulles International Airport that can withstand scrutiny. They will receive every order placed and be the sole distributor for overseas shipments. All items processed by this warehouse will transit as farming equipment and apparatus. Isn't it nice to have the Farm Bureau honor its roots and leave a paper trail only involving farm goods? Mr. Zanoska's global network will be in place to ensure that every delivery reaches the intended recipient or organization, as directed. Putting the right products into the right hands will leave no fingerprint trail to raise concern for our government agency.

The monetary side of the ledger will provide very high compensation for all parties involved in this distribution method. This will be implemented quickly as there are places in the world that require our attention. For Alan and me, this implied that NO was not an option.

Having the Farm Bureau as a partner could prove exceedingly helpful if my organization encounters a few challenges. Alan, I could tell he was not a man who would shy away from a very profitable venture. Alan never inquired at this meeting about who I represented or the contacts I had outside the U.S. I am sure he had done his homework within a few days of our meeting and found out everything about his new partner. AX Tech Corp's file was put on my desk within 24 hours of our meeting, so I would be up to speed on who I was working with...

The government representatives indicated that all information discussed tonight was classified, and any disclosure of said meeting with anyone would result in the FBI filing criminal charges that will not go away.

We will manufacture three satellite mobile phones specifically for this project. The phone will be 100% encrypted and safe to use worldwide. Only three numbers will be accessible by these phones, the three parties in this room.. They should only be used to clarify shipping orders or in any type of emergency. At this time, there is no timetable for exiting this arrangement. We anticipate using this delivery system for quite some time in the foreseeable future.

Zach tried to comprehend that his father had partnered with Victor's organization for seven years. What he couldn't fathom was why the mafia would kidnap their family. The only logical answer was the ransom payment value of over four million dollars; once the stones were cut and polished, splitting them in two would be a nice bonus for each party.

Cody was still trying to make sense of Victor's disclosure. He only knew that the FBI was not the mole leaking information to the mafia; Alan most certainly had a hotline that went directly to the source.

Victor added that this venture, which has been operating for the past seven years, has nothing to do with promoting democracy or U.S. principles and policies. Its sole purpose is to guarantee conflict and unrest outside the United States. Constant worldwide turmoil can be beneficial for businesses looking to increase their profits. Victor said the three key ingredients from every order we have fulfilled over the past seven years can be directly attributed to Power, Control, and Profits. The American people are sheep that get in line, thinking the Red-White-Blue has the best values and principles of any government in the world.

I am sharing these details because, after Alan requested that I provide Zach with the combination sequence, he has gone dark and remains unreachable. At this point, I do not wish to involve or notify our third partner. I would greatly appreciate it if, upon opening the safe, I were immediately contacted and advised on any items inside that have a direct connection to my organization. In return for this favor, I will share the last chapter of the fairy tale story in another call if you all decide to continue your research based on what I told you today. I know you'll find the ending to be very interesting. Victor disconnected the call, leaving the room speechless.

Chapter 55

Given what we just heard, Cody said that some very loose ends must be tied up before we can all rest easily. Not knowing what we'll find, let's have everyone be available early tomorrow. Zach, you and I need to head to Great Falls and see if that combination works and why it was provided to you. Susie and Karen, please check your phones for messages or instructions. Any sensitive information I need to share will be sent encrypted via email. Cody told Zach, "I will follow you home. Please keep the BMW near the speed limit; it wouldn't be a good time for 25 mph over the limit, which could lead to a reckless driving citation."

Following Zach north on the GW Parkway, Cody tried to process Victor's long-standing business relationship with Alan Turner. The only thing that made sense was that Alan was in debt or financial trouble with Victor or some other unrelated business deal. The kidnapping was real but staged for a purpose. He thought that if Alan knew beforehand that the Kidnap & Ransom corporate insurance policy would be footing the bill for ransom payment, no one would lose anything in executing the crime. Cody had a working knowledge of the law and knew that kidnapping and being an accessory to this crime carry some pretty lengthy jail time. He thought Zach, while driving, was running similar scenarios, and they would discuss them upon their arrival at the Turner home.

The cars pulled into the driveway and parked next to each other. Cody asked Zach if he knew if his sister and mother were home. Since they all had spaces in the eight-car garage, he couldn't tell who was in or out. One point he was certain of and conveyed to Zach was that, based on what they had both heard from Victor, Carly, and Peggy, it needed to be left out of the process until all the facts and information were obtained.

When they entered the house, it seemed very quiet, and they found out why when they entered the kitchen. On a notepad, which always seemed old-fashioned to Zach with the availability of text messaging, was a handwritten note from Peggy to Zach. Carly and I decided to take a last-minute yoga class back around 6:30 pm, and we can figure out dinner then if you're available.

Cody and Zach entered the study and saw the antique safe sitting off the side of Alan's desk. Zach mentions that the insurance company, which was the original buyer of the safe, is the name stenciled across the door in gold leaf. The cost of one of these in the 1920s was substantial, so every safe sold was customized with the buyer's name embossed in gold leaf on the door.

Cody said, "Before we crack the safe and see what's inside, please give me your theory on what we just heard." Zach said he did not know if Alan secretly gambled, which could explain his need for cash, or had gotten into serious financial trouble. Cody replied, "I had the same thought process, but with a bad business deal or investment gone bad."

At that point, Cody told Zach to spin the dial with a steady hand and see if it opened. After entering the combination provided by Victor, the safe opened fairly easily. What surprised them was that the door and walls were 8 to 10 inches thick, with the inside storage compartment about the size of an upright mailbox. Zach said he had done some homework on the safe manufacturer and found they marketed this unit as fireproof. They built the steel box and filled it with a liquid-type concrete that hardened, which caused the safe, as described in their literature, to be fireproof.

The safe contained only one bound multi-page document; Zach scanned it and said, "I wasn't expecting this." Cody asked rhetorically, "Will you share what you just read or keep it a secret?" Zach announced that the document gave him full power of attorney over all AX Tech Corp operations. He added the passwords to all the corporate operating systems. It appears the legal document was drafted by the company's corporate counsel, notarized, witnessed, and dated the day the team kidnapped Victor.

Cody told Zach that, assuming Alan was still rational and hadn't gone off the deep end, we needed to find him and try to understand what was happening. We now have more questions than answers based on Victor's comment that Alan has gone dark and seen this document.

Cody texted Susie to check her email in 10 minutes, sending her a task he needed to be done. He told Zach he wanted Susie to hack into the TSA's system at Dulles International and Reagan National Airports the day before the kidnapping, the day of the abduction, and the day after we kidnapped Victor. I want her to find out if Alan Turner flew out of the area or the country and where he went. This may provide a trail for us to follow and hopefully clarify what is happening.

Suppose you agree with my thinking, tomorrow morning. In that case, we should have Karen and Susie access AX Tech Corp's financial records using the provided passwords and assess the company's current financial situation. Let's both sleep on it and see if other avenues must be explored. See you in the office at 8 a.m. sharp.

Cody asked Zach to photograph the corporate passwords and put the document back in this relic of a safe. The last item Cody thought they should investigate was Alan's personal computer, which he had left behind to monitor his business emails and messages from the kidnappers. He remembered hearing Carly had been given the sign-in credentials to open Alan's laptop. Zach said he would get with Carly tonight and bring the computer tomorrow.

Cody told Zach it was too early in the game to run out and get some new CEO business cards made up with his name on them. Zach always enjoyed Cody's wit and humor, so he told him to have some decent coffee ready for their meeting tomorrow.

Karen, Susie, Zach, and Cody sat around the conference room table at 8 a.m. The alcohol beverage cart from yesterday afternoon was replaced with dark roast Colombian coffee and a dozen donuts from the local pastry shop around the corner. Susie started by saying, "So much for watching my sugar intake," as she bit into a Boston Cream donut.

She reported successfully getting into the TSA database, commenting that these records should be made public. The TSA firewall is so flimsy that any 10-year-old could easily access information. In filtering the dates provided by Cody, she added BWI (Baltimore Washington International), Dulles, and Reagan National to the airport search. That group would cover all the metro DC area for air travel. Susie advised the group that Alan Turner had not boarded a plane on any of those dates. Zach commented then, "Where did Alan disappear to?"

Cody and Zach shared their experience opening the old safe in Alan's study. They provided a summary of the document found inside the safe. Karen asked Zach if this had changed his tax bracket and made him rich. Zach indicated that business law was not his specialty, and having power of attorney over a closely held corporation should allow him to make any future decisions regarding corporate operations, including selling the company, if he so desired.

Cody jumped in and asked Karen and Susie to use their laptops to access AX Tech business records. Zach provided them both with screenshots of the usernames and passwords from the document located in the safe. Cody wanted them both to dig into the company's financial side and see what the balance sheet showed. He also asked them to focus on substantial transactions within the past few weeks.

Susie's high-tech laptop mirrors her screen onto the flat-screen TV mounted on the conference room wall. Cody and Zach sat back and watched as Susie pulled up numerous financial statements for their review. Zach was amazed at how nimble Susie was in navigating the database and said, "If I ever get audited, I hope someone with Susie's ability doesn't work at the IRS." Susie looked over and smiled when she said to Zach that she would visit him in prison if he got convicted of tax fraud.

Karen did have an accounting background, but never took the CPA exam. She commented that AX Tech looked financially sound. They had two substantial lines of credit with two national banks and borrowed from them on a regular basis. The loans acquired were always paid down in large installments, minimizing the interest paid on the lines of credit. The U.S. government generates the most significant amount of receivables paid to AX Tech. Based on what Victor told us yesterday, the small arms sold that are shipped overseas are buried fairly deep. I haven't been able to identify where they are accounted for yet.

Susie flashed on her screen a transaction of two million dollars, marked 'K&R' as payment of claim number 8 or 9 digits long. She said what was interesting was that the full sum of 2 million was coded to CEO Alan Turner's sub-account. When I filtered through the financial records using K&R, I found a payable expense of two million from AX Tech to a diamond broker in New York City. Alan did not pay the ransom out of his own funds, but he deposited the insurance company's reimbursement payment directly into his account.

Susie asked Karen about a dozen payable transactions labeled Hungary and NATO negotiations. Karen said it was very creative accounting, and if I had to guess, these amounts would make an excellent source of bribe money for the right Hungarian decision-makers. Susie added that all the funds identified, totaling over 13 million dollars, were run directly through Alan Turner.

Everyone agreed that AX Tech was financially sound and in no jeopardy of defaulting. The 13 million may be playing fast and loose from an accounting standpoint, but the cost could be justified to obtain a huge contract.

Chapter 56

Cody wanted to move on to Alan's laptop. Susie took charge and entered the passcodes provided by Carly. Susie instantly saw that the computer functioned at two levels: the top level they had entered and a sub-level someone with excellent IT skills had created. Susie admitted it might be extremely difficult to breach or even impossible to enter the sub-level. Karen requested access to view information through contacts, emails, and other social media sites, rather than being buried in the sub-level. Everyone was ready for a short break and left Karen doing something she was very good at: digging for more information.

Twenty minutes later, they all reconvened in the conference room. Cody asked Karen if she had found anything interesting. She said the vast majority of items were routine and day-to-day. There was one that dated back several months, and that seemed odd. Alan expressed an interest in cryptocurrency, but it appeared obvious he had little to no knowledge of that market. It may not be important, but he contacted a business acquaintance, indicating some urgency, and asked for their understanding of basic crypto investing, trading, transferring, and security. He wondered who the most reputable and largest crypto broker in the U.S is.

The unusual aspect concerns Alan's apparent interest in learning and opening a cryptocurrency account. No other references or trail show that he did anything to open an account.

Cody commented that the sub-account was likely where anything new dealing with crypto was parked. He then asked Zach if his dad had ever been interested in the crypto marketplace. Zach replied that this was the first time I had ever heard Alan's name tied to possibly opening an account or making any crypto investment. Susie said she would keep trying to peel back the layers and expose the sub-account, but wasn't optimistic. She added, From a professional viewpoint, I would like to meet the person who created this monster.

Cody announced, "Let's break for an early lunch. The local deli menus are on the side table. Please place a delivery order and charge it to the corporate card." I'll take a turkey club and chips – I need to call Victor with an update about the opening of Alan's safe; after his call yesterday, we owe him some feedback. Cody entered his office, shut the door for privacy, grabbed his cell phone, and dialed Victor. He answered on the first ring and said, "Hello, Cody, do you have anything to convey?" Cody told him everyone in the Turner family believed the safe combination had been lost over the years. He went on to say the numbers provided did indeed open the 100-plus-year-old safe. Cody could tell Victor was anxious to know what he was inside.

Cody explained the power of attorney executed to Zach without going into great detail. He advised Victor that nothing in the document left in the safe referenced his organization. Victor expressed relief upon hearing this news and appreciated

Cody's call with the update. Cody told him about the TSA search they had conducted to determine if Alan had traveled overseas upon his departure and where he went. He did not share with Victor how they had hacked into the TSA system, but said Alan Turner had never flown anywhere from the metro DC area airports.

Victor commented on what seemed to be Cody's excellent access to a great deal of information. I am sure you will not give up your research until

you answer all the open questions. Let me continue my fairytale story about a business associate who approached me a year ago and asked if they could obtain a new identity. No reason was given for the exact purpose or usage of these fake documents. This type of information is readily available through various resources. We felt a business obligation to this associate and complied with their request. When doing more research, you might include the name Albert Thomas. We still need to chat about the closing chapter of my fairytale when you have most of the puzzle pieces together. Cody sat at his desk and thought he was a pawn in a perilous chess game.

Cody texted Zach, asking if he was done with lunch, to walk down to his office to discuss a few things. Zach promptly said something must be up that you don't want to share with the team. Cody said you are close to being spot on. Zach expressed his concerns over the recent events, including his father's unknown whereabouts, the power of attorney document left in the office safe, and the business relationship between Victor and Alan established by our government. This is your family that will most likely be impacted in some manner if we keep pursuing answers to the how and why questions dealing with Carly and

Peggy's kidnapping. Let us not forget that you were also a target, but fortunately, rather than being a victim, you played a significant role in the resolution.

Zach told Cody that, outside his family, he trusted no one more than the person sitting in this room. Peggy's well-being may still be perilous without your team and their commitment. I don't think that, since Victor told us his fairytale, I wanted to believe my father had no knowledge or involvement. In the kidnapping. Facts like the flight status with no information point us in another direction. With Peggy's release, it would have been nice to feel that the ordeal was finally over. But by discussing this, we both know there's more to the story. In response to your concern for my family, we have no choice but to utilize our resources to obtain answers to these lingering questions. However, as this evolves, I will sit down with Carly and Peggy to share our findings, whether good or bad, right or wrong.

Cody told his friend he had to make the offer to let this go, but already knew from their relationship what the answer would be. He then shared his brief call with Victor, advising him of the document stored in the safe. When he mentioned to Victor that Alan Turner didn't show up on any TSA databases for recent air travel, Victor provided him the name "Albert Thomas." Ironically, Albert Thomas and Alan Turner share the same initials of A.T. We should head back to the conference room and see where this information takes us.

Karen and Susie had wrapped up lunch and focused on their laptops. Susie mentioned that, based on the crypto email to Alan recommending the largest crypto broker in the U.S., she researched who that broker was and hacked into their profile to access account information. She mentioned that it's much more challenging to see someone's crypto holdings and investments, but it's easier to find just the basic profile data. Susie said she could find no trace of Alan Turner ever establishing a crypto account with that broker.

Cody briefed Karen and Susie on his call with Victor. He asked Susie to re-enter the TSA network for the same period, applying filters for all three local airports and entering the name Albert Thomas. If we get a hit, try again with the crypto broker profile pages and see if an account exists under that name.

Within a few minutes, Susie said the TSA scanned Albert Thomas's boarding pass at Dulles International Airport for a one-way flight on Emirates Airlines to Dubai. Cody asked Susie to get as deep as she could into the crypto broker records using Albert Thomas's name. He then requested Karen to do some quick homework on Dubai for background information on why people fly there. Cody asked Zach if he knew of any business contacts that AX Tech dealt with that operated from Dubai. Zach indicated that the name and region had never surfaced since he worked at AX Tech Corp and that his father's opinion of the Arab world was very negative.

Karen excitedly announced that she had found two key reasons why anyone without family or business ties may be interested in Dubai. Everyone was eager to hear what drew people to travel there, and Karen continued with the first reason: Dubai is labeled as the most crypto-friendly place in the world for business. Dubai has few rules or regulations regarding the trading or taxation of cryptocurrency accounts. Then the second reason is that Dubai has no extradition agreement with the United States. If a person committed a crime in the U.S., Dubai would be a good place to hide because U.S. authorities cannot reach them.

Chapter 57

Cody said that with Victor's help, we know where Alan has gone. We should now focus on whether a money trail also leads to Dubai. Susie indicated that the cryptocurrency industry has been plagued by rampant hacking and illegal cryptocurrency transfers. She added that anyone with decent computing skills considers it easier than stealing currency, but just as marketable. Susie indicated that her best bet would be to probe Alan's laptop again for the information they sought, understanding that the laptop program layers offer challenges to peel back. Cody told everyone, Let's break for an hour and see if anything of substance was uncovered.

Zach followed Cody back to his office and said the TSA information and destination pretty much validated that Alan had some knowledge or part in the kidnapping plan. If this were to all blow over without any FBI involvement, Alan could return home, indicate the Hungary deal fell through, and say a power of attorney was left as a safeguard if his plane crashed en route. If the authorities found Alan had committed or been an accessory to kidnapping, he would face serious prison time and would never leave Dubai.

Cody responded that he couldn't argue with his logic about Alan; it was likely that Alan was a partner and, at a minimum, feeding the Mafia information and updates. Zach said again to Cody, "We are going down this rabbit hole until we find the answers, whether we like them or not."

Susie knocked on Cody's door with a look of frustration. Cody waved her in and said Zach, and he was just kicking around theories about the kidnapping. Susie indicated that more time and programs would be needed to crack the lower layers embedded in Alan's laptop. She shared the good news and was able to return to the profile layer of the crypto brokerage firm. She found an account that had been opened several months prior in the name of Albert Thomas. Being unable to access account holdings due to firewalls has been very frustrating.

Susie indicated to Cody and Zach that she could not uncover any reference to an account balance. Cody said he knew precisely what the balance was in his account. Zach said he could only guess, but then deferred and asked Cody for his answer. Cody, simple math from our meeting today indicates that $ 2 million from the insurance company ransom and an additional $ 13 million from Hungary's supposed negotiations or bribes total $ 15 million. He also noted that it should buy someone a fairly decent retirement overseas. Zach added that crypto is an investment, and there is a reasonable probability that the crypto coins purchased should go up in value over time.

He asked Susie to take all the time she needed to try to get deeper into Alan's laptop. Cody felt it still held the information to give them insight and answers. He then openly admitted that he was missing something fundamental, a piece of the puzzle that one had to find to complete the picture. Cody revealed his frustration and told everyone to sleep on it, come back fresh in the morning, and put their thoughts together to find the answers.

The next morning, the team reconvened at Cody's conference room table, their second home. Zach kicked the meeting off by saying there had been no communication from Alan last evening. He referenced, as Victor put it, that Alan is still dark.

Cody said he tossed and turned through a pretty much sleepless night. The item that had haunted him to check on suddenly popped up like a light bulb being turned on. He asked Susie to return to the TSA system and locate Albert Thomas when he scanned his boarding pass through security. Susie took a few minutes to announce that she had the data on her screen. What are the names of the persons scanned by TSA before Albert went through, and who was scanned after Albert? Cody said if Alan had an accomplice, they may have flown together. Susie informed the group that the person before Alan was Ahmad Rashid, who seemed to be from Dubai or that part of the world. Then she hesitated and said, "You wouldn't believe who the person next in line was after Alan, with a boarding pass - *TSA shows someone named Barbara Thomas got on that plane.*"

Chapter 58

Zach asked who the hell Barbara Thomas was. Cody said he was pretty sure he knew exactly who was traveling with Alan. Zach replied I can't wait to hear this because I have no clue. Cody asked Zach to call the HR department at AX Tech and ask for Beverly Hardesty, also known as Alan's administrative assistant. Cody told Zach to remember you CC her on the message to Alan on Peggy's release. I guess that she never replied, which was very out of character. Zach confirmed he had not gotten any reaction from Beverly to his message. After connecting to the HR department and identifying himself, they advised Zach that Bev was on leave of absence for a family emergency and her return date was unknown.

Cody said Victor made two IDs a year ago, but wanted us to find this fact independently because of the implications. We have enough of the puzzle to call Victor shortly and hear the last chapter of his "fairytale". That may bring some final closure to this odyssey.

Susie said she had one more piece of the puzzle to share. After our meeting broke up, I decided to reach out to my mentor at Stanford University, where I obtained my combined Master's/ Doctorate's degrees in computer science. Zach interrupted and asked if he needed to call her Dr. Susie. She winked back and said Of course you do, then continued by saying her mentor linked into Alan's laptop. After an hour or so, they had peeled back enough layers to find Albert Thomas's emails.

Would anyone like to know the last email that Albert Thomas sent? By this time, she had everyone's undivided attention. His email was addressed to a crypto broker in Dubai, requesting a transfer of one Bitcoin into a bank account operating in his name, also located in Dubai. Bitcoin's current value is in the $100,000 range.

Susie added that she researched how one stores crypto, or in this case, Bitcoins, and found that secure wallets that can only be accessed by the wallet owner are used. The security codes are between 20 and 25 characters long and virtually unbreakable. If one loses their wallet code, the account is frozen in cyberspace. Per Cody's rationale yesterday, we have to assume that his wallet contained Bitcoins valued at 14.9 million dollars, having moved just over $100,000 to an operating account.

She went on to say the funny part of encryption is when the person receiving the message has to have the authority or ability to decipher the message. The original message stored by the sender is not encrypted in any manner. I am trying to convey to everyone that I have Albert Thomas's 25-digit code for his secure crypto wallet in Dubai. His email provided the code to transfer the crypto into his separate operating account. This code enables us to make Albert Thomas an impoverished man.

Chapter 59

Cody said it's time to close the loop and call Victor. When I tell him what we have uncovered, he should share his final chapter. Zach knew that the question was directed at him to save him from hearing potentially damaging news about his father. The decision was made that Zach and Cody should contact Victor and share only pertinent information with the rest of the team. Cody dialed Victor's cell phone number from his office. Victor was cordial and was a little surprised to hear from him again so soon after their last chat. Cody advised Victor that he felt they had put the puzzle together and told him he had provided two sets of identity papers some time ago: one passport for Albert Thomas and the other for Barbara Thomas. Cody advised Victor that both passports had been used the evening they had kidnapped him. He indicated the destination was Dubai, departing from Dulles International Airport. He added that Barbara Thomas was Alan's assistant, Beverly Hardesty. That relationship had existed for over a year when Alan requested the identity papers. Victor indicated he was again impressed with Cody's access to resources and told him that if he wanted to change careers, he would make a position in his organization available.

Cody asked Victor for his final fairytale chapter, stating that no recording devices were being used. Victor said I know your word is good, even though we operate on different business models. Sit back, it will take a little time to recount all the details.

About two to three months ago, Alan contacted me on the secure phone provided by the Farm Bureau. He made a request that I didn't expect. Alan asked that our organization kidnap his entire family; a ransom demand was to be made, but it had to stay under five million dollars, which was his corporate insurance policy limits for kidnapping and ransom. Let me phrase it exactly as requested: that his children would all be released, but to create some reasons that his wife would "never be returned". He explained Alan's long-standing relationship with his assistant, Beverly, and indicated that any divorce proceedings would cost him half of his corporation and everything else he owned.

Believe it or not, disposing of people is not part of our organization's business model. We have been tagged as ruthless and dangerous, which is a good persona. The people we work with always need to respect and fear who you are! Given the income generated from small arms distribution and the protection afforded by the government agency as a worldwide distributor, I had to consider Alan's request seriously.

The challenge was to plan the perfect crime that would provide some financial reward for us, prevent us from being caught, and help Alan with his problem. Victor said it was challenging to plan and execute a crime that met these criteria. Once the decision was made to use kidnapping, I had to be sure we would leave no trace behind.

Victor stated that Alan supplied us with all the data on the family habits we needed to formulate our plan. My nature is to develop a plan and then delegate it to others to execute. I believe the payment in uncut diamonds doubles in value when polished, and the ransom drop-off in the park was unique. Despite my efforts, the FBI remains clueless today, and you, Mr. Cody Wall, have yet to share with me the flaw you uncovered in my perfect crime plan. Cody told Victor that maybe our mutual respect is built on the fact that you never know the answer to that question. Victor said it would haunt him, not knowing, but as long as the authorities, including Kim Ross, don't have your information, I am okay with the situation, but I am still extremely curious. Cody was surprised to hear Victor reference Kim's name in his response to him - *Touche.*

Victor said now, as I was getting to the end of my fairytale, Alan contacted me on our special phone every day after the kidnapping. He was the one who advised us of the coated chemical on the diamonds, which we used to buy some additional time to decide what to do with Peggy. For this reason, we only released the daughter. During this period, we wanted to see if the FBI was still ineffective in finding clues to the kidnapping. I knew I had to fulfill my commitment to Alan to ensure Peggy was "never returned."

As you must know, I have contacts all over the world. So, I contacted a Colombian cartel asking for a possible favor. My request was for a safe house for one female in Cartagena, Colombia, a lovely resort town on the water. This safe house would include a bank account and papers to support her living in the country without needing a visa. I would fund this venture using some of the ransom money from the sale of polished diamonds. Peggy's choices, once everything was explained to her by us, were minimal, as you can imagine.

Then Mr.Cody Wall came along and took my option off the table before it was presented to Peggy. Ivan, whom you corresponded with on the day of the kidnapping at the restaurant when he became functional, answered my special phone late in the afternoon. It was Alan calling. He advised Alan that some developments had occurred and informed him that I would be unavailable for several days.

Alan must have panicked upon hearing this news from Ivan and had an exit strategy in place to leave the country using the papers we provided him a year ago. Since Alan's departure, we have not corresponded. I expect Alan was informed of Peggy's release, which would lead him to believe the kidnapping was uncovered and his involvement possibly exposed.

Your offer of suppressing any evidence to the authorities and allowing us to keep the ransom money would never have prompted Alan's sudden and abrupt departure if Alan knew these facts. I guess you provided me with a backdoor solution to a problem I was trying to resolve regarding Peggy Turner's handling.

Believe it or not, Cody, I found the humor in the box left on the back seat of my Mercedes, especially after your call to my cell phone inside the box, which thankfully didn't blow my car and me apart. This fairytale I have conveyed should provide some closure for everyone; unfortunately, with this news, I expect not all of you were contemplating it. With that comment, Victor abruptly ended his call with the team.

Chapter 60

Cody said Zach had to decide on how to handle the information just provided by Victor. This concerns the crypto wallet and the funds Alan has in Dubai. He said this should not be a knee-jerk reaction to the information just provided by Victor, but a decision he is comfortable with for years to come.

Cody knew his best was on an emotional rollercoaster. To allow Zach time to decide what he wanted to do, Cody asked Zach if Susie and he were available on Saturday night. I have a date with Kim Ross for dinner at a French restaurant in Great Falls, and I would love to have you both join us for dinner.

Zach grabbed Cody's desk phone and hit Susie's extension, asking if she had Saturday night open, and it would be a double date with Cody and Kim. Her reply was, Sounds great, how fancy this restaurant is, and I want to dress appropriately. Zach told Cody we're in, and I will spring for a limo because he knew the red wine would flow as it always does when Cody dined out.

At L'Auberge Chez François, Cody has arranged for an excellent table by telling the maître d' when he made the reservation that he would order several bottles of wine, focusing on a 2009 Bordeaux vintage. The maître d' knew 2009 was a premium year for Bordeaux; hence, those bottles commanded a much higher price range on their wine list.

Kim felt very comfortable with Susie and sensed Zach was very much himself now that his mother had been released. True to his word, Cody ordered a 2009 Chateau Pontet Canet from the Pauillac region in France. The waiter was impressed, knowing this was over a $450 bottle of wine. The sommelier delivered and uncorked the wine and was pleased when Kim did the tasting, saying it was marvelous.

After some light discussion on the excellent menu, Kim asked if she could talk shop for a moment. Everyone paused and said, Please do so, Kim said she had been a little surprised after only Carly was released, and Peggy was not. The Bureau expected her captors would make new ransom demands or requirements to obtain Peggy's release. No such action. was taken, or messages were received from the persons responsible. Then, one morning at 10:15 a.m., a message was received saying Peggy had been or was being dropped off at the Masonic Memorial.

Kim said, "I am not prying into any of your business, but my inner sense tells me that Cody and Zach have their fingerprints all over Peggy's release." I don't want to know professionally, that would be a conflict of interest, but you can imagine my curiosity about how this all transpired. Cody's response to Kim, as a well-trained FBI field agent, is that you know no fingerprints would be left anywhere if any of the persons involved were always wearing gloves. This comment prompted a good laugh from everyone, and they all knew the subject was now closed.

Kim excused herself, saying the ladies' room calls before I climbed back into the limo. She added that it may be the best dinner I have ever experienced, and I hope Cody can write it off for tax purposes. As she departed the table, Zach told Cody and Susie he had given lengthy thought to Alan's involvement and would like to attend the Sunday morning meeting with the team to discuss his thoughts. Cody replied that the meeting is at 9 a.m. in the conference room, knowing the importance of bringing closure to Zach's family. As Kim returned from the ladies' room, the conversation changed to who had ordered the best meal of the night. The winner was the house specialty, Bouillabaisse.

At the end of dinner, and after the second bottle of Bordeaux was finished, Zach told everyone about Cody's family's house at Lake Anna in southern Virginia. He mentioned this would be an excellent place for them to spend a weekend before the summer ended. Everyone was on board with the idea and agreed to pick a date that worked for everybody's calendar. As they got up to leave, Zach asked an odd question, inquiring if the lake house still had the oversized tubes for two people to float on the lake. Cody winked back and said they only needed to be blown up. On the way out to the waiting limo, Cody asked Zach if they could chat in his office 30 minutes before meeting with the team tomorrow morning.

Chapter 61

Sunday morning in the DC metro area was the absolute best time to drive anywhere; all the party crowd from Saturday night was still sound asleep, churchgoers were attending services, and the brunch crowd wouldn't surface before noon. Zach arrived and walked into Cody's office a little before 8:30 a.m. and commented that last evening's dinner was very much needed and truly a great dining experience. Cody poured Zach a cup of his double espresso blend dark roast coffee. Cody announced he was about to experience a great cup of coffee with a serious attitude.

Zach told Cody he had two dilemmas he was wrestling with, the first was what to say or tell his sister and mother about Alan. The second was Alan's involvement in orchestrating this whole ordeal.

Zach then asked Cody for his thoughts on what he would do with Alan. Zach stated that sending Stoney overseas with his sniper rifle would be a fitting ending. Cody replied that we both know that in the long run, neither of us would live comfortably with that decision.

Cody said he had given this matter much thought and spent the next 10 minutes telling Zach what he would do to resolve his problem. Priority: drain the crypto account, set up a trust for

Peggy and Carly. Have Susie erase all travel-related documents for Alan, Beverly, Albert, and Barbara Thomas. Last item, we'll need Victor's help to send an email to Alan, never to return to the U.S. or face prosecution for his crime. Zach said to dial Victor, and Cody called Victor's cell phone number. When Victor picked up, Cody apologized for calling on Sunday morning. Victor replied, "You must have some pressing things to discuss." Cody indicated he needed to make him an offer; hopefully, he wouldn't refuse. Cody said he and Zach were sitting in his office, and this call was not being recorded. Victor was more than curious and told them he was anxious to hear their offer.

Cody explained that Alan's departure from the country was a loose end that needed to be tied up for both of them. He instructed Victor to contact the "Farm Bureau" and explain to your government partner that Alan has decided to leave his family and embezzle a substantial amount of money from his company to retire with his administrative assistant overseas. You will inform the Farm Bureau of any potential new negotiations required to modify the distribution system for shipments to foreign destinations from your warehouse at Dulles Airport. This should protect your interests going forward with the Farm Bureau.

Cody said to Victor, I am going to read you an email message I want you to generate and send to Albert Thomas from VK :

Albert, our mutual partner assisting us to distribute farm goods overseas, called and advised me that the Bureau / FBI investigating the kidnapping had uncovered evidence that may link my organization to this crime. Our government partner brokered a deal: if we could expedite the release of

the remaining hostage, the authorities would reclassify the crime from a priority one status to a more minor matter. I immediately initiated the release of that person to comply with their requirement.

You know that the crime involved does not have a statute of limitations for future prosecution. If our organization is ever charged with this crime, your involvement will be disclosed. If this situation were to play out, you would be spending your remaining days in a U.S. prison.

My recommendation to you would be to avoid returning to the U.S. for fear of arrest and prosecution. This message will be the last time we ever communicate. VK

Victor pondered the request and said it made good business sense to him, and he would do his part.

Chapter 62

Cody advised Zach that Victor's part was locked in. He said that Alan chose Dubai because this country has no extradition agreement with the U.S. This email should make Dubai Alan's prison cell, where he cannot leave. He moved around $100,000 of his $15 million in Bitcoin to an operating account. Susie has identified the Bitcoin wallet holding the balance.

Cody stated that Dubai is an expensive place to live, with the cost of living mainly driven by the oil industry's profits. Alan will have to find a way to exist when his operating account of $100,000 becomes exhausted, which shouldn't take all that long. Victor is okay to send my message to Alan, AKA Albert Thomas, clearly stating the possibility of an investigation, prosecution, and serious jail time. I doubt anyone will hear from Alan Turner again or see him try to re-enter the U.S.

Zach wanted closure and the potential of keeping Alan out of their lives for as long as any of them were still alive. Cody said there are no 100% certainties in the world, but this should be a good starting point to make that happen. Cody grabbed his coffee and asked Zach to brief the team on their final resolution.

In the conference room, Zach was on the verge of tears as he thanked the team for taking a huge personal risk to bring Carly and Peggy back. He explained in detail Alan's involvement and the reasons for his sudden departure from the country to the entire team. Zach outlined the planning and usage of the false identities and the amount of funds his father used to establish a crypto account in Dubai. Zach admitted that the burden of his father's actions would be his responsibility for quite a while.

Zach acknowledged the need for Cody's insight and opinions to work through this dilemma and bring closure. Zach said the principal decision was for Alan to believe he was exposed as the planner of the kidnapping. Knowing a lengthy prison sentence was highly likely, this would restrict his movements in or out of Dubai. Combined with the fake papers and passports we purged from the government's database, this should also hinder Alan's future movements.

Victor has agreed this morning to support our team in conveying to Alan his dire situation as a criminal at large for his involvement in Peggy's and Carly's abduction. Lastly, Susie, please use the crypto wallet code and drain the account; it must be sent to a trust that will be established for Carly and Peggy. Then delete all travel document records from the U.S. system on Alan, Beverly, and the two Thomases.

Susie, in an hour, the funds will be in a secure holding wallet, ready to transfer to your trust, leaving Alan destitute. Documents will disappear without any trace or means of recovery.

Zach then told everyone that our team's work should finally be over, and we could live with the knowledge that through our collective efforts, we had done a hell of a job.

Chapter 63

Alan calls Beverly. The cell phones we picked up in Dubai seem to work just as well as our old ones back in the States. I have no idea if the local authorities have listening devices in rental properties. Please meet me in the small park at the end of our block. I have some distressing news to share with you.

Beverly sees Alan on a park bench, and it's getting dark out with no one else in sight. The broker handling our crypto account called me and requested an urgent meeting. I just left his office, and he informed me that our crypto account was hacked and all our funds were transferred. Beverly said, Are you telling me we lost all fifteen million we set up in that account. Expect the $100,000 I pulled out to cover our expenses and find a temporary place to live.

Alan, the crypto account has no backing by anyone if the funds are mishandled or removed. Our crypto wallet address was said to be unhackable due to its length and complexity. That said, the account balance is now zero.

Beverly, we need to go back to the States and reestablish control of your company. Read this email I received from our friend Victor, who executed the kidnapping. The U.S. has flagged our travel documents, and we will both be arrested for our involvement in the abduction.

You're saying we are broke and live in a foreign country, we can't afford? Alan, I did all this for you so we could both be happy and financially set for life. Now I am thinking of acquiring a gun and blowing my brains out. Beverly, what's love got to do with it? You're twenty-five or more years older than me, and soon to be homeless. It's time for me to start looking for another employer.

Chapter 64

Zach announced to the team that his newfound wealth was being acquired in cryptocurrency, specifically in Bitcoin. The only major product he knew that someone could buy using Bitcoin was Tesla automobiles. After confirming access to his new crypto account, he wanted everyone on the team to drive a new Tesla automobile. Zach looked directly at Stoney and told him to pass this on to Bones and V, advising them that soon, they should be driving a new Tesla. Stoney said he doubted either one would turn down being gifted a new car.

Cody replied to Zach, "I love my Mustang. Still, the new wave is toward everyone owning an electric vehicle, Cody added, "I would like mine in bright blue with the dual electric motors putting out a comparable 500 horsepower. He added that that kind of power "might make Zach's BMW look like an ordinary family sedan!" The buzz in the conference room was "electric" as they discussed driving and owning a new Tesla.

Cody added one last comment for everyone to contemplate: if the team had wavered in their commitment to get Carly and Peggy Turner back, the outcome could have been devastating. I want you all to seriously consider keeping this team together, utilizing our collective talents to help others address issues they can't resolve. A team member may identify these situations, and then collectively, all of us can decide to get involved and work toward a favorable resolution.

Zach said that his newfound wealth would increase substantially if I also decided to sell AX Tech Corp. I will then commit the funds to cover all the expenses for this team to operate. Providing access to the best resources available to solve whatever problem the team wants to tackle.

Karen, Susie, Q, Stoney, and Zach said they were all on board, then asked Cody if he had a name in mind for this new venture. The answer seemed obvious to Cody, who said we would become "The Resolution Team."

Cody added, "We still need to tend to our day jobs, but trust me, when a situation becomes apparent, we'll know when our team *has to be activated to respond and resolve.*"